PRA... MAN

"Fast, furious, and thoroughly enjoyable." —Jeffery Deaver on *The Last Witness*

"Joel Goldman is the real deal." —John Lescroart on *Cold Truth*

"Highly recommended." —Lee Child on *Deadlocked*

"A page-turner that keeps going full speed until the very end." —Faye Kellerman on *No Way Out*

"Page for page, I loved it." —Michael Connelly on *Shakedown*

"A masterful blend of rock-solid detective work and escalating dread." —Robert Crais on *The Dead Man*

"Suspense at its very best." —Libby Fischer Hellmann on *Stone Cold*

ALL IN
JOEL GOLDMAN AND LISA KLINK

ALSO BY JOEL GOLDMAN

The Last Witness

Cold Truth

Deadlocked

Final Judgment

Shakedown

The Dead Man

No Way Out

Stone Cold

Chasing the Dead

ALSO BY LISA KLINK

Slaves to Evil

Evil to Burn

Reborn

ALL IN

JOEL GOLDMAN AND LISA KLINK

THOMAS & MERCER

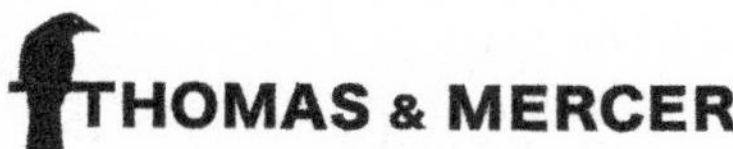

This is a work of fiction. Names, characters, organizations, places, events, and incidents are either products of the author's imagination or are used fictitiously.

Published by Thomas & Mercer, Seattle

www.apub.com

ISBN-13: 9781503944640

ISBN-10: 1503944646

Cover design by Marc Cohen

Printed in the United States of America

ONE

"The bet's to you, Mr. Kendrick," the house dealer said.

Alan Kendrick's brow creased for an instant, his eyes narrowing in a flicker of doubt, the fleeting combination a confession telling Jake Carter he was bluffing. It was the only thing out of control on a man who kept everything in check. Silver haired with a chiseled chin, he was immaculate and imperturbable, used to bending others to his will. Kendrick's tell was subtle and gone in a flash, the kind only a pro like Jake would recognize.

"Ten thousand," Kendrick said, tossing a red chip into the pot like he was tipping a bellman.

Jake was a professional gambler, making his living betting on the next card. The only thing more valuable for a pro than an ace in the hole was a whale, a player too rich to know or care that he was lousy at cards. Kendrick was Jake's whale. But Jake didn't want him to lose, not tonight. He wanted Kendrick to win and keep winning until Kendrick was convinced he couldn't lose, not just at poker but at anything Jake pitched to him. And that's when he would take Kendrick down, one piece at a time. For now, Jake would let him run. But Kendrick needed help squeezing out the other five men at the table.

Jake was the next bettor.

"Call, plus another twenty."

The game was at the Seventh Avenue Club, an invitation-only private card room in Midtown Manhattan catering to rich men trying to win other rich men's money. The room was paneled in dark mahogany, soft lights shining on prints of fox hunts, brass-buttoned leather chairs set around custom poker tables framed and topped with rare olive-ash burl veneers. A trio of beautiful young women dressed to distract in microskirts and loose blouses with plunging necklines tended bar and served the half-dozen tables, pouring single malt Scotch and handing out Cuban cigars. It was a boys' club for big boys.

The buy-in was fifty thousand dollars, chump change for a Wall Street hound like Kendrick but a good place to start for Jake, guaranteeing enough action to make the evening worthwhile. They were playing Texas Hold 'Em. Two hole cards, a three-card flop in the middle of the table, with a fourth and fifth card to follow, players combining their hole cards with the common cards to make their best hand, swapping chips, booze, and bullshit until there was a winner.

The last card had been dealt and they were in the final round of betting. One by one the other players folded. It was back to Kendrick, who studied Jake, smiling.

"What do you have that you're so proud of, neighbor?"

They lived in the same building—the Rexford on West Seventy-Second Street, the residents calling it the Rex—but they weren't really neighbors. Not with Jake living in a fifteen-hundred-square-foot two-bedroom on the fourth floor and Kendrick owning the twenty-thousand-square-foot thirty-fifth-floor penthouse. Same address, different worlds.

Jake's hole cards were a pair of kings. The community cards were another king, a pair of threes, a four, and a ten, meaning the only way Kendrick could beat his full house was to have the other pair of threes in the hole, the odds of that no better than 8 percent. Add in Kendrick's bluff and the odds were close to 0 percent.

Jake sighed.

"Hell, what I have is no worse than second place."

"There's no shame in second place, but there's no money in it either," Kendrick said. "All in."

Kendrick was the founder and chairman of the board of Kendrick Investments, a collection of mutual funds and hedge funds. He spent his days managing other people's money, getting it right often enough that he counted his own money in numbers that began with a *b* instead of an *m*. But buying low and selling high wasn't how he became a billionaire. To join that club, he had to cheat people who didn't know better. People who fell for his promises of guaranteed sky-high returns only to see their life savings disappear while he hid behind a phalanx of lawyers. People like Jake's parents and their employees in Lakin, Kansas, the hometown he'd left in a hurry when he graduated high school twenty years ago.

Jake didn't care whether it was Karma or luck that both he and Kendrick lived at the Rex. When the cards turned your way, you didn't ask why. You just played them. And that's what he'd been doing, first making sure he bumped into Kendrick often enough to strike up a conversation, finally leveraging that into an invitation to the Seventh Avenue Club. Tonight was the sixth week in a row that he'd joined Kendrick, careful never to win more or lose less than his whale, knowing that this was a long play and poker was just the first act.

Sitting at the table, Jake wasn't thinking about the hundred and sixty grand in the pot. He was focused on the money he was going to take from Alan Kendrick and give back to his parents and their employees. Fifteen million dollars.

Kendrick shoved his stack of chips worth two hundred and seventeen thousand dollars into the pot, then sat back with his hands clasped in his lap and his square-cut face a sea of calm. His tell was gone, replaced by the quiet confidence of the predator about to devour its prey. Pushing sixty, with a weekend sailor's tan, Kendrick had a glint in his steel-gray eyes and the makings of a smile leaking from the corners of his mouth that said, *Come closer, catfish, so I can gut ya.*

Jake could match the bet, leaving him enough for a cab fare if he lost. He peeled up the corners of his hole cards, giving them a final look, and shook his head, deciding it was time for Kendrick to win.

"It's all yours, Alan. Well played."

Kendrick nodded and pulled the chips toward him, his smile widening to a satisfied grin as he turned his cards over to show that he'd won with nothing more than the pair of threes in the community cards. Kendrick didn't care that showing his cards was a tacky move no real player would ever make.

"Yeah, I get that a lot," Kendrick said. "Let's call it a night."

It was past two thirty in the morning when Jake got home. The lobby was deserted except for Milo, the late-night concierge.

"How's it going, Milo?"

"Not too bad, Mr. Carter. Nobody's asked me to score front-row seats to *Wicked*. How was your night?"

"I did all right. Won more than I lost and—"

"You can't ask for more than that," Milo said, repeating one of Jake's rules of life.

Jake woke up the next morning reeking of cigars and wobbly from the Scotch. He wasn't hungover; he just had a slight case of brain fog. He scrubbed off the tobacco residue with a hot shower, finishing with a bracing blast of cold water to clear the fog, got dressed, and made his way to the kitchen, groaning when he opened the refrigerator. It was empty except for a wedge of moldy cheese and a small bottle of orange juice.

He grabbed the bottle and headed out in search of something to eat that wasn't mutating. The elevator was running slow, so he took the stairs, swallowing hits of OJ along the way, shouldering open the door to the lobby. The door smacked into something sturdy enough to stop it. Jake bounced off the door and doused himself with juice.

"What the hell!"

Jake squeezed past the half-open door.

"Watch it!" said a woman holding a box big enough to block his view of her from the waist up. She pushed past him and stepped onto the elevator, set the box down, and shot him a dark look, then muttered something he couldn't decipher except for "jerk."

"You're moving into the building?" Jake said, his voice rising like he was accusing her of breaking and entering.

She cocked her head. "You can always move out. I'll help you pack."

She was African-American, tall and slender, with well-toned muscles beneath smooth hazelnut skin. Her deep-brown eyes were flecked with amber, flashing as she glared at him, a look more captivating than intimidating. He gave her a crooked grin.

"Not likely, not now."

He held her gaze until she shook her head, huffed, and jabbed the button closing the elevator doors.

Ana Cortez, the morning-shift concierge, handed him some paper towels. She had copper skin, an inviting oval face, and a full body. She also had a husband who was a firefighter and a year-old son, which put her on Jake's flirt-but-don't-touch list. He'd seen the UPS guy try to hit on her once, the guy backing away wide-eyed like he'd been mauled.

"Here you go, Mr. Carter."

"Thanks, Ana," he said, mopping up what he could.

She pointed to the front of his pants, where the spilled orange juice had soaked into a wet blot. "You're lucky it was orange juice and not hot coffee."

"Yeah. That look she gave me was scalding enough. New tenant?"

Ana nodded. "She's subletting the Hamiltons' apartment. About time too. They own four other homes and only spent nine nights here last year, but the rent's so high they had trouble finding someone who could pay it."

"Is it just her up there?"

"Just her."

"How long is she staying?"

"It's open ended. She's on a month-to-month."

Jake frowned. "Are you kidding me? When did the Rex become the Residence Inn?"

"They can call it anything they want as long as they sign my check," Ana said, and walked back toward her desk in the lobby.

He followed. "What else do you know about her?"

Eyes narrowed and mouth pursed, she gave him a disapproving look he was sure she normally reserved for her child. "You know I don't share information about our residents."

"Of course not. And the stuff you just told me about her and the Hamiltons was what? A quote from the *Rexford Weekly Newsletter*?" He flashed a mischievous grin, launching the good-natured-rogue routine that had gotten him out of trouble on more than one occasion.

Ana, arms crossed over her chest, wasn't buying it.

"Mr. Carter, you can save your shiny white smile and your pretty-boy looks for some other woman."

"What about my manly physique and charming personality? Besides, why would I want another woman when I've got you?"

"You wouldn't know what to do with a woman like me. And I wouldn't care if you did, 'cause you got nothing on my man. Now let me get back to my desk."

"C'mon, Ana, tell me her name. That can't be classified information."

She planted her hands on her hips and glared at him for a moment before relenting. "Her name's Cassie Ireland."

"Okay, that's a start. What else?"

She let out an exasperated sigh. "You're a gambling man, aren't you, Mr. Carter?"

"That I am."

"And a gambling man appreciates a good tip."

"Always."

"Well, I don't know anything about her, but I got a feeling you roll the dice on that woman, you'll go home a loser for sure."

TWO

"Cassie! You're finally here, girlfriend! I can't believe it!"

Gina Kendrick swept into Cassie Ireland's new apartment, two glasses in one hand and a bottle of vodka in the other, and set them on a stack of boxes and embraced her. Cassie eased her back half a step and they exchanged air kisses.

"You made it happen. I don't know how you talked the Hamiltons into going month-to-month."

Gina waved her hand. "It was easy. No one tells my husband no, which means most people tell me yes." She looked around the spacious apartment, filled with the Hamiltons' antiques and traditional furniture, and turned up her nose. "Kind of stuffy, don't you think?"

"A little *Downton Abbey*," Cassie agreed, gazing around the expansive living room with its Central Park views. She poured them both glasses of vodka. "You suppose the Hamiltons would notice if we threw their stuff out and redecorated?"

Gina giggled into her glass. "Oh my God! We should so totally do that! I mean, look at this place! It reminds me of my grandma's house back home. Except that these antiques are worth a small fortune. But c'mon, really? This place is like a nineteenth-century landfill."

Cassie was an asset recovery specialist, often the last resort for victims of Armani-clad criminals like Alan Kendrick, who bought their way around the law. She worked for a man who called himself Prometheus. He liked that she'd grown up all over the world with her diplomat father and that she was rootless, never having lived long enough in one place to miss it.

She had been looking for a way into the Rexford ever since Prometheus gave her the Alan Kendrick job, telling her it was more important to do it right than do it fast. But doing it right had its own risks, including adding Kendrick's wife to the collateral-damage list. She might be an empty-headed, lonely, rich trophy wife on her way to a lifetime of luxury rehab stints, but Cassie had come to like her. And liking someone she had befriended in order to do her job wasn't just a risk. It was a mistake—one that she tried hard not to make, because it was the kind of thing that could land her in jail or get her killed.

She had used Gina to get to her husband, introducing herself at one of the many charity events Gina attended, turning the introduction into a friendship and the friendship into an apartment one floor beneath the Kendricks' penthouse.

"The furniture isn't the only thing from the nineteenth century," Cassie said. "You should see the security. There's a dead bolt on the front door, a smoke detector in the bedroom, and a sticker on the fridge that says to call 911 in an emergency. I'm going to need more than that. I've got some valuable pieces of jewelry—probably nothing as fine as yours, but they cost me enough that I want to take very good care of them."

"Alan's got more security in our place than a bank. I could find out who did ours."

"That would be great, though I wonder if they'd even take on such a small-scale job as mine. Your system's complex, then?"

"Oh God, yes. You should see it."

"Maybe I should. It'd be like touring a security showroom. I could pick out one or two layers that would do for me."

Gina clapped her hands. "Shopping! Why don't you come up tonight, and I'll give you the tour?"

"Are you sure? I don't want to impose."

Gina waved away her concern. "Alan's got a meeting," she added, framing *meeting* in air quotes, "which means he's either playing poker or getting laid or both, and I hate being home alone while he's out having a good time. And tomorrow night he's being honored at another one of those Man of the Year Award dinners, which cost him God knows how much money in donations and which means I'll have to plaster a shit-eating grin on my face and leave it there all night. You have to come up. I can't stand two crappy nights in a row."

Cassie smiled and hugged Gina. She hadn't planned on making her move so soon, but the awards dinner was the perfect opportunity she needed to do her job, and if things went well, neither Gina nor Alan would know what had happened until it was too late—and when they found out they'd never suspect her.

"Fantastic! We'll make it a girls' night."

After Gina left, Cassie settled into an antique French fauteuil armchair. It was in mint condition and, running her hands across the Rose Tarlow glazed cotton upholstery, she estimated it was worth ten thousand dollars, give or take. She'd recovered enough antiques over the years to appreciate the one she was sitting in. She closed her eyes and leaned her head back, running through her brief on Alan Kendrick.

Kendrick was a wealth manager, putting other people's money to work, more often for him than for his investors. A corporate predator, he used his hedge fund to buy troubled companies at distress prices, breaking them up and selling off the pieces at a hefty profit and sacking as many employees as necessary to cut costs to the bone. It was all perfectly legal except for the spying and prying his security people did to dig up the dirt that gave him the extra negotiating edge he needed.

Rare gems were his passion. Each time he closed a deal, he added one to his collection, most recently the Scarlet Star, a flawless, five-carat red diamond whose size and deep-crimson color made it one of the rarest diamonds ever found. Only he didn't buy the Scarlet Star to celebrate a deal. He accepted it as a gift from a CEO in appreciation of Kendrick's promise not to swallow his company and not to sell a sex tape Kendrick's security team had dug up featuring the CEO's daughter.

Now the CEO had a bad case of blackmailee's regret and wanted the video destroyed and the Scarlet Star returned, and if it weren't too much trouble he'd also like Kendrick's head on a pike outside the village gates. Cassie intended to oblige him, betting that Kendrick was the kind of guy that kept his treasures close at hand, where he could admire his collection and watch his dirty movies, and there was no place better for that than home sweet home.

Her cell phone rang, bringing her back to the moment. The name on the caller ID, Zoey Fletcher, made her grin. They'd been friends since they were eleven and enrolled in the international school in Tokyo, where Cassie's father was posted at the US embassy and Zoey's was an executive for British Petroleum. Zoey's blond hair and porcelain complexion were a sharp contrast to Cassie's dark skin and cornrows, but their immediate and lasting connection with one another ignored those superficial differences. Separated by their fathers' careers when they were sixteen, they'd remained best friends. Cassie never told Zoey what she really did for a living, sticking with her cover story that she was a security systems consultant.

"Zoey!"

"Hi there, girl. Where have you landed this week?"

"Still New York, but I've upgraded from the Marriott to a posh condo on the Upper West Side with spectacular views of Manhattan and the Hudson River."

"And I'm still stuck in Royal Tunbridge Wells with a not-so-spectacular view of Harry's balding head, my kids' runny noses, and my ever-widening arse every time I look in the mirror."

Cassie laughed, remembering when Zoey was kicked out of school for hacking into the registrar's office and changing everyone's grades to all As. In her twenties, she was deep into the hacker's world, until she fell in love with Harry and went straight and domestic.

"You're the luckiest woman I know. You married the man of your dreams, you've got two beautiful kids, and I'll trade butts with you anytime. And you're an hour from London, which makes up for a lot."

"How about we keep our butts and trade places instead?"

Cassie sighed. Zoey had the life she sometimes dreamed of having, especially after spending so many nights alone in unfamiliar places. "It's tempting, but I don't think either one of us could pull it off. You remember what happened the last time we traded places?"

Zoey snorted. "Ha! Do I ever!" It was the week they'd met. The teachers had all the students wear name tags so they could tell them apart. Zoey and Cassie had switched their tags at lunch. "The perfect crime, except we forgot that you are black and I am white."

"We didn't forget. We just never noticed."

"Ah. I think we spent more time in detention than we did in lessons. Those were glorious days. I've got to run, but I just wanted to say hello."

"I'm glad you did. I'll call you soon."

"Make it after the kids have gone to bed and Harry has fallen asleep in his armchair."

"I promise."

They hung up just as someone knocked at Cassie's door.

Cassie opened the door to a curvaceous Latina with a warm smile and a vase holding two dozen long-stemmed bloodred roses.

"I'm Ana Cortez, from the front desk," she said. "Welcome to the Rex. I'm sorry I didn't get a chance to introduce myself while you were moving in. These are for you."

Cassie accepted the flowers, smiling. "Why thank you. And don't worry about not introducing yourself." She turned and pointed to the boxes lining the entry hall. "I was pretty busy juggling all this stuff."

"Yes, you really had your hands full. And from the looks of things, you've got a lot left to do."

Cassie glanced over her shoulder at the boxes. The apartment had been vacant for months, and the dust motes disturbed by the movers were still floating in the shafts of sunlight beaming through the floor-to-ceiling exterior glass walls. She sighed. "I'll say." She drew in the roses' scent. "These certainly help, though. Thank you so much. Much warmer welcome than that moron who nearly flattened me in the lobby. Did you see that?"

"Yes, ma'am, I sure did."

"I hope the rest of my new neighbors are more polite. Who was that guy?"

Ana hesitated, taking a breath and letting it out. "We're really not supposed to talk about the residents, but I suppose it doesn't matter under the circumstances."

Cassie arched an eyebrow. "What circumstances?"

"His name is Jake Carter, and he's the one who sent the flowers."

THREE

It was eight o'clock when Cassie arrived at the Kendricks' door carrying a bottle of champagne and a box of chocolate mousse–filled cupcakes from Molly's in the West Village. Her gaze darted from the security camera surveying the hallway to the small lens mounted by the door. She pressed the buzzer on the intercom, then heard the clickety-clack of Gina's heels approaching. The door swung open.

"You made it!" Gina said, bussing Cassie's cheeks. She was dressed down, wearing jeans and a University of Nebraska T-shirt, the glassy look in her eyes and the whiskey scent on her breath telling Cassie that she'd gotten an early start on the evening. "And you brought treats! OMG! Molly's Cupcakes! They are the best! Girl, we're gonna get fat and slappy tonight!"

Cassie grinned. "You know it!"

Her grin faded when she glanced at the security keypad by the door and saw that it was a Cronus model that employed a biometric fingerprint ID. Worse, Cronus used a tomographic motion-detector system, which was a lot harder to outsmart than the passive infrared variety.

Gina grabbed her wrist, pulling her into the apartment. "C'mon. We can't let those cupcakes get stale."

She led Cassie through the entry hall, past the living room, through the dining room, with seating for thirty, and into the kitchen, with its three separate cooking stations, warming ovens, and refrigerators. Gina put Cassie's bottle of champagne in one of the refrigerators, then removed another bottle chilling in a crystal ice bucket and grabbed two champagne flutes.

"Let's go to the movies!"

They sat side by side in two of the twenty plush, padded leather recliners in the home theater, watching a double feature of *Bridesmaids* and *An Officer and a Gentleman*, laughing and crying and washing down cupcakes and popcorn with champagne.

"This has been a lot of fun," Cassie said after Richard Gere carried Debra Winger out of the factory. "We have to do it again."

"Not before I show you all our security doodads, or whatever the hell they're called. We've got invisible motion sensors that can see through walls. At least I think they can. Can they?"

Cassie was relieved that Gina had finally broached the subject. Her plan had a much better chance of working if Gina thought she was the one orchestrating events.

"It sounds a little sci-fi to me. Thanks for reminding me. Between the cupcakes and Richard Gere, I almost forgot."

Gina brightened, popping up and taking Cassie by the hand. "I'll give you the tour and then you can go home."

Cassie followed Gina through all nineteen rooms, listening as Gina pointed out the features of Kendrick's impressive high-tech fortress. There were Cronus keypads at every entrance, and microcameras buried in the crown molding in every room, except the bathrooms, the master bedroom, and Kendrick's office. Gina's claim about invisible motion detectors meant that Cronus had mounted small security nodes inside the walls that bounced radio signals off each other, creating a motion-detector net throughout the apartment. If an intruder blocked or disrupted those signals, the alarm would sound.

For Cassie, the two most important features were in Kendrick's office—the control panel for the entire system, and the entrance to Kendrick's panic room. The office was dominated by a massive mahogany desk with stubby legs carved into snarling lions' heads, the king of the jungle guarding the master of the universe, a black leather high-backed chair adding a touch of throne. The control panel was concealed in a recessed compartment built into the credenza behind Kendrick's desk, and the entrance to the panic room was disguised by a section of the floor-to-ceiling bookcases. Cassie smiled when Gina showed her the Cronus keypad for the panic room, hidden in the hollowed-out core of one of the books on the shelf—a biography of Diamond Jim Brady.

Gina turned her back to Cassie, tapped in the alarm code, and opened the door. They stood together in the windowless room, which was lined with locked display cases filled with glittering stones, none of which were the Scarlet Star. The three-foot-high Winston & Stevens safe mounted in one corner made Cassie cringe. The manufacturer claimed its electronic lock had over a million possible combinations and that it could stand more than twenty hours of manual manipulation. Cassie wouldn't have more than a few hours to crack it while Gina and Kendrick were at the Man of the Year dinner, not nearly enough time to run through all the possible combination permutations even with an auto dialer, but enough time, she hoped, to drill the safe.

Good as it was, Kendrick's security system was vulnerable to the one risk that couldn't be programmed out—humans. Someone who would inadvertently give away the keys to the kingdom. Cassie was counting on Gina to be that person.

They were in Kendrick's office, having just left the panic room, when Cassie faced her. Every job had make-or-break moments and this was one of them.

"There's something I need to tell you, Gina."

"What?"

"I haven't been entirely honest with you. I told you I'm a business consultant, that I advise clients on the integrity of their systems."

"And you don't? What are you? A thief?" she said, laughing. "Are you going to rob Alan and me?"

Cassie smiled. "No. Actually, it's the opposite. I'm here to make sure you don't get robbed."

Gina wrinkled her nose and crunched her eyes. "I don't understand."

Cassie pulled a business card from her pants pocket and put it on the table. "This is who I work for."

Gina picked up the card. "Global Security. What's that?"

"We do security audits for insurance companies that insure high-risk clients. And your husband is a very high-risk client because of the value of his precious-gems collection and your artwork. We do unscheduled, unannounced audits to test security. We don't tell the insurance company or the insured until we deliver the report to make certain we see things as they really are. You have a good alarm system. Hidden cameras, motion sensors . . ."

Gina retreated, putting distance between them, doubt creeping into her eyes.

"You mean all this time you've been pretending to be my friend just so you could move into the Hamiltons' apartment and then get me drunk enough to show you how to break into our panic room? Are you going to move out tomorrow now that you've made a fool of me?"

"Pretending to be your friend was part of my job, and I hated it because we became friends, real friends. My company transferred me to New York because we have a lot of clients here. I couldn't live in a hotel forever and you were the one who suggested I take the Hamiltons' apartment. And I'm not moving out until the Hamiltons kick me out."

Gina's lips were quivering, her eyes darting around as Cassie watched her struggle with the possibility that she had been manipulated into suggesting Cassie move in one floor below. Cassie was counting on everything Gina had told her about her life with Alan—how he limited their social life to the high and mighty, treating her as nothing more than arm candy—to overcome her anger. Pretend or not, Cassie knew she was the closest Gina had come to having a friend since Alan married her, rescuing her from life as a waitress at a Wall Street diner. Cassie may have deceived her at first, but now she'd come clean, something Alan would never do. Cassie hoped that would be enough for Gina to accept her explanation, because the alternative was too painful.

Gina nodded, beginning to relax, letting her arms ease down to her sides. "Alan always gets the best."

"But there's a flaw in your security, isn't there?"

Gina swallowed, her face reddening. "Me. I showed you where this room is and how to get inside."

Cassie went to her, put her arm over her shoulder. "Yes. You did, but it's okay because nothing happened. And now you know how careful you have to be."

"Please don't tell Alan. He'll kill me."

"I'm not going to tell a soul."

Gina's eyes widened. "You're not? What about the insurance company?"

"Not them either. It's bad enough that I took advantage of our friendship. I shouldn't have done that." Cassie shook her head. "I should have told them to send someone else as soon we became close."

"But you have to tell them something, don't you?"

"I do. I'll tell the insurance company that I tried to get you to tell me about the panic room but you wouldn't."

"Oh my God. Thank you so much."

"You don't have to thank me, because the way things turned out, you helped me do my job."

"How?"

"Well, I'm pretty certain that you'll never tell another soul about how to get into the panic room."

"Not even if they tortured me!"

"So you see, you've actually made your security system even stronger than it was before."

Gina smiled. "I guess I have, haven't I?"

"And if you don't tell your husband about tonight, he'll never know."

Gina raised her hand and took an oath. "Trust me. I'll never say a word."

"I do. What's the code for the master panel?"

"Same as for the front door. We use the same code for everything. Alan says that's okay because he's always changing it. Is that a bad thing?" Gina dropped her chin like she was expecting to be scolded for a mistake, even if it wasn't hers.

"No. Makes sense," Cassie assured her, although she would never dream of using the same code on multiple devices. "But changing the password so often can make it hard to remember the right code."

Gina rolled her eyes. "Tell me about it. Alan makes me repeat it out loud until he's sure I've memorized it. But an hour later I can't remember it."

"But you didn't have any trouble entering the code a few minutes ago."

Gina winced. "I cheated."

"What do you mean?"

She opened the biography of Diamond Jim Brady, pulled out the Cronus keypad, and removed a lavender-colored Post-it stuck on the backside of the keypad, on which she'd written the password. She handed it to Cassie, whose eyes lit up. She'd never seen such a simple key to a kingdom.

"I know it's a stupid thing to do," Gina said, "especially now, but I was afraid I wouldn't remember the code and if there was an emergency

I wouldn't be able to get into the room. I also keep the code in my phone, but I don't always have my phone with me. Please don't tell Alan. He'll kill me."

Cassie shook her head. "I won't tell him."

"I guess I shouldn't do that anymore, huh?"

"Well, it's not the most secure system. Let me think about some options. We'll keep it between the two of us."

Gina let out a sigh of relief. "Oh my God, that would be so great. I've been so worried that Alan would find out."

"In the meantime I need you to open the master panel for me so I can run some tests." Cassie handed her the Post-it. Gina entered the code and scanned her thumbprint, smiling like a schoolgirl about to be rewarded with a gold star. "Perfect! Do you know where your circuit breaker box is?"

"In the utility room off the kitchen."

"Great. I need you to turn off the power. I'll let you know when it's time to flip the power back on."

Gina placed the Post-it on the back of the keypad and headed to the utility room. Cassie removed the code, photographed it with her smartphone, and put it back before taking a closer look at the master control panel. The Kendricks, like many rich people, couldn't be home every time someone needed to get into their apartment, and they weren't about to hand out their alarm code. The system was set up to allow them to enter an alternate code that expired after a set time for those occasions and, if they chose, to turn off the biometric sensor. Knowing that Kendrick frequently changed the code, Cassie created her own code as a backup and set it to expire at ten o'clock tomorrow night.

But the code wasn't enough. She'd still have to get past the biometric sensor. Fortunately, the system also allowed for the entry of additional thumbprints. Cassie scanned in her own print and set it to expire at the same time as her alternate code, though erasing her print didn't mean that it was gone forever. With the right software, a lot of information that was lost could be found. But recovering her thumbprint wouldn't expose her, because her prints weren't on file anywhere in the world. Prometheus had made certain of that.

She had a final backup. Kendrick's system was wireless. The FCC restricted the frequency ranges for wireless alarm systems, including video cameras and motion sensors, to specific parameters. Gunnar Agnarsson, her hacker guru, had sent her a handheld device the size of a package of cigarettes that would jam any wireless device operating within those frequencies within a radius of twenty meters. There would be dead silence from all sensors and cameras within range of the jammer, and the system wouldn't know that anything had happened, supposedly allowing her to walk through Kendrick's apartment as if she weren't there. The emphasis was on *supposedly*, since Gunnar had only tested it on his own equipment, and Cassie wouldn't be able to test it on Kendrick's unless her codes and thumbprint failed.

While the jammer might get her past the alarm, it wouldn't get her into the panic room. That was why she'd created her own backup alarm code and entered her thumbprint into the system.

The lights went out, and, as Cassie expected, the control panel remained lit, powered by a separate source. She tested Kendrick's code, her alternate code, and her thumbprint on the panic room and the master control panel, pleased that everything worked, and then yelled to Gina to turn the power back on. When Gina returned, they heard a bellow from the front hall.

"Gina! Gina!"

"Oh, Christ! Alan's home!" Gina closed the credenza, put the desk cover back, and smoothed her shirt and finger-combed her hair. "How do I look?"

"Like a wife who's glad her husband is home."

"Gina! Goddammit, where the hell are you, woman!"

"Crap! He's drunk. I hate it when he comes home drunk. All he wants to do is fuck, but he's usually too far gone to get it up, and then he starts crying like a little boy."

"Alan Kendrick crying like a little boy—I'd pay good money to see that."

"What can I tell you? He's a man, and when you get right down to it, men are weak and pathetic."

"Gina! Gina!"

"We better get out there," Cassie said, "before he starts crying."

Cassie stayed a step behind Gina down the hall to the entry, until stopping cold, her jaw hanging open, when she saw Jake Carter holding Kendrick upright.

Gina rushed to Kendrick, and she and Jake half dragged him to the first sofa they could find and laid him out.

Gina knelt beside him, holding his hand to her face. "I'm here, baby. I'm here."

Kendrick raised his head. "I think I'm gonna be sick." And he was immediately right, coating Gina with remnants of dinner and booze and sending Jake jumping back out of range.

"You again," Cassie said, glaring at him.

He grinned. "Twice in one day. What are the odds?" He glanced back at Gina and Kendrick, who was now busy convulsing with dry heaves. "Ain't love grand?"

FOUR

The elevator doors closed after them, but before Cassie could press the button for her floor, Jake pulled the stop button, blocking her from the control panel.

"Don't worry," he said. "I'm harmless, and the concierge is watching and listening. Isn't that right, Milo?"

Milo's voice crackled through a speaker on the control panel. "Yes, sir, Mr. Carter. I'm right here. You need anything?"

"No, we're good." Carter spread his hands apart, his gesture saying, *See, I told you so*, and shined his best grin at her. "Hidden camera."

Jake was impressed that Cassie kept her face neutral and her stance relaxed, arms loose at her sides. Cool as she could be, neither intimidated nor threatening but ready for whatever might happen.

"What do you want, Mr. Carter?"

"It's Jake, same as the name on the card that came with the flowers."

She took a slow, measured breath, the effort telling Jake that he was getting under her skin but that she wasn't about to let him know it. More to like.

"What do you want, Jake?"

"To start over. That's how it works in rom-coms, right? We meet cute, hate each other at first, but get over it and live happily ever after."

"Kittens are cute. Running someone over is rude."

Jake covered his heart with his hand. "For which I've apologized by sending you flowers, and I think that gets us back into the cute category."

Cassie began to smile but stopped and turned her head to one side until she composed herself. Jake took that as progress. He'd settle for nonverbal encouragement, since she gave no sign of being ready for the spoken variety.

"Listen, Jake," she said, facing him, keeping her voice neutral but firm, leaving no room for argument. "I appreciate the gesture, but I'm not looking for whatever it is you have in mind."

Jake studied her for a moment. He'd given her a chance. Time to get down to business.

"Fair enough. Hey, Milo?"

"Yeah, Mr. Carter."

"Kill the camera."

Milo laughed. "Sure thing, Mr. Carter. Catch you later."

Jake kept his eyes on Cassie, picking up the narrowing of her eyes, the subtle tensing in her biceps and thighs and the slight uptick in her breathing. Her autonomic system didn't believe that he was harmless, but the stone-cold look in her eyes told him she might be the dangerous one.

"Step away from the control panel," Cassie said. "We're done here."

Jake held his ground. "Okay, so cute is out. Let's switch gears. Which one of them are you after? Gina or Alan? Or do you want both of them?"

His question knocked Cassie back, her short, quick gasp telling him he'd caught her off guard.

She shook her head, raising her eyebrows. "I have no idea what you're talking about. Gina and I are friends. She helped me get my apartment and invited me to come up tonight to celebrate moving in."

"Nice bluff, but your reaction gave it away. Don't feel bad. The body can be an unfaithful bitch. But here's the real problem. Your reaction doesn't fit with your profile."

Cassie folded her arms across her chest. "Pardon me?"

"You're a systems consultant for Global Security, whatever that is."

"Global Security is a—"

"Not Global Security. I read the 'About' section on the website. I'm talking about being a systems consultant. Talk about two words that mean less together than they do separately. It's probably code for overpaid, but I guess that's what you get with a Harvard MBA and a raft of recommendations on LinkedIn."

She narrowed her eyes. "You investigated me?"

There was something about Cassie that had taken hold of him. It wasn't just that she was beautiful. She was, but New York was full of beautiful women, many of whom turned his head, just not 360 degrees. Ana had warned him not to press his luck with her, but that only made her more intriguing, especially now that he suspected she was playing the same game he was with the Kendricks. He was at heart more riverboat gambler than probability stats nerd, and nothing got his blood pumping like going all in on a long shot.

Jake shrugged. "I wouldn't call it an investigation. I googled you and . . . I may have paid for one of those instant background checks. Cost me twenty bucks. No criminal record or unpaid taxes or traffic tickets, so that's definitely in your favor."

"I can't believe you did that."

"Well, you did cost me a bottle of orange juice."

Cassie lowered her arms to her sides. "You can buy a lot of orange juice for twenty dollars. You could've spent it on learning some manners."

He wiggled a finger at her. "But it did pay for this conversation. And how you ended up in the penthouse apartment of one of the richest men in America in the middle of the night on the very day you move in is a puzzle. And the way you reacted when I asked you about that—well, that's a puzzle within a puzzle."

Cassie gave him a curt smile. "And your answer to the puzzle is that I'm somehow after Gina or Alan."

"Better than even odds. So, yeah, that's my answer."

She cocked her head. "You know something? I'm standing here wondering why you would accuse me of something so absurd, and the only answer I can come up with is that you're delusional and are off your meds."

Jake smirked. "Oh c'mon, Cassie. You can do better than that."

"In fact I can. You were out with Kendrick until the middle of the night getting him throw-up-and-fall-down drunk. Sounds like you're the one trying to reel him in. For what—insider-trading information?" Cassie folded her arms over her chest and raised an eyebrow. "I suppose I should warn Gina, don't you think?"

"And ratchet up their security? I'd think that was the last thing you'd want them to do."

"Really?" Cassie opened her phone and began punching numbers on the keypad, one hand on her hip, head cocked and chin tilted at Jake like a dare.

Jake smiled closed-mouthed, admiring her even more, his hands raised in surrender. "A bluff and a raise. Good for you. Good for you. I fold."

Cassie shut down her phone. "You play poker?"

"For a living."

"Then take my advice. Find another line of work."

Jake grinned, unlocked the stop button, and pushed "34" on the control panel. The doors opened a moment later. He watched as Cassie walked away, calling after her.

"You still owe me a bottle of OJ."

Cassie stopped, shook her head, and continued on without answering or looking back.

FIVE

Jake Carter was a complication Cassie didn't need. She didn't know what his angle was—only that he had one—but she didn't care so long as he didn't undermine her relationship with Gina or give Kendrick a reason to tighten his security. He was one more reason to get in and out of Kendrick's apartment as soon as possible without leaving any trace leading back to her.

She had been mostly truthful when she told Gina that she wasn't leaving the Rex, omitting the unless-she-had-to part. She longed for a place to call home, and she could do a lot worse than the Hamiltons' apartment, though she knew that living there happily ever after would be difficult if even a whiff of suspicion that she had robbed Kendrick came her way. No matter her denials, Gina would suspect her. She might not tell her husband out of fear of what he would do to her, but she'd never trust Cassie again. And even if all of that worked out, Prometheus wouldn't like her staying on. She'd talk him into it, though, telling him that the prestige address was an important part of her cover. If the job went well, he'd give in to keep her happy. If it went south, he wouldn't have to tell her to pack her bags.

Cassie spent the next day getting ready, pulling together everything she would need, mentally rehearsing each step, planning as much for what would go wrong as what would go right, because something always went wrong. That evening, using binoculars, she watched from her balcony as Alan and Gina Kendrick emerged from the Rex and walked to their waiting limo. Gina, in a low-cut red gown that could have been painted on, would have stood out even without binoculars from a height of thirty-four floors, the driver staring at her as he ushered her into the backseat, Kendrick grinning at him as if to say, *In your dreams, buddy*.

It was late May and wouldn't be dark for an hour. Cassie gave herself two hours after that to finish the job. It should take longer than that to serve the rubber-chicken Man of the Year dinner and make the speeches, but she didn't want to risk Gina bailing out and coming home early.

The building plans she'd studied showed surveillance of the stairs leading to the roof similar to that in the elevators and outside Kendrick's front door, leaving her only one option: climbing up from her balcony to Kendrick's, the bottom of which was twelve feet above the floor of hers and which was ringed with a four-foot-high wrought-iron fence. The Carrara marble–tiled balcony floor was six inches thick, and the bottom rail of the fence, which would be the closest grab point, was four inches above the surface. The wrought-iron rail around her balcony was also four feet high, meaning it was eight feet ten inches from the bottom rail on Kendrick's balcony. She was five feet eight inches tall, with an additional overhead reach of two and half feet. If she stood on her railing, arms raised, she would still be eight inches shy of Kendrick's railing, but she wasn't about to stand on her tiptoes and jump in any event, especially while carrying a backpack stuffed with thirty-five pounds of safecracking gear.

Instead of making that suicidal leap, she would use a rope pulley system. Designed for rescuing stranded mountain climbers, it was perfect for balcony-to-balcony breaking and entering. All she had to do was throw one end of the rope, weighted with a pulley, over the top of the rail on Kendrick's balcony, hoping its momentum would carry it through its vertical rails and back down to where she could reach it. She'd learned to use the system on another job, when she was climbing mountains instead of balconies.

Under cover of darkness, Cassie hugged the wall and leaned out over her railing, swung the rope three times, and launched it at the rail above, hearing the pulley clang against the iron before falling back to her. Her next toss made it over the top. The pulley swung neatly through the rails and back down into her gloved hands.

She anchored the system at the base of her railing and hoisted her backpack onto her shoulders. Smiling to herself, she thought about how far she'd come from slogging through business case studies at Harvard to being the bullet Alan Kendrick would never see coming. No way could she ever go back. Tugging on the rope to make certain it was secure, she pulled herself to Kendrick's balcony railing. Dressed in black with a watch cap pulled down over her forehead and hidden in shadows, she was nearly invisible.

She chose the sliding glass door that opened into the master suite because it was closer to Kendrick's office and the panic room and because there was a security pad on the wall only a few steps from the door, giving her plenty of time to enter the code and her thumbprint before all hell broke loose. The bedroom had one other important advantage. When Gina gave her the tour of the apartment, she hadn't seen signs of any hidden cameras, glad that Kendrick didn't want images of his naked posterior preserved for posterity. Even so, she'd keep her head down in case she was wrong about the cameras.

She picked the lock on the sliding door and set the timer on her watch for twenty-five seconds, knowing from her research on the Cronus system that she had thirty seconds before the alarm would summon the police. She opened the door, triggering the alarm's nerve-jangling beeping, and crossed the bedroom to the security keypad. Three seconds gone. Keeping her breathing steady, she entered the alternate code she'd programmed the night before. The beeping didn't stop. She tried it twice more. Eleven seconds gone. Nothing. Heat rising from her chest to her neck, she entered the code Gina had given her. Same result. She checked the photo she'd taken with her cell phone to confirm the code. Tried it again. The beeping didn't stop. Twenty seconds gone. Sweat beading under her watch cap and dripping into her eyes.

Shit! Kendrick had changed the code and shut out her alternate code. Why? Had Jake gotten to him? Had Kendrick discovered her thumbprint and blocked it as well? Twenty-three seconds gone. Breathing faster, her mouth dust dry.

She pulled the jammer from her pants pocket and fumbled with the controls, cursing herself for not practicing with it while wearing gloves. She grabbed the fingertips of the glove on her free hand with her teeth and ripped it off. Twenty-eight seconds gone. Her heart pounding. Flicked the jammer control.

Silence.

Twenty-nine seconds gone.

She took a deep breath, then another, then a series of smaller breaths, reeling herself back under control. The alarm was off, but unless she could figure out Kendrick's new code, she wouldn't be able to get into the panic room. There would be no point in giving up and trying again another night, as she doubted Gina would fall for another security audit requiring her to divulge another alarm code that Kendrick could change before Cassie had a chance to use it.

Waving the jammer in circles around her, she made her way to Kendrick's office. She set the jammer on his desk, opened the Diamond Jim Brady biography, and removed the Cronus keypad, expecting to find a lavender Post-it with Kendrick's latest password written in Gina's curlicue script. But there was nothing there. No Post-it with the old code or new.

Kendrick might not have given Gina the new password. Gina could have forgotten to write it down, or maybe she hadn't had time to hide it in the book, or maybe she'd had a change of heart and told her husband what had happened. The reason didn't matter to Cassie. She was just as fucked.

Cassie laid the book on Kendrick's desk, crossed her arms over her midsection, and clenched her chest, crushing the fleeting panic rising from her gut. *Just do the goddamn job! There's always a way. Now find it.*

She dug through Kendrick's trash basket and rifled his desk drawers for his new password, slamming the last drawer shut when she came up empty. The password Gina had shown her had ten characters, six of which were a mix of upper- and lowercase letters, two of which were symbols and two of which were numbers. Even if the new password used the same distribution, she wouldn't live long enough to try all the possible combinations.

Standing in front of the bookcase, Cassie took three deep breaths, filling her lungs and emptying them in a steady cadence. The effect was calming, clearing her head. She was wrong. The fact that Gina hadn't followed her usual procedure didn't mean she hadn't recorded the new password. It only meant that the password wasn't where Cassie expected to find it.

The only hopeful possibility was that Kendrick had given Gina the password, but she hadn't had a chance to hide it in the Diamond Jim Brady biography. In that case Gina would have made certain to write it down, not trusting herself to remember it later. And she would have hidden it someplace Kendrick wouldn't stumble across it. In an apartment riddled with hidden cameras, she would have chosen one of the few spaces not under constant surveillance. That limited Gina's options to the master bedroom, bathrooms, and closets.

Using the jammer like a shield, Cassie returned to the master bedroom. She rejected it as a possible hiding place because Gina shared it with Kendrick.

They each had their own closet and bathroom. Gina's bathroom and closet were bigger than every apartment Cassie had lived in before moving into the Hamiltons' unit. The bathroom fixtures were gold, the countertops cut from slab granite. The shower could seat six, and the Jacuzzi was big enough for a deep end. The closet had floor-to-ceiling racks and shelves and a center island filled with cabinets and drawers. Experimenting with the wall switches, Cassie discovered that the clothes racks could be raised and lowered for easier access. She almost didn't notice the flat-screen TV built into one corner.

Even in all that space, Cassie knew what every woman knew when it came to hiding things from their men. Cassie found Gina's maxipads in a bathroom cabinet, but the code wasn't in the box. Gina's birth control pills were in a drawer next to her sink. Cassie popped the container open and there it was—a lavender Post-it with the new password.

It was 9:50 when Cassie entered the panic room. She had an hour and ten minutes left on her timetable. She surveyed the glass cases, making certain that Kendrick hadn't added the Scarlet Star to his private display, then focused on the keypad embedded in the door to the safe that controlled the electronic lock. She tried the same code, frustrated when it didn't work. Alan had trusted Gina with the code to get into the panic room but not into his safe. Cassie's heart sank because now it would be impossible to finish the job without leaving proof there had been a robbery.

She removed a chisel and hammer from her backpack and used them to pry the faceplate off the keypad. With a small metal hook, she fished out the solenoid wire from the interior of the keypad. When the correct code was entered, it would send a current through the solenoid wire to the locking mechanism, telling it to retract the steel bolts that held the door shut. To bypass the code, Cassie would send a small current directly through the wire to unlock the safe, a trick she'd learned from Renaldo Reis, a handsome young safecracker in Brazil who had seduced her by teaching her his safecracking skills, among other talents, making for a memorable weekend in Rio de Janeiro.

She stripped the cover off a section of the solenoid wire, split and braided the ends, and attached them to a nine-volt battery, experiencing a true aha moment when the safe refused to open. The aha was that Reynaldo had been full of shit, because the safe he tested it on was a piggy bank compared to this one. Though, in fairness, he was all that he claimed to be in bed.

She reached into her backpack and took out a plasma torch, pulled on goggles, and switched to Kevlar gloves. She opened the flow of pressurized argon gas from the tank and flipped on the electrode inside the nozzle, unleashing a thirty-thousand-degree-Fahrenheit jet of bright-blue flame. Training the flame on the safe, she burned a hole through the front wall, the half-inch-thick steel glowing bright yellow as it melted. Then she burned a second hole next to the first and turned off the torch.

Cassie emptied the remaining contents of her backpack on the floor, picked up a borescope—a flexible metal arm with a camera on the end—and connected it to her laptop. She inserted the borescope into the first hole she'd made and watched on her laptop as its LED light illuminated the interior of the safe, stopping when she saw the back of the electronic keypad and maneuvering the camera until she found the tiny red reset button.

Holding the borescope steady, she threaded a long, thin piece of metal into the second hole. She jabbed the wire at the minuscule button twice, missing it each time.

Cassie sat back for a moment and closed her eyes. "Calm down," she ordered herself. "There's no rush." But, of course, there was. She took a deep breath and started again, watching her laptop screen, edging the wire toward the reset button, brushing against it and slipping off, finding her way back until it was poised dead center over the button. She nudged it ever so slightly and gently pushed the button, heaving a sigh of relief when the keypad beeped.

"Gotcha!"

She reset the code to 123456 and pressed "Enter." The keypad beeped again, accepting the new code. She withdrew the borescope and the wire, turned the handle on the door, and opened the safe. It was ten fifteen. Forty-five minutes before her self-imposed get-the-hell-out deadline. Plenty of time left.

There were half a dozen small black velvet bags hanging on one wall, each containing rare precious gems, but after she examined their contents only two interested her. One held the Scarlet Star. She rolled it around in the palm of her hand, marveling at its deep-red color, before swapping it with a fake, sealing it in a small plastic pouch, and stowing it in a side pocket of her backpack. The second held a two-carat jadeite gemstone, a pure form of jade with an intense green color so rare it sold for three million dollars per carat. She tucked the bag into the same pocket as the Scarlet Star. Since Kendrick would know he'd been robbed, she wanted him to think the jadeite was the only precious stone that was stolen so that he wouldn't look closely at the fake Scarlet Star.

The top shelf inside the safe held ten DVDs in hard plastic cases, each marked as a master disc. One at a time she inserted them into her laptop long enough to see that they were sex tapes and that one was of her client's daughter. She took all of them, not wanting to draw undue attention to its theft. She didn't know whether there were other copies, but this was at least a start.

Tightly banded bundles of crisp hundred-dollar bills were stacked like building blocks on the floor of the safe. Thumbing one bundle, she did a quick count. It was a hundred thousand dollars. There were twenty-five blocks. She tossed five into her backpack, clearing enough space in the safe to reveal a laptop hidden behind the blocks. Nobody locked a laptop in a safe and buried it under two and a half million dollars in cash unless whatever was on the hard drive was worth a lot more.

Cassie booted it up and shook her head when she discovered it wasn't password protected. Kendrick must have figured with all the layers of security between a thief and the laptop, one more layer wasn't necessary. She scrolled through the hard drive index, pulling up a few documents and grinning when she found duplicate sets of stock transactions, one marked private and the other public, along with e-mails detailing several of Kendrick's insider-trading windfalls. Though she'd seen only a limited sample of everything on the laptop, Cassie suspected she'd found the mother lode of evidence that would send Kendrick away forever.

She stuck a flash drive into a USB port on the laptop and began downloading everything on the hard drive instead of stealing it. She wanted Kendrick angry about the gems and money she'd stolen, not scurrying to cover his ass because his laptop was gone. Prometheus would get the flash drive to the authorities, and while Kendrick was still filling out his insurance claim there would be a knock at his door—and it wouldn't be from Publishers Clearing House telling him he was the big winner. The display on the laptop counted down the remaining time before all the files would be downloaded. Seventeen minutes. Still plenty of time.

Sitting cross-legged on the floor, Cassie stuffed as much additional cash into the backpack as she could. A million dollars' worth of hundred-dollar bills weighed around twenty pounds. She managed to cram two million into her backpack, boosting its weight to fifty-five pounds.

She'd leave it to Prometheus to decide what to do with the jadeite and the cash, knowing that some of the money would help finance jobs for people who couldn't afford their services and some of it would go to charity. At least that's what Prometheus always told her. Never having seen his financial records, she had to trust him, because the alternative would make her sick or, worse, force her to go after him, and that was a fight she didn't know whether she could win.

The timer on the downloading process hit five minutes to go. *Almost home free*, she thought—until an earsplitting, pulsating siren began wailing, reverberating throughout the apartment. The jamming device had failed! But why would that set off the alarm? There must be motion detectors inside the panic room, which meant there could also be cameras.

The door to the panic room began to close, another automatic security-system response. Cassie threw her backpack into the opening, stopping the door and leaving just enough room for her to slip past if the pressure on the backpack didn't rupture the argon tank nestled among the stolen cash, incinerating her and the money. But she couldn't leave yet, not until the download was complete.

"C'mon! C'mon!" she pleaded with Kendrick's laptop, drumming her fingers against her thighs and keeping her head down and away from any cameras, glancing up long enough to see the glowing red light of a hidden camera beaming at her from the back of the safe. "Son of a bitch!"

She jumped to her feet, ran into Kendrick's office, and opened the master control panel, not breathing until it accepted his new password and her thumbprint. A minute had passed since the alarm sounded. Cronus promised its clients that either the cops or its own security force would respond in less than five minutes to an alarm, meaning she had no more than four minutes before a SWAT team broke down the door.

Cassie pressed the button to turn off the alarm, but the siren kept blaring. There had to be a way to override the alarm, but she didn't have time to figure it out. She tapped a button labeled "Cameras," which pulled up a diagram showing the position of each camera, then clicked on the one inside the safe. The screen immediately switched to the camera's feed, showing where she'd been sitting moments ago. She paused the recording, clicked "Rewind" and then "Play," and gasped when she saw herself pocketing the jewels and the cash.

"Fuck me!"

She clicked the "Erase" icon, allowing the video to run far enough back at high speed until the door to the safe was closed, and paused the camera. Hoping that did the trick, she glanced at her watch. The alarm had been sounding for over five minutes. She was way out of time.

She hustled back to the panic room and pulled the flash drive from the laptop, relieved that the download had finished. She shoved the panic room door as hard as she could, gaining just enough room to kick her backpack out of the doorway. She bolted into Kendrick's office, grabbed her backpack, and ran for the balcony.

Once outside, she heard the wail of police-car sirens. Peering over the rail, she saw squad cars blocking each end of the street. Overhead came the *whup-whup* of an approaching helicopter, its spotlight cutting through the dark and heading right at her. Hands tight on the rope, her backpack grinding into her spine, she raised one leg, then the other, over the rail and slid back to her balcony. In a series of rapid-fire movements, she disassembled the rope and pulleys and threw herself to the ground as the helicopter spotlight danced past her, then skittered into her apartment as soon as the chopper passed.

SIX

Jake strolled into the lobby of the Rex shortly after midnight and found himself in a swarm of residents and cops. Milo wormed his way through the crowd, tugging on Jake's sleeve, out of breath.

"Hey, Mr. Carter, you won't believe what went down here tonight!"

"I have a feeling you're right," he said, craning his head as he scanned the crowd, finding Cassie leaning against a wall on the far side of the lobby, a bemused look on her face.

"There was a robbery! A big, motherfucking, blow-the-lid-off robbery!"

Jake couldn't take his eyes off Cassie. "You don't say."

"I do say, and you'll never guess whose apartment got hit."

"Kendrick's."

"Damn, Mr. Carter! How'd you know?"

Jake looked at him. "Just playing the odds, Milo. A lot of rich people live here, but if the robbery was as big as you say it was, it had to be Kendrick because he's the richest of us all."

Milo laughed. "Well, he's a little less rich now than he was when he woke up today."

"Have the police arrested anyone?"

"Not yet. At first they thought whoever did it was still in the building, but they searched all the common areas and didn't find anyone. Then they started knocking on doors, asking the residents if they could search their apartments. Well, you know how that went over. Everybody started calling their lawyers. Anybody who walked in from the street they're keeping down here."

Jake pointed to Cassie. "What about our newest resident, Ms. Ireland?"

"She came in just ahead of you."

Jake watched as an overweight detective in a badly fitting suit approached Cassie and showed her his badge.

"Catch you later, Milo," Jake said, and made his way to Cassie and the detective, cupping Cassie's elbow when he got there. "There you are," he said to her. "I wondered where you'd gone."

Cassie looked at him, her eyes steady, one brow slightly raised. "And I was wondering the same about you."

Jake ignored the detective, knowing both of them were bluffing, deciding whether to check or raise. With a half smile he placed his bet.

"That call I got from Charlie, I couldn't get him off the phone. I thought you were going to wait for me."

She sighed, giving her head a slight shake, annoyed. "I got tired of waiting, and besides . . ."

"Besides what?"

"You know I've never liked Charlie."

They held each other's gaze, their eyes dancing, until the detective interrupted.

"And who are you?"

"Jake Carter. I live on the fourth floor."

"And you and Ms. Ireland were out together."

Jake slipped his hand into Cassie's. "We had dinner and then took one of those long romantic walks around Manhattan."

The detective arched an eyebrow at Cassie. "That so?"

Cassie curled her middle finger, digging the nail into Jake's palm. "Yes. We had a nice time."

"Huh, then I guess you won't mind letting us have a look around your apartment, since it's directly below the unit that was robbed and the thief might have used it to get in and out of the victim's unit."

Cassie's jaw dropped. "Do you think that's what happened? Oh my God, I could have been robbed too! When can I go check? And what if I'd been home?"

The detective nodded. "Yeah, that would have been real terrible. You mind if we go have a look?"

"No, of course not. I want to find out what happened."

"I'll come with you," Jake said.

The detective held up his hand. "Steady, pal. Just me and the lady."

Jake put his arm around Cassie's shoulders, reassuring her. "I'll wait for you down here."

Ten minutes later they were back, the detective's disappointment written in his downturned mouth.

"Everything okay?" Jake asked Cassie, taking her by the arm.

"Yes. Fortunately, no one broke into my apartment."

"Great. Detective, would you like to see my apartment? It's only on the fourth floor, but I've got great views of the buildings across the street."

The detective shook his head. "Maybe next time."

As soon as the detective walked away, Cassie pulled her arm free, but Jake held on, sliding his hand into hers once more.

"What are you doing?" she asked.

"I thought you could tell. I'm holding your hand."

She tried to tug her hand out of his but he held tight. "I'd rather you didn't."

"An evening's date may only last a few hours, but an alibi lasts forever. If you haven't noticed, that detective is pretending not to watch us. You don't want to give him a reason to keep pretending, do you?"

Cassie gritted her teeth for an instant before melting into a smile. "No, I don't suppose I do."

"Me either." Jake put his hands on her waist, pulled her toward him, and kissed her, feeling her stiffen, then relax as she kissed him back. Jake eased away, inhaling. She smelled as good as she tasted.

The elevator opened behind them. Jake wrapped his arm through hers and led her onto the car, and kissed her again. When the doors closed, she pushed him away, her eyes fiery as she raised a pointed finger at him. Jake wrapped his hand around her finger and whispered.

"Cameras. Remember," he said, punching the button for the thirty-fourth floor with his other hand. "The cops will check the video."

Cassie forced a smile, sliding her hand behind his neck. She leaned in, her mouth next to his ear. "Kiss me again and I'll kick your balls so hard you'll spit them out."

"And that would be a tragedy for both of us."

She stifled a laugh, dropping her chin to his shoulder. "You're irrepressible. Are you like this all the time?"

"Only when I'm awake. You'll get used to it."

Cassie didn't respond, but she didn't resist when he held her closer, maintaining their embrace until the elevator stopped on her floor. Jake walked her to her door. She opened it and turned toward him.

"Thanks," she said.

"For what? The alibi?"

"I don't need an alibi."

"Of course you don't. That's why you played along instead of telling the detective to arrest me for stalking you."

"I went along with you because that was safer than seeing what you'd do if I didn't."

"Am I that unpredictable?"

"So far."

"And you thought I was a lousy poker player."

She smiled. "You run a nice bluff, I'll give you that."

"Then why did you thank me?"

She ducked her head, then raised her eyes. "For a nice bluff."

He smiled in return, his eyes boring in on hers. "I'm not bluffing now."

She shook her head. "I'm sorry but we're not playing the same game. This is as far as we go."

"Tonight?"

She forced her answer. "Ever." And closed the door.

SEVEN

Jake left a message on Kendrick's cell phone the next day but didn't get a return call. Five more unanswered messages left him with the queasy certainty that his whale was getting away, though Kendrick didn't strike him as the kind of man who would go to ground over a robbery.

He knocked on Cassie's door a few times, even sliding a note under the door with his cell phone number on it asking her to call him, but she was ignoring him too. He was pretty certain she had something to do with the robbery, and if she did it was her fault Kendrick had cut him loose. If so, he should be furious with her, but he wasn't. Why? He doubted she had shimmied up from her balcony to Kendrick's and made off with a fortune. More likely she had done the advance work for someone else, using her friendship with Gina to scout Kendrick's apartment. Why else would she have let him be her alibi? And why had he thrown her a lifeline that could turn into an anchor around his neck if she was involved? And why would he go all in with a woman like that? He knew the answers to all his questions. Some risks were just worth taking.

A week after the robbery he stopped at the concierge desk to chat with Ana.

"Have you seen Cassie Ireland lately?"

"Why? She dump you already?"

"What?"

"Don't play coy with me, Mr. Playboy Poker Player. I've seen the elevator video of you two locking lips the night of the robbery. Guess you're not such a good kisser."

"I'm a great kisser, just underappreciated. She hasn't moved out, has she?"

"No. So maybe if you keep trying she might give you a second chance."

"Thanks for the moral support. Anything new on the robbery?"

She shrugged. "Like they would tell me anything."

"A need-to-know basis, huh?"

"And I don't need to know, except for these." Ana opened a drawer and pulled out several copies of a grainy black-and-white photograph of someone dressed in dark clothing, a watch cap pulled low over the brow, head turned upward barely enough to capture the eyes, and even that part of the image was blurred. "One of the detectives gave these to me. He said it was from Kendrick's surveillance cameras. Supposed to be the robber."

"Why did he give them to you?"

"He asked me to pass them around to the staff and see if anyone recognized the robber. Like that's possible with a crummy picture like this, so I stuck 'em in the drawer."

Jake picked up one of the photographs. He made his living studying his opponents' eyes. Though the image was blurry, he'd bet even money he knew whose eyes they were.

"I see what you mean. Mind if I keep this?"

"What do you want it for?"

He shrugged, not wanting to tell her it could be his winning hole card. "A souvenir. Who knows? It may be worth something one day when they catch the thief."

"No way they gonna do that. Anybody who could get past all the security the Kendricks had in their apartment and get away with nobody seeing anything is way too smart for New York's finest. I can tell you that for sure."

Before Jake could reply, a platoon of men and women wearing navy-blue windbreakers with "FBI" stenciled on the back marched into the lobby.

"Can I help you?" Ana asked.

"Yes," the agent leading the parade said. "By staying out of our way."

He handed her a copy of a search warrant and motioned the rest of the agents to the elevators. Jake read the warrant over Ana's shoulder. It was for Kendrick's apartment. Cassie got off one of the elevators as the agents were piling on. She nodded at Ana and Jake as she walked past without saying a word.

"Hey, Cassie, you should take a look at this," Jake said, holding up the search warrant, keeping the photograph tight against his thigh.

She stopped and turned toward him. "What is it?"

"A search warrant for Kendrick's apartment. Looks like Alan has been a very bad boy."

Cassie smiled, her lips closed, her eyes dancing. "And bad boys deserve to be punished. See you around," she said, and walked out the door onto the street.

EIGHT

ONE MONTH LATER

Cassie sprinted past the Rex's rooftop swimming pool, weaved around a faux Michelangelo statue of David in the sculpture garden, and hurdled a marble bench before skidding to a stop at the roof's edge, hands planted on the waist-high wall. It was near midnight, the city lit up from Harlem to Chinatown, her breath coming in quick bursts, the unmistakable voices she heard from the balcony of Alan Kendrick's penthouse directly below giving her a chill. She slid her backpack off her shoulders and peered over the wall, her worst fears realized.

"Do you want to die tonight?" Kendrick asked, looking at Jake, who was dangling upside down over the balcony, a muscle-bound thug holding him by the ankles, Kendrick's acid tone suggesting it didn't matter to him one way or the other.

Jake curled upward as best he could, shaking his head. "Not especially."

Cassie smiled at his nonchalance. She didn't expect anything less, though the beads of sweat she saw running off his face told a different story.

"Then tell me where I can find that bitch."

"Which bitch?"

Kendrick nodded at the thug, who let go of one of Jake's ankles, causing him to cry out.

"Shiiiit!"

Cassie's heart climbed into her throat. She pulled her rappelling gear from the backpack, slipped into the harness, and cinched one end of the rope around the marble bench, confident it wouldn't budge against the combined flying force of her 120 pounds and the dead-dropping weight of Jake's 180-odd pounds. Then she reached into the backpack again, removed a second coiled rope, and knotted one end to the bench and the other in a large lasso, holding it tight against her thigh.

"Still feel like being a smart-ass?"

"No, definitely not," Jake said, his words tumbling out in a torrent. "Just tell the Hulk to pull me up."

Kendrick nodded at the thug a second time, and the thug grabbed Jake's free ankle. Cassie breathed easier at Jake's sigh of relief.

"His name is Hugo, and he doesn't like it when people call him the Hulk."

"Okay, please ask Hugo not to drop me."

"That all depends on you. Cassie Ireland robbed my apartment, and you gave her an alibi. Tell me where I can find her, and Hugo will pull you up. Now where is she? I'm not going to ask you again."

Cassie didn't wait for Jake to answer. She climbed on top of the wall and jumped out into space in a sweeping arc, holding the rappelling rope in one hand, swinging the lasso with her other. In midflight she whipped the lasso around Jake's head and over his shoulders, yanking it up to his waist and tightening it just as Hugo let Jake go. Still in flight with legs widespread, she slammed crotch-first into the goggle-eyed Hugo, clamping her legs around his enormous head and driving him back a couple of steps. She did a backflip, seized the railing with both hands, and snapped Hugo over the rail.

Hugo's dying wail faded in the distance as Cassie righted herself and knotted the end of Jake's rope around the bottom balcony rail. Saucer-eyed, Kendrick tore a gun from his jacket. She whipped around, driving a powerful kick into his belly, and ripped the pistol from his hand as he crumpled to his knees. Cassie kneed him under the chin, whiplashing his head and knocking him out.

She leaned over the rail. The wind had picked up, swaying Jake back and forth, his arms clamped tight to his sides by the lasso.

"Nice night, huh?" she said.

"Getting better every second. Though you do realize that ape almost took me with him when you drop-kicked him off the balcony, right?"

"He probably just wanted to kiss you good-bye."

"You going to leave me hanging or reel me in?"

"No way I'm leaving behind a perfectly good rope."

Bracing herself against the base of the railing, she pulled him up and onto the balcony, tilted him upright, and, holding him close, cut the rope.

Jake held on to her until his legs stopped wobbling, burying his face against her neck. "Thanks."

"Anytime."

They stepped away from each other. He stroked her cheek, eased his hand under her chin, and lifted her lips toward his. She closed her eyes as he kissed her, pressing her body against his. Breathing heavily, she pulled away, took him by the hand, and led him inside to the master bedroom. She unhooked her harness and let it drop as she unzipped and stepped out of her black leather bodysuit. Naked, she licked her lips, enjoying the ravenous way Jake looked at her. She undressed him, slowly at first, then faster and faster until, wrapped in each other's arms, they sank onto the bed, overcome by need.

Jake was on top, inside her. They moved in unison, her back arching as she cried out, and her eyes fluttered open, only for her to find herself alone in her bed with her thighs clamped around her body pillow. Panting and frustrated, she kicked the pillow to the floor and rolled onto her side, clutching the sheets, moaning.

"Oh. My. God!" She sat up, ran her fingers through her hair, and took a deep breath and let it out slowly. "What is the matter with me?"

She reached for her phone and called Zoey Fletcher, counting on Zoey to assure her that her crazy dream was nothing more than a crazy dream.

"Is everything all right? Do you have any idea what time it is?"

Cassie looked at the clock on the nightstand next to the bed. "It's 8:00 a.m. your time. Don't tell me I woke you."

"With two kids to get dressed, fed, and off to school? Hardly. I've been up for two hours, but it's three o'clock in the morning in New York. What's up?"

"I had a dream you won't believe."

"Was there sex?"

"Oh, yeah."

"Hang on a sec. Harry," she called to her husband. "You'll have to take the kids to school today. Okay, kids. Off you go and make sure your dad doesn't get lost. Love you! Okay. I'm back. Let's hear it."

Cassie recited an edited version of her dream, changing Kendrick's name and leaving out the part about the robbery.

"A lasso? Can you believe that?" Cassie said.

"Damn the lasso. I'm more interested in the sex. Who is this guy?"

"His name is Jake and he lives in my building."

"Does he know you want to screw him senseless?"

"Oh God, no."

"Then where's this coming from? Have you been out with him?"

"No, but he's been flirting with me."

"What do you know about him? And don't tell me you didn't look him up. I know you too well for that."

"You do know me too well. That's why I called you. He's thirty-eight and he's from a small town in Kansas. That's a state in the middle of the country."

"I know where it is. I've seen *The Wizard of Oz*."

"His claim to fame is that he starred as Professor Harold Hill in his high school's performance of *The Music Man*."

"Harold Hill was a con man. What about Jake?"

"He's a gambler, a professional poker player."

"Well, that's close. So what are you going to do about him?"

"I don't know. I haven't seen him in the last few weeks."

"Why not?"

"He hasn't been around. Besides, with my schedule I don't have time for a relationship."

"That hasn't stopped you from dreaming about him."

"I know."

"Do you miss him?"

Cassie hesitated. "Yeah."

"You haven't said that about anyone since Gabriel."

"I know."

"Then you've got a problem."

"I know that. What do I do?"

"A girl like you and a bloke like Professor Harold Hill—either use your lasso or run like hell."

NINE

Later that morning Cassie decided to go for a run. Ana was on duty at the concierge desk.

"Morning, Ms. Ireland. I heard the good news."

Cassie stopped, wrinkling her brow. "What good news?"

"That you signed a new lease on the Hamiltons' apartment. Guess you'll be with us for the next year."

"Looks like it."

Ana lifted an eyebrow and gave her a sly, girl-to-girl grin. "I'll bet Mr. Carter will be glad to hear that."

Cassie felt her cheeks flush. She never should have let Jake kiss her in the lobby, let alone kissed him back. Anyone on the staff that hadn't seen them kiss had no doubt heard about it, maybe even watched the replay.

"I wouldn't know. I haven't seen him in several weeks."

"Well, he's been out of town, but he'll be back any day now."

"Good for him."

Cassie hurried out, stopping on the sidewalk to tighten the laces on her running shoes. Her life had been a series of short stays at anonymous addresses ever since she met Prometheus, and she had good reasons for changing that. She'd promised Gina she would stay. The more she realized how vulnerable Gina was, the more important her promise became. With the ongoing police investigation into the robbery, staying would be less suspicious than leaving. The Rex fit with her cover, and having a base of operations was easier than living out of a suitcase. And as much as she tried to deny that it mattered, staying would keep her closer to Jake.

**

She'd called Prometheus a week ago to tell him that she'd signed the lease.

"I'm sending my jet," he'd told her. "Be on it tomorrow morning at six. We'll talk about this when you get here." He left no room for argument.

The plane's window shades lowered automatically as it taxied out onto the runway the next morning and remained closed throughout the flight, cutting off her view of anything that might hint at his location. She'd never left the grounds of his estate on any prior visits and never saw anything that identified where it was. The most she could say for certain was that it was a six-hour flight from New York and that it was in the Tropics. She'd studied maps and researched flight times and could do no better than to place his island somewhere south and west of Barbados, though she couldn't find one that fit her calculations.

By midafternoon she was sitting with Prometheus on his veranda enjoying the breeze coming off the ocean and the endless view to the cloudless horizon. He was in his seventies. His shaggy white hair hung to his shoulders, accentuating his narrow face, and his lanky frame was confined to a wheelchair. Despite age and infirmity, he had a deep, commanding voice and penetrating dark eyes that evoked more power than any able-bodied man she'd ever known. He never offered his real name or explained why he couldn't walk, and she knew better than to ask.

Hibiscus, orchids, and bougainvillea surrounded the house, along with unkempt grasses and shrubs maintained in a natural state, suggesting the grounds had always been that way. His home was modest, the floorboards creaking and the roofline sagging. As a tropical hideaway, it fell somewhere between Gilligan's Island and Bali Ha'i.

"Where are we?" she asked him.

"You ask that every time you visit me."

"And you've never given me an answer."

He cocked his head. "And you know why I haven't."

"Yes. So that I can't tell anyone."

"Then why do you keep asking?"

She stood, folding her arms across her middle, staring out to sea before turning back to him. "Because I don't like not knowing. When I get off your plane, it's as if I've stepped through some kind of dimensional rift into another world and this tropical island paradise of yours is all there is. It's . . . it's . . ."

"Disorienting?"

"Yes. And a little claustrophobic, if that's possible in paradise."

He thumped the armrest on his wheelchair. "You think my island is claustrophobic, try living in this damn chair. I told you it would be like this from the beginning and you agreed, did you not?"

Cassie nodded her head, a student again. "Yes."

"And do you regret Gabriel Degrand recruiting you away from that miserable Wall Street worm Howard Platt six years ago?"

She shook her head. Hearing Gabriel's name made her ache even after all this time. She had been his Gina, someone he manipulated in order to do his job.

"I thought I was going to be a whistle-blower."

"And if that's all you'd been, you wouldn't have been able to get a job at Starbucks, let alone on Wall Street. Gabriel and I turned you into someone far more useful and valuable."

"I've sometimes wondered if you orchestrated everything—if you used Howard Platt to get me and not the other way around."

Prometheus shrugged. "Being overestimated is an occupational hazard, but I've learned not to fight it. People believing you have power can be as useful as actually having it. Either way, you accepted."

"You needn't remind me."

"You know what we are. We're the last resort for people who have lost their most valuable possessions and have nowhere else to turn, whether because the justice system has failed them or because they can't risk going to the authorities. If you have a problem with that, maybe you're not—"

"I don't have a problem with that."

"All right. So is it how we work that bothers you? It seems simple enough. I offer you an assignment. It's up to you whether to accept. If you do, you recover the assets. How you do it is your business. I arrange for the return of the assets. I charge a fee of ten percent of the asset value, with a minimum fee of one million dollars, twenty-five percent of which is yours. Your money is deposited in the untraceable foreign account of your choice."

"Did you bring me here just to give me a refresher course in what we do?"

Prometheus bristled, his jaw tightening for an instant before softening, his voice steady and firm. "I brought you here to remind you of one of the most important reasons we are able to do what we do."

Cassie hung her head. "Get in and get out. No attachments."

"Attachments to people, places, or things will color your judgment. They will take your mind off the job. You will make decisions because of the way you feel and not because of what you must do. Gabriel knew that, but he ignored the rule and it cost him his life."

Cassie's words caught in her throat. "That's not fair. He recruited me after the Platt job and you hired me. We fell in love. That wasn't wrong."

"Then you should have told me and I would have terminated both of you. He died saving you. That you avenged his death changed nothing."

"Would you have preferred that he let me die?"

"I would have preferred that he didn't have to make the choice. I don't remind you of him to cause you more pain. I do it to remind you of why he died. No attachments. This is the way you must live if you are to continue being useful. This is the life you chose."

"It's only an apartment lease. You went to all the trouble to create my Global Security cover story but you didn't give me a place to live. Even people who travel all the time have an address, and the Rex fits with my cover."

"And those are your only reasons?"

"No. I sent you the flash drive with the documents from Kendrick's computer."

"Along with the gems and the cash. Yes. Job well done."

"And you made sure those documents found their way to the FBI. That's why they raided Kendrick's apartment."

"As you knew I would."

"Gina Kendrick is going to suspect I had something to do with the robbery," Cassie said, explaining how she'd persuaded Gina to give up the secrets to the security system. "So, if I suddenly move away, she'll tell her husband or the police or both and we lose control of the situation. The next time I show up in New York, we could have a problem."

"Nothing that couldn't be handled, but yes, it would be better if that wasn't necessary. So, I'll ask you again. Is there any other reason you signed that lease?"

"What other reason could there be?"

He pressed his hands together in a steeple. "None that would be wise."

"The Rex is an address. Nothing more."

Prometheus stared at her. His scrutiny made Cassie uneasy but she resisted the urge to squirm.

With a slight nod, he gave her his answer. "Then go back and keep it that way."

**

Cassie jogged east on Seventy-Second Street until she reached Central Park, where she took her usual route north. She circled the reservoir before making her way back along the east side, cutting across Terrace Drive to the west side. When she got back to the Rex, the street in front of the entrance was blocked by three black SUVs with government license plates. Uniformed police officers held back a growing throng of onlookers. Reporters were jockeying for position. Their cameramen monitored the images on their equipment.

She elbowed her way through the crowd until she reached the police line. Alan Kendrick, hands cuffed behind his back, emerged from the lobby flanked by two men, each holding him by the arm. He walked with his chin up, staring straight ahead, expressionless. One of the men opened the back door to an SUV and pressed Kendrick into the car. The convoy pulled away. Reporters ran to their cars to follow and the crowd dispersed.

Cassie found Gina in the lobby surrounded by more reporters. Gina was shaking her head and putting her hands up in front of her chest, trying to keep the reporters at bay. Cassie caught her eye, but Gina glared at her and looked away. Cassie's throat tightened. She was afraid that Gina blamed her for Kendrick's arrest.

Ana watched Gina and the reporters from behind the concierge desk with a smoldering look on her face. Cassie approached her.

"Ana, I'll get the elevator. You get Mrs. Kendrick."

Ana nodded. "You got it."

When the elevator opened, Cassie stepped inside out of sight of the reporters and held the door. In another moment Ana had bulled her way past the reporters and ushered Gina into the elevator. She then wheeled around to face the mob, arms crossed, as the elevator doors closed.

Fists clenched and shaking, with tears running down her cheeks, Gina squared around at Cassie.

"You did this."

TEN

Jake had been certain he would win back his parents' and their employees' retirement money playing poker with Alan Kendrick. But Kendrick had quit playing, and Jake didn't have a plan B. He wasn't a con artist and he wasn't a thief, but he was patient. A guy like Kendrick couldn't stay away from the table forever, and when he was ready to play, Jake would be waiting. In the meantime he needed another game.

Las Vegas and Atlantic City had been out ever since the World Series of Poker a few years ago. Anonymous and untrue whispers that he'd cheated his way to the final table hadn't been enough to get him banned, but the casinos let him know they didn't want his action. The few times he'd gone back, they made sure he couldn't get a sniff of a high-stakes game.

He'd been tempted to stick around New York to see what might happen with Cassie Ireland, even if she was the reason he'd lost his grip on Kendrick. There was no denying that their kiss had been more than a kiss, but when he couldn't get so much as a hello, he decided it was time for a change of scenery.

He'd spent the last two weeks playing poker on the Latin American tour, winning enough in Rio that he could afford to spend the rest of his trip being a tourist. That's when Esteban Soriano, an old poker rival, tracked him down and invited him to try the pizza at a restaurant a friend of his owned in Buenos Aires—and the private game he ran in the back. Soriano had dropped off the circuit a few years ago and they'd lost touch, but Jake was intrigued enough to make the trip.

The restaurant was plain and simple—wooden tables covered with white butcher paper—but the stone dough *fugazetta* pizza was fantastic. And it went well with the moscato wine. The waiter, a teenage boy with dark bangs hanging over his brown face, handed Jake his bill.

"How about that," Jake said. "Eight hundred forty-seven thousand five hundred eighty-two pesos for a slice of pizza."

"Senor Soriano say to tell you it's the best pizza in Buenos Aires, that's why it cost so much."

Jake laughed. "I'm glad I didn't order a second slice."

He handed the waiter his brand-new credit card, issued by the Saurez Bank Group. The waiter swiped the card on the processor attached to his iPad and Jake used his finger to scratch his signature on the screen.

Jake looked at the menu. A slice of pizza cost twelve pesos. The buy-in for the poker game about to start in the storage room behind the kitchen was one hundred thousand dollars, which in Argentine pesos exactly matched Jake's bill.

"Go sightseeing when you're dead," Soriano had told him. "Play poker so that you know you're alive."

Smiling and shaking his head, he dropped fifty pesos on the table and walked through the kitchen—fragrant with the smell of rising dough, melting cheese, and sweet onions—and into the storage room, where the air was crisp, cool, and dry.

The room was a concrete square illuminated by bare fluorescent tubes suspended from the ceiling. A barstool and a small, round, chest-high table were positioned along one wall, giving whoever sat in the chair a place to set a drink and an overhead view of the poker table in the middle of the room. The table consisted of a thick, round slab of hardened black mesquite buffed to a high sheen and mounted on a pedestal base. There were eight chairs—seven for the players and one for the dealer. White, red, blue, and black chips were stacked and waiting in front of the players' seats. Half a dozen wrapped decks of cards were fanned out in front of the dealer's chair.

Jake was the last to arrive. He surveyed the other players. Four were middle-aged men—some lean, some not—all wearing fine clothes and Rolex watches. They were clustered in one corner, talking loudly and laughing. Jake pegged them as well-heeled regulars at Soriano's game.

The only woman was tall and sleek with silver-streaked black hair and was dressed in tight black leather pants and a billowing black blouse. She looked to be in her late fifties and was handsome in the way of women who'd lived well. Her eyes were dark and her look intense when she glanced at Jake. He gave her a slight nod and she smiled in return, her gaze softening. She carried herself with the cool confidence of a player.

The remaining player was a man thirty years her junior. He had slick, brushed-back hair and a smooth olive complexion, more Mediterranean than Latin American. Dressed in Armani, he stood apart from the others, absently twisting a platinum ring with an emerald-cut sapphire. Jake guessed the sapphire weighed at least five carats. He caught the man's eye. The man gave him a quick look before he turned his attention to the woman, the hint of a sneer telling Jake the man had decided he was unworthy.

Soriano met Jake at the door, clasping his hand, an iPad with a credit card processor tucked under his arm.

"Hello, my friend."

"You gave up the Latin American Poker Tour for this?"

"I got tired of taking your money. Besides," Soriano said, patting his wide, round belly, "I'm prosperous enough."

"And if I know you, Esteban, your rake from the private games you're running will keep you that way."

"Sí," he said with a laugh, pointing to his gray hair and tugging at his thin beard. "I'm too old to be risking so much. I'm like the whore who became a madam. Now I just watch the players and take their money, and I only keep 5 percent of each pot—a modest rake, don't you think?"

"Let's call it the upper end of modest. What's the story with the Suarez credit card?"

"Nobody carries the kind of cash we play for, so everybody wants to play on credit. But I'm not in the collection business."

"But the Suarez bank is."

Soriano shook his head. "They like collecting even less than I do. You and the other players gave Suarez wire transfer instructions for your personal bank accounts. Those instructions are embedded in the credit card." He held up his iPad. "Should anyone require additional funds, all they have to do is swipe their card and the wire transfer is instantaneous."

"Why Suarez? Do you get an iPad for every account your players open?"

Soriano grinned. "I get something better than an iPad—protection. The owner of the bank has many important friends. He makes sure no one bothers me or my games and that my guests have no difficulty moving their money in and out of the country without paying any of our exorbitant taxes."

"Is that why I had to deposit a hundred and ten thousand dollars in my Suarez account before they'd issue the credit card?"

"The bank's accommodations are not cheap."

"So I'm paying ten thousand dollars in protection money for the privilege of playing in your game? How is that a good deal?"

"Consider it a business expense. Deduct it from your American taxes . . . if you pay them."

"Every penny."

Soriano clapped him on the back. "Then don't give it another thought. If you don't win ten times what Suarez is charging, we'll both be disappointed."

"You're right about that. I was surprised when I got your call. It's been a while."

"Too long, my friend. I'd heard that you were in Rio. I'm glad you could make it."

"Your timing was good. The game I'd been working in New York dried up, so I thought I'd try my luck south of the equator."

"Bad for you but good for me. An American is always a good draw for my games, and one with your reputation is an even better attraction.

"This game came together very quickly because of that one," Soriano said, tilting his head at the man that had dismissed Jake with a glance. "He asked a friend of mine where he could find a high-stakes game, and my friend asked me to set it up. It is what friends do."

"Who is he?"

"Theo Kalogrides. His father is one of the richest men in Greece. He made his fortune in shipbuilding but has many interests. My friend tells me that Theo is blessed with his father's money but none of his brains or charm."

"But can he play poker?"

"We shall see. He is said to have a temper."

"What about the woman?"

"She is my sister, Mariposa. She's a master chef, very good with a knife in or out of the kitchen, and a good poker player. Her restaurant is down the street. There's a six-month wait for reservations."

"And the others?"

"Successful men who enjoy the game. Raul—the tall, skinny one—is a lawyer. Standing to his right is Tomas, the best plastic surgeon in Buenos Aires. Ignacio, the one with a belly to match mine, is his brother-in-law. His first wife died and left him a rich man. The handsome one is Mateo. He owns the most valuable real estate in the city. He would also like to own my sister, but she isn't selling."

Jake made his living in high-stakes private games with people who could afford to lose a lot of money. Games like that were hard to find. Soriano's invitation had turned into a golden ticket to the chocolate factory. Jake patted him on the back.

"If I'd have known you were running a game like this, I'd have moved down here a long time ago."

Soriano beamed and turned toward the others.

"Welcome, my friends. Let the game begin. No-limit Texas Hold 'Em, World Series of Poker rules. All bets in American dollars. Introduce yourselves, and good luck to everyone."

ELEVEN

Soriano climbed onto the barstool. Two men entered from the kitchen. One was past seventy, slight, and stoop shouldered, with sunken eyes and a narrow chin. He took the dealer's chair, unwrapped a deck of cards, and began shuffling. The other was middle-aged, with a barrel chest, powerful arms, shaggy black hair, and a smashed, pulpy nose. He stood next to Soriano, a two-legged Rottweiler on a short leash.

Jake had played in a lot of games with rich kids like Theo. They'd pretend to shrug off dropping six or seven figures in one night because it was another way of reminding themselves and the world how rich they were. Jake never bought the shrug. Even if the money didn't matter, winning always mattered, especially if the money was Daddy's dough. Trust-fund babies had a hard enough time proving themselves. Getting their ass kicked in a poker game never helped.

He took a seat opposite Theo, who was thumbing his chips, checking the count before the game started—a rookie move telling Jake that Theo wasn't as experienced as he wanted Jake to believe, valuable information in a game that was more about the players than the cards. Then again it could be an act. Jake had played the bumpkin enough times to know how useful it could be to encourage your opponents to underestimate you.

And there it was. This was poker, a game in which everyone lied, no one could be trusted, and a fortune could be won or lost. And that's why Jake loved the game.

Mariposa sat on Jake's left. Raul sat on her other side. The dealer was between Raul and Theo. Tomas, Ignacio, and Mateo filled the seats between Jake and Theo, who was still worrying his chips.

"They all there?" Jake asked Theo.

Theo narrowed his eyes, then set the chips on the table. "I never doubted it. I just like the feel of the chips in my hand."

Jake decided to poke him, check the thickness of his skin. "I guess you Greeks haven't heard of Kenny Rogers."

Theo leaned back in his chair, smiling. "'The Gambler.' You'll excuse me if I don't take a country singer's advice about when I should count my chips."

Jake nodded. "You might want to rethink that before we're done."

Theo lost his smile. "Maybe you should be more concerned about me counting your chips before the night is over than the words to a silly cowboy song."

They stared at one another long enough that Jake picked up a slight, almost imperceptible tic in Theo's left eye. More good information.

The dealer interrupted, breaking the silence. "Everybody antes a hundred dollars on each hand. Small blind is one thousand dollars and the big blind is double that."

Jake let the game come to him, studying the other players, watching for any tells that would tip their hands, evaluating their tendencies. Mariposa was aggressive but smart, taking modest risks, pouncing if she sensed that someone was bluffing.

Raul and Ignacio stayed in hands as long as they had decent cards, folding at the first sign of trouble. Tomas didn't know when to fold, constantly scratching a chip against the table, handing his credit card to Soriano every hour or so. Mateo chatted away as if he was barely paying attention but didn't miss a thing, steadily building his stash of chips.

Theo was reckless, using big bets to drive the others out of a hand, confusing luck with skill. He laughed and joked when he won, his eyes lit up like a child's, and sulked when he lost, casting accusatory glances at whoever won the hand, twice demanding a new deck of cards. Theo had asked for wine early in the evening and Jake's server from the restaurant had kept his glass full. The more he lost, the more he drank, and the more he drank, the uglier he became, finally cursing Mariposa when she won yet another hand, matching her two aces to the pair in the flop.

"You goddamn bitch. You must've pulled those aces from between your legs."

Soriano's enforcer stepped toward the table but stopped when Soriano put his hand on his shoulder.

Mariposa reached for the chips in the pot, acting like she hadn't heard.

"Goddamn cunt," Theo muttered.

"El hombre pobre," Mariposa said, pushing her lower lip out in a sad face.

The others laughed, nodding their heads.

"What'd she say?"

No one answered.

Theo slammed his palm on the table. "What the fuck did that bitch say?"

Jake knew enough Spanish to know that Mariposa had called Theo a poor man, a mild insult but more than enough to push him closer to the brink.

Jake glanced at Mariposa, who had pulled a small switchblade from the folds of her blouse and was palming it in her lap, blade open, her eyes icy. Soriano's hand remained on his enforcer's shoulder. Theo had twice insulted his sister, and no one would blame him if he let his man beat the crap out of Theo, but he was letting it ride. Soriano caught his sister's eye, shaking his head. She closed the blade and pocketed the knife. Their restraint convinced Jake that Soriano's cut of Theo's losses—or Jake's winnings—was worth more than his sister's honor.

Soriano translated. "She said she wishes you better luck."

Theo glared at Mariposa, who tilted her head and gave him a coquettish smile.

"Sí," she said. "I was lucky, senor. Perhaps it is your turn now."

"It better be."

Theo won the next three hands. Jake watched both him and the dealer closely for any sign that either was cheating but saw none. It was, he decided, the run of the cards, and it was enough to calm Theo. When the cards turned the other way, he didn't complain about having to use Soriano's iPad to wire-transfer more money to his Suarez account. By two in the morning, Theo was down a million dollars, most of which Jake had won.

The button had passed to Jake, meaning he was presumed to be the dealer for purposes of the bet, allowing him to be the last bettor throughout the hand, which was a considerable advantage. Seated to his left, Mariposa had to put in the small blind of one thousand dollars, and Raul had to put in the big blind of two thousand dollars.

"The pot is right," the dealer said, shuffling the deck and dealing two cards facedown to each player.

Because he was seated to the left of Raul, Theo was the first to bet after the hole cards had been dealt. He smiled broadly as he peeled back the corners of his cards.

"Fifty thousand."

Tomas and Ignacio folded. Mateo called, matching the bet. Jake considered his hole cards—a nine of clubs and an eight of spades. Weak cards, but not weak enough to let Theo run him out of the hand, at least not until he had a better sense of whether Theo was bluffing.

"Call," Jake said.

Mariposa nodded and added her chips, not saying a word. Raul folded.

The pot had grown to more than two hundred thousand dollars.

The dealer laid three community cards faceup in the middle of the table: ten of clubs, ace of hearts, and seven of clubs. Jake watched Theo's reaction to the flop. If Theo was holding a pair of aces, the appearance of a third would have triggered a paroxysm of joy he'd never be able to suppress, but his expression was intense, not joyful, and there was no twitch in his eye.

Jake had picked up Mariposa's tell early in the game. Her jaw muscles tensed when she suppressed a smile, but her cheeks were smooth now. He decided that she wasn't thrilled with her cards. Mateo sighed, quiet for the first time, his face sagging as if he'd run out of gas and things to say at the same moment.

Mariposa's position to Jake's left meant that she was the first bettor for as long as she remained in the hand. She rapped her knuckles on the table.

"Check."

It was Theo's bet. Jake watched his eyes as they darted around the table. He could check or bet small, hoping to keep the remaining players in the game, or make another big bet to drive them out. That he was taking so long to decide told Jake that the wine was slowing Theo down.

"Check," Theo said.

Mateo did the same.

Jake's hand had developed into a potential straight, with seven, eight, nine, and ten unmatched. But it wasn't a straight yet. "Check."

The dealer placed a fourth card faceup on the table, a queen of diamonds. Theo's eye twitched, convincing Jake that Theo's hole cards were a pair of queens, meaning he now had three of a kind.

Mariposa bet ten thousand dollars. Jake figured that one of her hole cards was a club and that she was hoping to draw to a flush with the three clubs on the table. It was the only way she could hope to beat trip queens. Unless she'd been holding a pair of aces all along and concealing it especially well.

This time Theo didn't hesitate. "Come on. I thought we were here to play. Call your ten and raise another fifty."

Mateo let out another long sigh and shoved his cards toward the middle. "Fold."

Theo turned to Jake. "You're not going to pussy out too, are you?"

Jake wasn't that much older than Theo, maybe seven or eight years, but the difference was enough that Jake thought of him as a kid—a spoiled rich kid who was daring him to stay in the game. That probably worked on the guys Theo usually played with, and Jake wanted Theo to think it was working on him as he ran the numbers.

A straight would still beat trip queens. He needed one of eight cards to make the hand: a six or a jack. He would be conservative and assume that one of those had been dealt to another player, leaving him seven potential outs in the remaining thirty-six cards of the deck. That gave him a 19.4 percent chance of success.

It was a low-percentage risk he decided to take. Theo was running out of chips. Jake wanted to push him into buying more to see how committed he was to his hand.

"Hell no. Call and raise another fifty."

Mariposa shook her head. "Not me. I'm out."

Grinning, Theo called Jake's raise, pushing the pot to three hundred and thirty thousand dollars.

The dealer turned over the final card. There it was, the jack of hearts. Jake had his straight. Even better, Theo was unlikely to guess he had it, based on the community cards. Poker was a game of skill more than luck, but you needed both. Jake had gotten seriously lucky on this hand. Other gamblers might attribute this to wearing their lucky shirt or chewing their lucky gum. He took it for what it was: pure chance, beyond anyone's control. He frowned slightly, not wanting to overplay his supposed disappointment but showing Theo what he wanted to see.

Theo drained his wineglass and wiped his mouth with the back of his hand. He picked up a stack of black chips and dropped twenty of them into the pot, leaving him with only fifty thousand.

"Two hundred thousand."

Jake considered the growing pile of chips on the table. "You want me to think you have three queens, but I don't think you do."

"And you want me to think you've got something better, maybe trip aces, but I think you're bluffing."

Jake nodded. "Maybe I am. Call," he said, putting in his chips. "And raise another two fifty."

Soriano climbed down from his chair and stood next to his sister. The room was dead silent. Jake's bet had moved the pot to just under a million dollars. Theo handed his Suarez credit card to Soriano.

"How much would you like, senor?"

"Half a million," Theo said, staring at Jake. "You can't bluff me."

"I didn't think so."

Soriano tapped on the iPad. His face paled as he tapped again and again.

"What's taking so long?" Theo asked.

Soriano set his iPad on the table. "I am sorry, senor."

"Sorry? What are you sorry about?"

"Your bank would not approve the transfer."

Theo jumped out of his chair and grabbed the iPad. He swiped his card and punched in the amount, but the transaction wouldn't go through. His face darkened as sweat broke out on his forehead.

"Dammit!"

He opened his cell phone, called a number, and walked to the far corner of the room, his back to the others. Though Jake didn't understand

Greek, he could tell by Theo's enraged tone and wild waving of his hand that there was only one explanation. His father had cut him off.

"My bank's computers are down," he said when he returned to the table. He shoved the rest of his chips into the pot, along with his sapphire ring. "The ring will more than cover the last bet. All in."

Still standing, he turned over his hole cards, revealing the pair of queens to go with the third one on the table. He glared at Jake with his hands on his hips, his body stiff.

Without a word, Jake slid the seven out of the flop, placed his eight and nine next to it, then moved the ten and jack into place beside them. "Straight. Jack high."

Theo stared at the line of cards, wide eyed and slack jawed, as the horrible truth dawned on him. "No," he choked out. "That's not—"

"Mother of God!" Soriano said.

Mariposa took Jake's face in both hands, kissing him on the lips. Jake stood and began to sweep in the mountain of chips.

Theo clamped a hand on his arm. "You cheated. Nobody gets that lucky!"

Jake pulled his arm free. "But I did."

"No!" Theo turned on the dealer. "You must have stacked the deck."

"That's enough. Gonzalo," Soriano said to his bodyguard. The big man stepped between Theo and the dealer. "I run an honest game."

"Yeah? Maybe you were in on it together. 'Let's invite a rich guy and steal all his money.'" Theo started grabbing handfuls of chips from the table and stuffing them in his pockets. "This is my money!"

Gonzalo grabbed Theo from behind, holding his wrists together with one hand and bending him over the table. Soriano pulled the chips from his pockets. Mariposa stood next to him, holding her knife blade open at her side.

"Good night, senor," Soriano said. "Better luck next time."

"You don't know who you're fucking with," Theo shouted. "I'm not done with you, Carter. Or the rest of you."

Gonzalo hustled Theo out.

Jake picked up Theo's ring. "It's a little showy for my taste." He handed it to Mariposa. "It will look better on you." He turned to Soriano. "Whatever it's worth, just make sure the money ends up in my account—after you and your bank friends take their cut, of course."

Soriano wiped his face with a handkerchief. "I hope you get a chance to spend every penny."

Jake wrinkled his brow. "He'll cool off, and his daddy will buy him a new ring."

"I'm not so sure. He lost two million dollars plus whatever the ring is worth, and he was humiliated when his bank cut him off. That can make a man very dangerous. And it won't be hard for him to find you."

Jake nodded. "Then I'll make it hard."

TWELVE

Gina really looked like she wanted to hit her.

From the instant Cassie saw the FBI putting Alan Kendrick in a car, she was afraid that everything she'd done to conceal that she had robbed him, as well as her precautions to shield Gina, were unraveling. The poisonous look Gina had given her when Cassie found her in the lobby of the Rex swarmed by reporters confirmed that disaster was close at hand. Now that Ana had helped her slip Gina into the elevator and the doors had closed, there was only one option. She had to lie to her well enough that Gina would trust her again.

She stepped in quickly and embraced Gina as the elevator rose. Gina stiffened and tried to pull away, but Cassie held her tight, whispering in her ear, "I'm so sorry you're having to go through this, but please don't make it worse for you and Alan. I know that you blame me, but promise me that you won't hate me forever until we can talk. Your friendship matters too much to me for it to end this way. There's a camera in the elevator recording us and you can bet the FBI will see it. And they've probably bugged your apartment, so we can't go there. My place is safe. We'll talk there. Okay?"

Gina stopped resisting, resting her head on Cassie's shoulder and nodding. "Okay."

"Good."

Cassie let her go and pushed the button for the thirty-fourth floor, and then was relieved that Gina followed her into her apartment. They sat on a sofa in the living room facing one another.

"Can I get you something to drink?" Cassie asked. "I opened a bottle of Pinot Grigio last night that I'd hate to waste. It was on somebody's top ten list of best wines for last year."

Gina shook her head. "I'd love a glass but I haven't had a drop since the FBI searched our apartment."

Cassie arched her eyebrows. "Really? That's when most people start drinking more, not less."

"Yeah, I know, but you can't imagine what this has been like. Alan won't tell me anything about what's going on. He says that's for my own good. All I know is that the thief took some jewels and some cash. And Alan is going crazy trying to figure out who did it. His security guys are going through everything."

Cassie's throat tightened for an instant. She'd been careful not to leave a trace, but Gina's comment about Alan sparked a concern that she might not have been careful enough.

"Isn't that a job for the police?"

"Not if your name is Alan Kendrick. He says the cops are just a bunch of hourly grunts who get paid even if they don't catch whoever did it. He keeps making those if-it's-the-last-thing-I-do speeches, and he means it. But you know what I don't get?"

"No. What?"

"Why would getting robbed make the FBI come after Alan?"

Cassie knew the answer but couldn't tell her. All she could do was add one more lie to the others she had told Gina. "Who knows? Maybe one has nothing to do with the other."

"Maybe, but I feel like everything is spinning out of control. As much as I would like a drink, I'm afraid if I start I won't stop, and then I'll lose whatever little control I have left. And now that Alan's been arrested . . ." Gina's voice trailed off. She lowered her head, staring at her hands, and then looked up at Cassie, her face pinched, her eyes watering. "And now that Alan's been arrested, I'm so terrified."

"And you blame me."

"What am I supposed to think? You tricked me into showing you how to get into our panic room, and the very next night we were robbed. And then a week later the FBI showed up with a search warrant, and now, three weeks after that, my husband is in jail."

Cassie had been raised to believe that lying was one of the worst things a person could do. Yet she'd chosen a life where her success depended on being an excellent liar, where manipulating someone like Alan Kendrick was all in a day's work. She could live with that because Kendrick deserved what he got. Gina's suffering was harder for her to accept because Gina's only mistake was marrying an asshole. She promised herself to find a way out for Gina if she could.

"I suppose that makes sense, except for one thing."

"What?"

"My job was to prevent you from being robbed. My boss has been screaming his head off at me ever since this happened."

Gina tilted her head to one side, her mouth turned down. "You told me you worked for Global Security."

"I do."

"Then why hasn't the insurance company ever heard of Global Security?"

Cassie's gut churned. Gina may have been the weak link in Kendrick's security system, but she was also the weak link in Cassie's plan.

"Which insurance company are you talking about?"

"Our homeowner's insurance company. I asked the claims adjuster if he'd ever heard of Global Security and he said no."

"I would have been surprised if he had. First of all, Global is a security-consulting firm. Insurance companies are our clients. Second, your claims adjuster works for the insurance company that has the primary coverage for your loss, not the company that hired us."

"I don't understand."

"Your husband's collection of precious stones is worth tens of millions of dollars. Plus you've got all that fabulous artwork. No single insurance company is going to take that entire risk. That's where reinsurance comes in. Other insurance companies agree to take on different levels of the risk. Your company may only be liable for the first million. Other companies divide up the rest, and they all share in the premiums your husband pays. One of those companies hired Global. There's no way in the world your adjuster would know or care about any of that."

Gina sat back, taking a breath, slowly shaking her head. "I've never heard of reinsurance. Alan never told me anything about that."

"Alan never told you anything, did he? Wait here." Cassie retrieved her laptop from the kitchen and handed it to Gina, along with her business card. "Open up the browser and go to the website on my card."

Gina typed in the information. Her eyes widened as she reviewed the website. "Wow. It's just like you said."

"You've got your phone. Call the number on the card and ask for me."

Gina closed the laptop, blushing. "No, no. That's not necessary."

"Please. I insist. You've got enough to worry about. I don't want you to worry about me too. Put your phone on speaker."

Gina sighed. "Okay, but I feel really foolish." She tapped the number into her phone and smiled when her call was answered.

"Global Security. To whom may I direct your call?"

"I'd like to speak with Cassie Ireland."

"Ms. Ireland is away from the office. Would you like her voice mail?"

"Yes. Please."

Cassie's recorded message came on a moment later. "Hi, you've reached Cassie Ireland. I'm sorry I can't take your call right now. Please leave your name and number, and I'll get back to you as soon as I can."

Gina giggled. "Hi, Cassie. I'm sorry for what I said in the elevator. Bye." She closed her phone. "Boy, I feel like such a dope."

Cassie took her hand. "Forget about it. I do have to ask you something, though."

"What?"

"You said that you asked the claims adjuster if he'd heard of Global. Did you ask him if he'd heard of me?"

Gina lowered her eyes, shaking her head. "No. I wanted to leave your name out of it. I was afraid he'd say something to Alan and—"

"You didn't want Alan to know that you'd shown me the panic room." Gina nodded. "Don't worry. That will always be our secret."

THIRTEEN

Soriano and Gonzalo drove Jake back to his hotel and walked him to his suite, the bodyguard searching each of the three rooms before allowing them to enter.

"Is that really necessary?" Jake asked.

"An angry man—no, a humiliated and angry man with money and a powerful father—has a long and swift reach," Soriano said.

"Maybe so, but it looked to me like Daddy cut him off. That's why he had to throw in his ring."

Soriano shrugged. "That was then. Who knows about tomorrow? The Greeks can be very touchy about family honor. And you are my guest. It would be terrible for my reputation if anything happened to you."

Jake grinned. "And I would hate for your reputation to suffer on my account."

"There's a nonstop Aerolineas Argentinas flight to New York tomorrow night at eleven. I suggest you take it. Until then, do as you wish but be careful. Gonzalo will be close by."

Gonzalo checked the locks on the sliding door to the balcony. Jake started to tell him that wasn't necessary since his suite was on the twentieth floor but stopped, remembering that Alan Kendrick's apartment had been on the thirty-fifth floor. When Gonzalo planted himself in an easy chair, folding his beefy arms across his massive chest, Jake looked at Soriano.

"Really? He's going to sit there all night?"

"As I said, he will be close by. Safe travels, my friend."

Being threatened by sore losers was an occupational hazard for Jake. He didn't dismiss their threats. He just calculated the odds of someone coming after him as being low, relying on his long experience of cooler heads prevailing the morning after. Some professional gamblers carried guns, but not Jake. He knew the odds were that his gun would be used against him. Still, he didn't relax until his flight took off from Buenos Aires the next evening, soon falling asleep.

He landed at JFK at eight the next morning. Two hours later he'd showered, changed, grabbed his unopened mail, and walked through the door at his favorite coffee shop, Cup of Joe, a few blocks from the Rex. The low-key vibe and the overstuffed furniture arranged like a large living room were just what he needed. The owner, Pete Sciarelli, a pudgy corporate-world refugee whose midlife crisis had given birth to Cup of Joe, greeted him like the good friend he'd become.

"Hey, stranger. What's it been, a month?"

Jake plopped into an easy chair next to a table stacked high with magazines. "More like a couple of weeks."

"Yeah, and another day longer I'd've had to lay off Brianna." He turned to the bar, where a slight, brown-haired, blue-eyed barista was filling a porcelain mug. "Hey, Brianna, your boyfriend's back."

Jake shook his head. "Give the poor girl a break."

"Can I help it if she's got a crush on you?"

"I'm twice her age and she's not my type."

"Yeah, so what is your type, gambling man?"

Jake pictured Cassie glaring at him furiously when he cornered her in the elevator, muscles tense and ready to . . . How did she put it? Kick him in the balls so hard he would spit them out. He found himself smiling. She was definitely his type. Brianna appeared at his side, setting a mug on the table next to Jake before he could respond.

"Cappuccino with an extra shot, just the way you like it, Jake," Brianna said.

Jake handed her a ten-dollar bill. "Keep it. All of it. Don't give your boss a dime. He owes you for all the harassment you have to put up with."

Blushing, she ducked her head, murmured something inaudible, and retreated to the bar.

"Hey," Pete said, pointing to the magazines. "Latest issues of *Forbes*, the *Economist*, *Scientific American*, and *National Geographic*. All the crap you like to read. Why can't you be happy with *Sports Illustrated* and *People* like everyone else?"

Jake chuckled. "I meet a lot of interesting folks in my line of work. Got to stay up on a lot of different stuff."

"That's what you get for sitting around a poker table with a lot of highfliers."

"Got to talk their language."

"So they don't notice when you take their money?"

Jake laughed. "Something like that."

He was distracted by the appearance of an all-too-familiar face on the flat-screen TV on the far wall. Alan Kendrick was coming out of the federal courthouse, flanked by lawyers. Jake spotted Gina trailing along behind him in a conservative, navy-blue suit that was probably intended to disguise the fact that Kendrick had a hot, young wife. It wasn't working.

"Brianna, can you turn that up, please?"

The reporter's smooth voice carried across the room.

"Charged with more than forty counts of securities violations, wire fraud, and blackmail, Kendrick pleaded not guilty. The judge set bail at five million dollars and required Mr. Kendrick to surrender his passport."

Kendrick and his entourage stopped midway down the courthouse steps. He looked serene and confident, as if he hadn't a care in the world and didn't know what all the fuss was about. His lawyer, who'd made a fortune defending Wall Street's mightiest, waited until a ring of microphones surrounded them.

"Alan Kendrick is innocent of the charges that have been brought against him. This case is part of the government's ongoing witch hunt against the men and women who have made this country great, creating jobs—"

"That's enough," Pete said. "Mute that asshole. Can you believe these guys? I don't know who's worse. Guys like Kendrick who steal the money, or the lawyers who help them get away with it. That's why I got out. I couldn't take wading in their bullshit."

Jake let out a short, humorless laugh. "I told you my parents got ripped off by a Wall Street scumbag, right?"

"Right."

He nodded at the TV. "That's him."

Pete gaped. "No shit?"

"No shit."

Pete grinned at him. "So this is great! The asshole got busted." He waved to Brianna. "Two double espressos. On the house." He turned back to Jake. "Are your folks going to testify? Bring them by!"

"No," said Jake. "I don't know what Kendrick's case is about, but he made sure my parents couldn't be part of it."

"How'd he do that?"

"They signed an agreement when they hired Kendrick to invest their retirement money and the company's profit-sharing money. It had all the standard language about accepting the risks of investing in the open market, yada, yada, yada. And an arbitration clause."

Pete winced. "Binding?"

"Yeah."

"Did they know they were giving up their right to sue the guy?"

"You have to know my folks," Jake told him. "They couldn't imagine dragging someone into court. Sitting down and talking it over seemed like a perfectly reasonable way to solve any problems."

"They could still arbitrate," Pete insisted. "If he acted in bad faith . . ."

Jake shook his head. "That's tough to prove. Kendrick put their money into high-risk venture capital deals even though they told him that they only wanted to be in conservative blue chips. They lost everything. Even if they wanted to try arbitration, they'd have to come to New York for however long it dragged out. And if they lost they'd have to pay the legal fees for both sides. They can't even afford their own lawyer, much less Kendrick's personal army."

"Espresso?" Brianna held out the two small cups uncertainly, not wanting to interrupt.

Pete took one and downed it in a single gulp. Jake didn't especially want his but took it anyway to be polite. Pete clapped a hand on Jake's shoulder and assured him, "Well, your folks can still celebrate when the asshole goes to jail."

If he goes, thought Jake. He had mixed feelings about the prospect. While it would be undeniably satisfying to see Kendrick behind bars, it would also complicate his own plans to win back his parents' money. But Jake figured he'd get his chance. He put the odds against Kendrick ever seeing the inside of a prison cell at 7 to 1. Tops. He decided not to share these thoughts with Pete. The guy was trying to make him feel better.

"Yeah. I'm sure they will."

Pete left to greet another customer. Jake sifted through his mail, stopping when he saw a brochure from his travel agent, Sheila Hanks, about a twelve-day Mediterranean cruise on board the *Shangri-La*, a cruise ship that according to the brochure was "the most luxurious vessel on the seven seas." He wondered why she would bother him with that, especially since the ship sailed in two days, until he opened the brochure and read about the Grand Slam Poker Challenge, which would take place during the cruise. It sounded tempting, but he was looking forward to mornings at Cup of Joe and whatever else struck him the rest of the day.

He put the brochure in his "toss now" pile and was working his way through the rest of his mail when his cell phone buzzed, telling him he had a text message.

Theo came for his ring. Watch your back. Soriano.

A photo of Mariposa was attached. She was missing the ring finger on her right hand.

FOURTEEN

No fear. First rule of poker. Fear makes you weak, makes you fold too soon or stay too long. Doesn't matter if you do the wrong thing. What matters is if you do it for the wrong reason.

Jake knew the rule. Had learned it watching other players. Seen what fear had done to them—how cracks crept into their poker faces, how tremors rippled from cheek to jowl, and how eyes flickered and froze. Figured out that if he was afraid of what might happen at the table, he didn't belong there. The key was his ability to run the odds on any hand at any moment in the play and decide whether he could live with all of the outcomes. He could accept being disappointed, but not being surprised. And that's why he'd never been afraid at the table.

On the street, with Theo coming after him, was another story. Fear could make him weak or strong depending on how he handled it. Use the fear to stay alert, run the odds, and play smart. Do that and he'd figure out a way to handle Theo. Let Theo get into his head—make him question his judgment, scare him into taking the wrong risks—and he'd lose more than a finger.

Walking briskly back to the Rex, mail tucked under one arm, he glanced up and down the sidewalk on both sides of the block and swept the street traffic for anyone that looked out of place, then shook his head. "Like anyone could look out of place in New York," he said so loud that a passerby gave him a quizzical stare.

Jake ran the numbers. Odds that Theo wasn't kidding when he said this wasn't over—100 percent. Odds that Theo wanted a pound of flesh to go with his money—100 percent. Odds that Theo would find him in New York—100 percent.

Odds that he was a match for Theo in a fight? Jake paused, letting people pass by him on either side. He hadn't been in a fight since high school, when a bully tried to sucker-punch him. Acting on pure instinct, he stepped in and under the swing and kneed the bully in the nuts, leaving him crying for his mama. Smiling at the memory, he knew he wasn't without skills, but a man who'd cut off a woman's finger wasn't a schoolyard thug. Odds in a fight with Theo? Not good.

He began making calls, continuing nonstop until he was back in his apartment. The last call was to a private number given to him by a man with whom Jake had played more than a few hands of poker. The man had been on a vicious losing streak until Jake figured out that another player, someone close to the man, had been cheating him. Jake called the cheater out. The man got his money back, thanked Jake, and told him to call if he ever needed a favor.

A week later the cheater's body was found in a garbage dump. The next time they played, the man told Jake that it wasn't the money, it was the disloyalty that he couldn't accept. Jake had known that the man was connected but thought that made him more colorful than dangerous. It was the last time they'd spoken. He had hoped never to need the favor, but that moment had come.

The man answered.

"It's Jake."

"You looking for a game?"

"No. A favor."

"Give me five minutes. I'll call you back."

Exactly five minutes later his phone rang. Caller ID said "Unknown." The man wasn't taking any chances.

"I got a special phone for favors. The kind I only use once. What do you need?"

Jake told him. The man listened.

"How soon?"

"Tomorrow morning."

"You sure you want to go this route? There's other ways. I could take care of the problem for you."

Jake was certain of that but he wasn't interested in a permanent solution, especially one that would cause him nightmares for the rest of his life and turn the favor into a debt that could never be repaid.

"Yeah. I just need some time to figure this out."

"Fair enough. Here's what you do."

The next morning Jake followed the instructions he'd been given, returned to his apartment, and packed his bag. He locked his apartment and waited for the elevator. The door eased open. Cassie was alone in the car. She was wearing dark slacks with a pale-green blouse and a waist-cut jacket, a roll-on suitcase at her side. They stared at each other, mouths half-open, eyes cautious, until the door began to close. Cassie grabbed it, holding it open.

"It's okay," she said. "I won't bite."

Jake stepped inside, letting the door close, and the car resumed its descent.

"Kinda takes the fun out of it, don't you think?"

Cassie ducked her chin and turned and shook her head, unable to suppress a smile.

"Are you ever serious?"

He waited for her to look at him, then held her gaze, his eyes intent, giving her a crooked grin. She gave in, her smile widening and her eyes lighting up. She put her hand to her mouth, shaking her head again.

"How do you do that?" she asked.

He furrowed his brow. "Do what?"

"That. That look you gave me. What is it—your pick-up-a-girl-on-the-elevator look?"

Jake shrugged, feigning innocence. "Don't know what you're talking about."

"Oh, stop pretending you aren't flirting with me."

"Who said I was pretending? Maybe the next time I shove a note under your door asking you to call me, you will."

She folded her arms over her chest and cocked her head. "Maybe."

The elevator reached the ground floor. She got out first, and he followed her into the lobby.

"Hang on a second," he said. She stopped and turned toward him. "Where are you headed?"

"Tokyo."

"Business?"

"Yes."

He nodded, smiling again.

"What's that silly grin for?"

"Nothing. I'm wondering if I should come along just in case you need another alibi."

She raised one eyebrow. "I'll call if I do."

Jake pointed to his bag. "Don't you want to know where I'm going?"

"No."

He watched her walk away, mesmerized. Looking through the Rex's revolving door, he saw Ana on the sidewalk, holding open the rear passenger-side door to a black Lincoln Town Car. Cassie slid into the car and disappeared behind tinted windows.

Jake hadn't moved when Ana returned.

"Don't worry, Mr. Carter. She'll be back."

"Am I that obvious?"

"Well, if you're going to stand there till she does, be sure to pick your tongue up before housekeeping vacuums the floor. She tell you the news?"

"What news?"

"No more month-to-month. She signed a full-year lease."

Jake grinned.

"How about you? Where are you off to this time?"

"Thanks for asking. Vegas. Anybody asks, that's where they can find me."

FIFTEEN

The morning after posting bail, Alan Kendrick sat next to his wife on a small sofa in their master bedroom. Using a black marker, he wrote on a small dry-erase board balanced on his knees.

The government has bugged our apartment.

Gina bit her lower lip and nodded.

I'm going to tell you what we're doing today and I want you to agree.

Gina took the marker and the board from him.

I'm scared.

They took turns rubbing out what the other had written and adding their own messages.

Don't be. Everything is going to be okay.

What's going to happen?

I'll tell you as soon as I can. In the meantime you have to trust me. I love you.

Gina's eyes filled and she began to tremble. Kendrick pulled her close and wrapped his arms around her. When she stopped shaking, he got up and wiped off the dry-erase board. He walked into her closet and returned with a golf outfit for her.

"Honey," he said, "my lawyer told me to stay away from the office for a few days. He said I should go play golf until things quieted down."

Gina scrunched her brow, her mouth half-open. "But—"

"I know you don't play, but now's your chance to learn. I don't want us to stay cooped up in here, and the minute we walk out the door the press is going to be all over us. The club is private. We can get away from all this craziness for a while."

Gina nodded and cleared her throat. "That sounds great. It's a nice day and it would be good to be outside."

Kendrick clapped his hands. "That's my girl." He pulled her to her feet and kissed her.

The New Hook Golf Club was located in New Jersey along the Hudson River directly across from Manhattan. With a million-dollar initiation fee and annual dues of one hundred thousand dollars, the golf club made certain its members were in the upper 1 percent of the 1 percent. In addition to all the luxurious amenities the rich expect, members could reach the golf course by ferry from Manhattan or by helicopter, docking or landing on a spit of land sticking out into the Hudson that wrapped around the backside of the green on the twelfth hole.

As he expected, the paparazzi trailed Kendrick's Mercedes all the way to the club's entrance, where a pair of muscled staff members enforced the no-trespassing sign. Looking in his rearview mirror, Kendrick grinned as he left behind the string of cars, his expression changing to grim determination when a single car—a government-issued Crown Victoria—followed him onto the club's grounds.

"Goddamn FBI," he muttered.

Two agents riding in a golf cart followed them around the course, never more than a couple of hundred yards away. Kendrick and Gina played at a leisurely pace. Kendrick was patient and gentle with Gina as she floundered with her clubs. No one complained or asked to play through, because Kendrick had reserved the course to himself for the day. They finished the twelfth hole and before continuing on stopped at a snack bar and grill located between the marina and the helipad and ordered lunch. The FBI agents followed them inside.

"Can I buy you gentlemen something to eat?" Kendrick asked. "I'm afraid they don't take cash."

The agents glared at him and left without a word. Kendrick chuckled as they returned to their golf cart.

"Go to the bathroom and stay there until I come for you," he said to Gina.

"Why? What's going on?"

"Just do as I say." She stared at him. "Go on. We don't have a lot of time."

She shook her head, drew a deep breath, and let it out as she pushed back from the table. A moment later another woman came out of the bathroom and took Gina's place at the table. She bore more than a passing resemblance to Gina and was dressed identically to her. Kendrick nodded at her and went to the men's restroom, where a man who could pass for his double and wearing the same clothes was waiting. The man left and joined the woman who had taken Gina's place.

The two impostors left the snack bar, climbed into the golf cart, and drove straight toward the heliport just as a Sikorsky S-76C helicopter shot across the river and touched down. They ignored the FBI agents' shouted orders to stop as they pulled up beneath the spinning rotors and jumped from the golf cart into the chopper. The Sikorsky shot back into the sky, leaving the agents staring helplessly as the helicopter shrunk from view.

Kendrick watched from a window at the back of the snack bar as the agents returned to their cart. One called in his report and the other drove their golf cart toward the clubhouse. When they were gone, Kendrick opened the door to the women's bathroom.

"You can come out now."

Gina joined him. "Who was that woman? Why was she made up to look like me? What's going on?"

Kendrick took her by the elbow and herded her outside toward the marina. "She's a struggling actress who just played the role of a lifetime."

Gina shook her arm free. "How is playing me the role of a lifetime?"

Kendrick smiled, putting his hands on her arms. "Please, honey. Give me a few more minutes and I'll tell you everything." Gina studied him, hesitating. He leaned in and kissed her on the mouth. "Trust me."

Gina ducked her head for a moment, then looked at him. "Okay."

A few moments later a Cobalt 336 cabin cruiser pulled up to the dock. The pilot idled the engine while another man reached out to help Gina climb aboard as Kendrick gave her a boost. She was about to take the man's hand when she stepped back.

"Where'd that woman go? The one that looked like me."

"Doesn't matter," Kendrick said. "Just get on the boat."

"I heard a helicopter landing. Did she get on it?"

Kendrick sighed, his patience slipping away. "Yes. She got on the helicopter, and now you're getting on the boat."

Gina crossed her arms over her chest, scanning the golf course. "Where are the FBI agents?" Kendrick didn't answer. Gina's eyes lit up. "The woman was a decoy!" She paced in a half circle. "There must have been a man dressed like you. The FBI agents must think we're on the helicopter. That's why they left." She stopped and faced Kendrick, one hand over her mouth. "Oh my God, Alan! You're jumping bail!"

He cocked his head, half grinning. "I prefer to think of it as a well-earned vacation."

"But, but . . . the FBI will come after you." Her eyes filled, the words catching in her throat. "Your lawyer said the government didn't have a case. You told me you were innocent, that you hadn't done anything wrong."

"And I haven't, but the Feds don't care. The US attorney is going after everybody on Wall Street who ever made a dime. They'll put me away because they can. It doesn't matter that I'm innocent."

Gina shook her head, wiping her eyes with the back of her hand. "I don't know. I don't know." She took a deep breath, stiffening. "Run if you have to, but I'm not going with you. I don't want to spend the rest of my life as a fugitive."

Kendrick embraced her, nuzzling her neck, murmuring. "Baby, baby . . . I can't do this without you. My lawyer says he'll work something out, but he needs leverage. This is my leverage. I'll come back when he makes a deal. I may have to pay a fine and do community service, but everything's going to be okay if you'll just trust me and come with me. It's only for a little while." He pulled away, his hands on her shoulders. "Please, Gina. I need you now more than ever."

Gina sniffled. "Promise we'll come back soon."

"Cross my heart."

"Okay."

"That's my girl!"

They climbed aboard. The pilot backed out of the slip and headed for open water. An hour later they were in international waters, where they pulled alongside a five-hundred-twenty-five-foot, five-story yacht. Gina stared, open mouthed.

"Whose boat is this?"

Kendrick put his arm around her waist. "It's not a boat. It's a yacht, and we can take it around the world if we want."

"But who does it belong to?"

He shrugged. "Me."

"You never told me about it."

"I was saving it for a special occasion, and today certainly qualifies. Let me show you our quarters."

Kendrick led her to the two-story, six-room master suite on the fourth and fifth decks. He slammed the door behind them. Gina jumped at the sound and spun around.

"What was that for?"

Kendrick grabbed her by the arm and dragged her into the bedroom, where he threw her onto the bed. She gaped at him wild-eyed, her breath coming in spurts as he towered over her.

"Tell me everything you know about Cassie Ireland."

SIXTEEN

Cassie wasn't going to Tokyo. She was going to Tallinn, the capital of Estonia, to recover a stolen Kandinsky from Andrus Vesik, a mobster who controlled Tallinn's docks. Vesik had hung the Kandinsky in his office, which was also where he kept a pair of Neapolitan mastiffs he'd trained to attack anyone who entered the office if he wasn't there. He forgot to train them not to guzzle ten pounds of ground beef laced with fifty grams of acepromazine. Cassie removed the painting from its frame, rolled it into a hard plastic tube, and patted the sleeping dogs on their heads on her way out.

She took a ferry from Tallinn across the Gulf of Finland to Helsinki, one of her favorite cities. She loved the stylish Art Nouveau architecture and the old-world feeling in Senate Square, the oldest part of the city, where she left the Kandinsky at a prearranged drop. She never saw the person who picked it up but had no doubt that the exchange was completed. Working for Prometheus was all about trust. If she had to look over her shoulder, they had a problem.

Cassie had a reservation at the Hotel Kämp, Helsinki's most luxurious hotel, and planned to spend the day in the spa getting steamed, massaged, and rejuvenated. She waited until she was in her suite to check in with Prometheus.

Every government, business, and cybercrime gang in the world wanted a hack-proof online network, but no geek, nerd, or genius had written the code for that holy grail. No one except for Prometheus, who described it to her as quantum cryptography, a process that generated onetime keywords known only by the two parties who used them to exchange secure messages.

Using her cell phone, Cassie logged on to Prometheus's network, entered her key, and sent him a message confirming that she'd made the drop. He replied by attaching an encrypted file containing only an image of her and Jake taken in the lobby of the Rex the night of the robbery. They weren't kissing but they were inches apart, their heads close though tilted slightly to opposite sides in a way that was unmistakably intimate, her mouth slightly open, eyes raised to his, Jake's half-lidded gaze drawing her in. She struggled to recall the moment but couldn't, though she was forced to admit that it had happened. Had she been so unaware?

Any thoughts of her planned rejuvenation vanished. Her stomach sank and for a moment she felt light-headed. Sending her the image was Prometheus's way of accusing her of lying about her reasons for signing the lease at the Rex. She wasn't surprised that Prometheus had the photograph, not if he'd been suspicious of her. He might have had someone investigate her, who snapped the picture, or he might have hacked into the Rex's video system on his own and pulled this freeze-framed shot. She stared at the phone, deciding whether to call him and what she would say if she did, when her phone rang, startling her so that she dropped it, catching it with her other hand. She tapped on the phone, answering the call.

"Yes?"

"What do you know about this man?" Prometheus asked.

Cassie knew there would be no point in lying even if he didn't already know everything she would tell him.

"His name is Jake Carter. He lives in my building. He's a professional gambler. I met him through Gina Kendrick. He plays cards with her husband. They may be friends or he may be trying to see how much of Kendrick's money he can win or both. The photograph was taken in the lobby the night of the robbery. A lot of the residents had gathered there while the police searched the building. I had just gotten back from taking a walk. An NYPD detective was questioning me. Carter interrupted and volunteered that we had been together all evening."

"He gave you an alibi. Why would he do that?"

"I don't know. After the detective walked away, he said that the detective was still watching us and that we had to make the story believable, so he kissed me. I don't know whether the photograph was taken before or after."

"After. From the look on your face it must have been quite a kiss."

Cassie hesitated a moment. "He caught me off guard. Why are you doing this?"

"Why do you think?"

"Because of the lease."

"Hardly. I don't approve, but it's your burden and you know better than to make it mine."

"Then why send me the photograph?" He didn't answer and then she understood, another knot twisting in her gut. "Jake Carter is a target."

"More precisely he's your next target, unless that kiss is going to get in the way of doing your job."

Cassie stood and paced the room. Prometheus wasn't going to accuse her of lying, because doing so would mean he no longer trusted her. Instead, he was going to give her a chance to prove her loyalty by making her choose between him and Jake. It wasn't exactly *Sophie's Choice*, but that didn't mean it was an easy decision. She didn't know how she felt about Jake—only that she'd like to find out. Maybe Prometheus was doing her a favor by giving her the assignment and letting her see what kind of man Jake really was. There was only one way to find out.

"Not a chance. What did he do?"

"Cheated our client out of two million dollars at the poker table. And it's not the first time. He apparently also cheated his way to the final table at the World Series of Poker several years ago. He's been persona non grata at the big casinos ever since."

Jake a cheat? The thought made her angry, not just at him but at herself for being such a poor judge of character. Though it did explain why he'd been playing cards with Alan Kendrick instead of cleaning up in Atlantic City.

"When and where?"

"A few days ago in a private game in Buenos Aires. All you have to do is recover the money and send it on to me through our usual channels."

"Your minimum fee is a million dollars. The client will still end up short a million."

"My dear, you should know by now that it isn't always about the money. And a word to the wise—a good kiss can hide a lot of faults."

Cassie hung up and continued pacing through her suite. The quick and dirty way to handle Jake would be to track down his bank account, hack into it, and withdraw the two million dollars. While that might satisfy the client, it wouldn't hurt Jake. He'd sue the bank for not protecting his account and he'd win. The bank would be out the money, not Jake, and some poor bank employee would probably be out of a job. Not Cassie's idea of justice.

She had another problem with that scenario. She'd always enjoyed being the bullet the bad guy never saw coming, but this time she wanted Jake to know that she was the bullet. That is, if Jake really did cheat the client out of his money.

Cassie saw herself more as Robin Hood than Robin the Hood. Alan Kendrick was a perfect example. But while Andrus Vesik had stolen the Kandinsky, she didn't know whether the client hadn't stolen it from someone else. She relied on Prometheus to make those distinctions, but even he wasn't infallible. If Prometheus was wrong about Jake, she would not forgive herself for being the bullet. Maybe she was rationalizing, or maybe that kiss was skewing her thinking. Either way, she wouldn't take Jake down unless she was certain he deserved it.

After Jake had slipped a note under her door with his phone number, she put him in her contacts on her phone. She was about to call him when she stopped. She couldn't just call him up and say, *Hi, Jake. Did you rip some guy off in a poker game? And—oh, yeah, about that kiss . . .* She needed a plan and that required more information, starting with where she could find Jake.

Cassie looked at her watch. It was midmorning in New York. Ana would be on the front desk. She scrolled through her contacts for the number. Ana answered on the first ring.

"It's a beautiful morning at the Rexford. How may I help you?"

"Hi, Ana. It's Cassie Ireland."

"Oh, hey, Ms. Ireland! How you doin'? You callin' all the way from Tokyo? What's the weather like on the other side of the world?"

Cassie always made it a point to know what was happening in whatever place she claimed to be. "It's hot, if you can believe it. The rickshaws are barely moving. Listen, I'm expecting a package. Has anything shown up for me?"

"No. I haven't seen anything, but I'll keep an eye out."

"Thanks. Oh, by the way, Mr. Carter was headed out of town the same day I left. Any idea where he went?"

Ana snickered, making Cassie feel foolish and her ruse about a package sound lame.

"Yeah. He said anybody asks where to find him, tell them he's in Las Vegas. Why? Is he expecting a package too?"

Cassie couldn't help smiling. "You didn't buy the whole package thing, huh?"

"I've been on this desk too long for that. But I'll be honest, Ms. Ireland. When I saw what happened between the two of you the day you moved in, I thought no way is that ever gonna work. But after the way he kissed you that night in the lobby and the way you looked at him, I told my husband I'm not so sure."

"Don't get ahead of yourself, Ana. There's nothing going on. I just need to talk to him."

"Okay, okay. Not my business. Say, did you hear about Mr. Kendrick?"

"No. Hear what?"

"He jumped bail. Ran out on a five-million-dollar bond and took his wife with him. Been all over the news here."

Cassie's breath caught in her throat as she wondered whether Gina had gone with him hand in hand or with Kendrick twisting her arm behind her back.

"Wow. I'm sure the police will find him."

"Don't count on it. A man with that kind of money can hide out where nobody can find them. You say hello to Mr. Carter for me."

"I'll do that," Cassie said.

SEVENTEEN

The cable networks were giving Kendrick's disappearance wall-to-wall coverage. Cassie jumped back and forth between their websites, live-streaming the reports. No one knew anything except that Kendrick and Gina had disappeared and made fools out of the FBI. She was about to call Gina's cell phone when a reporter for CNN said that he had tried, but the number was no longer in service.

A wave of nausea hit Cassie, her stomach accusing her of being responsible for Gina's predicament. She hoped Gina would reach out to her so that she could make things right.

There was nothing she could do at the moment, so she refocused on finding Jake and called Gunnar Agnarsson. Prometheus had introduced her to him, and she spent six weeks at his farm outside of Reykjavik learning how to hack into computer networks. She'd never be in his league and was glad that he was always on call. She told him what she needed. He said he'd get back to her in an hour. She took a shower, and by the time she was dressed he'd left her a message to call him back with thirty minutes to spare.

"Where is he?" she asked.

"Your Jake Carter is an interesting fellow."

"How interesting?"

"He's registered at the Bellagio in Las Vegas, where he's run up quite a bar tab and had a decent run at the tables."

"What's so interesting about that?"

"He's also done the same thing at a hotel in Reno and another one in Lake Tahoe. All at the same time."

"You're kidding."

"Not my nature. He's also been enjoying himself in Atlantic City and at casinos in Connecticut and Mississippi. Also at the same time he's been living it up in Nevada."

"How can he do that?"

"He didn't. I checked the security videos for the times when he checked in at each place. Sometimes he's tall. Sometimes he's short. Sometimes he's white. Sometimes he's black. Once he was even a woman."

"His identity has been stolen. Those people are cleaning him out."

"Doubtful. They've each used different credit cards in his name, three of which were issued by the same bank. Given the amounts of money they're spending, at least one of the credit card companies' fraud teams would have flagged the cards and contacted him, and there's no sign of that."

Cassie thought for a moment. "Then he must be laying a false trail."

"Six of them by my count. What did he do? Steal the crown jewels?"

"No. Just enough money for someone to come after him."

"You?"

"There's no way he could know that. Has to be someone else. I've got a number for him. I'm going to call him and I want you to trace the call."

"Give me a sec . . . okay. I've got you. Ring him up and I'll have him too."

Cassie found Jake's number and hesitated again. What had Jake gotten himself into? He was charming, handsome, and more of a rogue and wiseass than was good for him. All of which could land him on the wrong person's bad side. Prometheus's client wanted his money back, and no one was better suited to make that happen than Cassie. So why hire someone else to do the same job? Didn't make sense. She unblocked her phone so that Jake's caller ID would let him know that she was calling and tapped his number.

"Alibis R Us. Don't confess until you talk to us."

Cassie gritted her teeth, simultaneously annoyed and amused. Even on the run he hadn't lost his sense of humor.

"Seriously? If I look up 'beating a dead horse' in the dictionary, will I see your picture?"

"Better me than the horse. Stop gritting your teeth. It's bad for your molars."

Cassie relaxed her jaws and shook her head. "Okay. How did you know I was gritting my teeth?"

"You've had my number for over a month and yet you waited to call me until you're on the other side of the world. You weren't interested in where I was going the last time I saw you and you don't think the alibi shtick is nearly as funny as I do. That makes you gritting your teeth an odds-on bet. So, how's Tokyo?"

Cassie sighed. The man was impossible—attractive and desirable, but maddeningly impossible.

"Right on all accounts. Tokyo has been warm during the day but it cools off at night and is very nice. How is it where you are?"

"Vegas is always hot, except in the casinos, where it's always cool and there are no windows, clocks, or seasons. Just pretty women and free drinks. Tokyo is what, seventeen hours ahead of Vegas?"

"I'll take your word for it. I always calculate the difference based on what time it is in New York."

"So, while I'm sitting by the pool at the Bellagio, you're up in the middle of the night in Tokyo calling me. I like that. What's up?"

Cassie was impressed. He was quick.

"Nothing really. I been thinking about—"

"How you promised to kick me so hard in the balls I'd spit them out if I tried to kiss you again?"

Anyone else and it would have come off as angry. Jake turned it into a punchline, making her laugh.

"Yes. That was pretty awful, wasn't it?"

"Awful doesn't touch it, but America is the land of second chances and I've got a pocketful of those. You can have as many as you'd like."

Cassie felt the tension drain from her neck and shoulders—the last thing she expected or wanted, especially since she knew he was lying to her.

"Fair enough. I'll take one as soon as we're both back in New York. What's your schedule?"

"I don't have one. Just seeing how far my luck will take me. What about you?"

"Oh, with work I never know. I could be home tomorrow or wake up to another assignment and be off again."

"Sounds grueling. Why not take some time off? Give yourself a break."

Her phone vibrated with a text from Gunnar. *Got him!*

"Maybe I will. But I'm going to hold you to that second chance."

"I'd be disappointed if you didn't. Travel safe," he said, and ended the call.

Cassie called Gunnar. "Where?"

"Rome. And I don't know how he got there."

"What do you mean?"

"There's no record of him leaving the US. He's not traveling on his own passport."

Cassie's head was swimming. "He laid half a dozen false trails that took you half an hour to expose—"

"Which is sloppy work for a pro but not bad for an amateur. He must have been in a hurry. But he did a fine job of slipping out of the country. Fake papers aren't easy to come by on short notice. He must have a good friend somewhere. Maybe CIA or organized crime."

A job that had started out simple was rapidly becoming difficult and potentially dangerous. Jake had gone to extraordinary lengths to conceal his whereabouts, further convincing her of his guilt. Yet he'd made a huge mistake, leaving his cell phone on so that anyone who had his number could track him down, further proof that he was in way over his head.

"Find out what's going on in Rome that would attract a gambling man like Jake Carter."

"I'm on it."

Her suite had a balcony with a view across Helsinki and the distant sea. She stepped out onto it, a cool wind chilling her, as she sorted through her conflicting emotions. She was furious with Jake. He hadn't just cheated her client at cards. He'd cheated her. Deceived her into thinking he might be someone he wasn't—a man she could care about. That she had allowed that to happen made her angrier with herself than she was at Jake. And if that weren't bad enough, she was scared about what might happen to him if she didn't find him before whoever else was chasing him did.

Her phone chimed with another text from Gunnar. *Click this link and you'll find him.* The link was to the website for the Grand Slam of Poker tournament to be held on board the luxury cruise ship *Shangri-La* during an eight-day Mediterranean cruise. Jake's name was on the list of participating pros. The cruise originated in Rome and was departing today. No chance to make that. She studied the itinerary. The next stop was Monte Carlo.

She sent a reply to Gunnar. *Get me on that ship!*

"The man is unbelievable," she said, and started packing.

EIGHTEEN

High over the Atlantic on a red-eye flight from JFK to Rome, Jake did a Google search for "*man on the run*." He found the lyrics to a song by the Little River Band warning him to steer clear of the devil and the dice. Theo wasn't the devil, but the image of Mariposa's mutilated hand was enough to convince him that leaving the country was the right decision. As for dice, there was no chance he'd walk away from gambling. Working nine to five wasn't in his DNA.

He shook his head, still not quite believing what he'd done. If Theo came looking for him at the Rex, Ana would send him to Vegas, where Theo would find a false trail leading him all over the country. Jake had made hotel reservations for consecutive nights, beginning in Las Vegas and continuing on to Reno and Lake Tahoe and then to a casino in Biloxi, Mississippi, and ending in Atlantic City.

To make the trail more believable, Jake had asked gambling friends in each city to check in to that city's hotel under his name and leave word of his next destination when they checked out. His friends suggested hotels where they knew a cooperative desk clerk that would check them in as Jake even though they didn't have matching IDs and who would note Jake's next destination in his guest records. Jake overnighted a credit card to each of them to pay for the room, adding that they should also treat themselves to a great meal and a fine bottle of wine. He'd accumulated a stash of credit cards over the years in search of one whose travel rewards he could actually cash in. This was the best use he'd ever made of them.

Most importantly, he told his friends to stay away from the hotels once they checked in and to rely on automatic checkout to avoid a second visit to the front desk, and not to try to otherwise impersonate him. He texted each of them the photograph of Mariposa to underscore the risk and to make certain they were willing to help. None of them hesitated, all of them ready to roll the dice for a friend.

Jake had no idea whether the false trail would slow Theo down or frustrate him enough to give up, only that his credit card bills would set new records. Laying a false trail was something he'd only read about in novels. Giving away his credit cards in order to do that was the first ruse that came to his mind. It had sounded clever at the time. Now he wasn't so certain. He'd made clear to his friends the risk they were taking and done everything he could think of to protect them. Still, it nagged at him that he might have been more clever than wise, especially considering the stakes. If anything happened to his friends, he couldn't see how he could live with himself.

Traveling under a phony passport was the second part of his plan. It had worked for James Bond and Jason Bourne and he hoped it would work for him. Especially since it was a federal offense. He'd googled that as well. Committing a felony punishable by up to twenty-five years in prison tilted the odds against a winning hand.

One thing at a time, he told himself, and the Grand Slam poker tournament was the next thing.

Jake knew he'd have to play under his own name because there was a good chance that some of the other pros would recognize him. He was willing to take that chance because the odds that Theo could track him to, and then get to him on, the cruise were slim. Nonetheless, he'd be sure to keep an eye out for him whenever they touched land. And when he was ready to go home, he'd reenter the country using his phony passport and hope no one in customs would notice.

According to the rules posted on the ship's website, all participants in the tournament had to have qualified by winning satellite events in person or online, unless they were granted an exemption by the promoter. Jake knew the drill. The promoter wanted big-name players who would draw passengers to the cruise, and they weren't going to come unless all their expenses were paid and they didn't have to qualify.

Jake didn't know whether he was still a draw. Even if he was and lingering rumors from the World Series of Poker hadn't cut him out of that circle, it was too late for his name to induce anyone to book the cruise. Too late, that was, until he saw that Henry Phillippi was the promoter.

Jake knew Phillippi by reputation. He'd started out as a pit boss in Vegas, moving up in management until financial irregularities discovered during an audit at the last casino he'd managed had prompted him to pursue other opportunities. He found work running poker rooms on cruise ships, eventually starting his own company managing shipboard casinos and promoting poker tournaments at sea. Since all the gambling took place in international waters, the games weren't subject to any governmental regulation, making it the perfect place for Phillippi. If anyone would overlook the rumors, it would be him.

Before leaving New York, Jake e-mailed Phillippi, asking if he could sign up for the tournament. Phillippi answered immediately, telling Jake he'd reserved a VIP stateroom for him, not mentioning any of Jake's concerns.

When Jake got through customs, he saw a dark-haired young man holding a sign with his name on it.

"I'm Jake Carter."

His greeter, no more than twenty-five, glowed with a face-stretching smile and excited wide eyes. "Mr. Carter! I am Maurizio. The

Grand Slam Poker Challenge welcomes you to Rome. I shall take you to the *Shangri-La*," he announced with a strong Italian accent, carefully pronouncing each practiced word.

Jake couldn't help smiling back. "Then let's go."

Maurizio took his suitcase and messenger bag and led him outside to a black S-Class Mercedes. *Very nice*, thought Jake. Some tournaments sent a shuttle bus to pick up players at the airport. Some left them to fend for themselves. The Grand Slam was a classy affair.

Soon they were cruising along the highway toward the port city of Civitavecchia.

"Where do you live?" Maurizio asked.

"New York."

"Ah, that is where I wish to live someday."

For the rest of the forty-five-minute trip, Maurizio quizzed Jake about New York. Jake was happy to sing the city's praises, grateful for the chance to think about something other than Theo and prison.

As they reached the port, he saw three cruise ships docked along the breakwater. The largest of these was the *Shangri-La*, its eighteen decks looming like a white mountain over the terminal building.

"Wow," said Jake. "Look at the size of that thing." Jake's experience with ships was limited to a three-day booze cruise in the Caribbean, and he didn't remember much of that.

Maurizio shifted into tour guide mode. "The *Shangri-La* carries five thousand eight hundred and twenty passengers and crew."

Jake gave a short laugh. "That's more than twice the entire population of my hometown."

The driver smiled. "My home too."

He opened the door for his passenger and unloaded his luggage from the trunk.

"This is for you," Maurizio said, putting a lanyard around Jake's neck.

An ID card labeled "Shangri-La VIP" with Jake's name and the photograph he'd included with his registration hung from the lanyard.

Jake handed him two twenty-euro notes, almost fifty dollars US. Maurizio tried to give them back.

"You don't have to—"

Jake wouldn't take the bills. "Save it for New York."

He hung his messenger bag over one shoulder and pulled his suitcase into the port terminal. It was a massive structure, three football fields from one end to the other with a two-story ceiling, bare except for the security screening stations near the entrance and the array of ticket agents on the far wall. Passengers stood in long lines, shuffling slowly forward, waiting their turns.

Before he could find his place in the security screening line, an attractive blond-haired woman with a dazzling white smile approached him, her hand extended.

"Hello, Mr. Carter. I'm Eliana. I'll escort you through security and to your stateroom."

Jake shook her hand, looking at the hordes of less fortunate passengers. "You mean I don't have to—?"

She smiled. "No, sir. Our VIPs wait for no one."

With Eliana at his side, Jake breezed through security. Another crew member materialized out of nowhere and took Jake's bags, promising that they would be in his stateroom when Jake arrived. Once on board, they emerged into a huge open atrium. A four-story waterfall cascaded into a blue-tiled pool surrounded by lush greenery. Late-afternoon sun streamed in through the glass roof, casting a golden glow and reflecting off hundreds of sparkling crystals embedded in the floor.

She led him to a corner stateroom at one end of the sixteenth deck. Standing outside the door, she handed him a black, hard rubber bracelet with a digital screen.

"Put this on. It's your digital companion for the duration of the cruise. Wave it in front of your door to unlock your cabin. Any charges you incur will be scanned to it. And it will keep track of your winnings—or losses—at the tables. You can sync it to your bank account to access funds as you need them. If you win the tournament, the prize money will be transferred instantly to your account."

Jake slipped it on. It reminded him of a high-end fitness bracelet.

"Doesn't sound very secure. What if I lose it? Will someone else be able to get in my room or my bank account?"

"The bracelet has a preset password so you can get into your room." She pointed to a button next to the screen. "Use that to set your own password. Enjoy your cruise and best of luck in the Grand Slam."

Jake nodded and waved the bracelet across the door handle. He heard a click and tried the door. It swung open. He turned to thank Eliana, but she was already halfway down the corridor.

NINETEEN

Jake walked into a living room furnished with a sofa and two easy chairs. A fifty-inch flat-screen television hung on one wall above a fully stocked bar. An enormous fruit basket sat on the coffee table. Arrangements of exotic flowers were set out on end tables at either end of the sofa. Two bottles of wine and a basket of gourmet snacks were lined up on the counter in the minikitchen.

He crossed the room to the balcony and stepped outside, where a table and two chairs were bolted to the floor. When he came back inside, a small man with light-brown skin and jet-black hair wearing a uniform of black pants, white shirt, and black jacket stepped out of the bedroom. He bowed his head slightly at Jake.

"Hello, Mr. Carter. My name is Amado. I'll be your personal butler."

"My butler? I get a butler?"

"Yes, sir. You get a butler, and I am him."

"Call me Jake. Pleased to meet you." He held out his hand.

"As am I, Mr. Carter." Amado nodded and quickly shook hands. He spoke with a British accent, although his features suggested that he was from the Far East. "I've taken the liberty of unpacking your things."

Jake followed him into the bedroom to find his clothes hanging in the closet and folded neatly in the dresser drawers.

"That's great. Thanks."

"My pleasure, sir."

"Is there a butler code of conduct that says you can't call me Jake?"

"Yes, sir. And the penalties for violating the code are quite stiff," Amado said, smiling.

Jake liked that. "Well, I'm glad the code allows a sense of humor."

"Only when appropriate, sir. And we're never to be funnier than those whom we serve." They both chuckled. "I'll attend to the upkeep of your stateroom and your personal effects, including laundry and tailoring services. I'll keep your room stocked with the food and beverages of your choice. I can bring your breakfast in the morning and arrange for room service at any time you like."

"Who's going to tuck me in at night?"

"You'll have to make your own arrangements for that, sir. However, I can make reservations for any shipboard activities and services as well as any shore excursions."

"I'll keep that in mind, but I'm playing in the Grand Slam, so I don't know how much time I'll have for extracurricular activities."

Amado smiled. "That should be very exciting"—he started to say "Jake" but corrected himself—"sir."

Jake was pleased to find a potential point of connection other than master and servant. "Are you a fan?"

"I enjoy the game."

"Do you play?"

Amado turned his head. "Not very well, I'm afraid."

"Maybe I can give you some pointers."

"I wouldn't presume to ask." He straightened. "If you need me anytime day or night, simply press the call button." He pointed to a small black button on the bedside table. "Or in the living area." He led Jake out to the main room and indicated a similar button on the wall near the minifridge, which, at four feet tall, wasn't so mini.

"Will do."

"Is there anything else I can do for you, Mr. Carter?"

Jake shook his head. "I'm good for now. Thanks."

Amado dipped his head and quietly let himself out of the suite.

The *Shangri-La* set sail just after seven. Jake stood on his balcony and watched the lights of Italy fade into the night. A warm July breeze ruffled his hair. The tension in his neck and shoulders drained from his body the farther they got from shore. He felt safe for the first time in days, sailing across the Mediterranean, out of Theo's reach.

A chime interrupted his reverie. It took him a moment to realize he had a doorbell and someone was ringing it.

Jake recognized Henry Phillippi as soon as he opened the door. Phillippi's photograph had been plastered all over the tournament brochure and website. He was of average height, with an average build and average looks, except for a nose that must have been rearranged by someone else's fist a long time ago. Everything about him was average except his clothes—straight from *GQ*—and the way he carried himself with the smooth confidence of a master of the universe—or a master con artist.

"Henry Phillippi," he said, clasping Jake's hand for a quick, hard squeeze before walking past him into the suite. He stopped in the middle of the room, hands on his hips and beaming like he'd built the ship with his bare hands. "Not bad for last-minute, huh?"

"And you can't beat the price. Thanks for taking care of me."

"Hey, my pleasure. A player with your rep will take the tournament buzz up another notch." Jake didn't respond, afraid of which reputation Phillippi was talking about. Phillippi raised his palms. "No offense, but I heard about what happened at the World Series."

Jake stiffened. "It was bullshit. I didn't cheat."

Phillippi waved off his protest. "Never said you did. The trouble for guys like us is that it's damn near impossible to get rid of the taint once someone shits on us."

"So that audit in Vegas, it was bullshit too?"

He shrugged, sweeping his arm around the room. "After a while what people know or think they know about the past doesn't matter anymore. What matters is the here and now."

"So you dropped by to let me know that you're running a clean game and that I better play it straight—just in case. Am I right?"

Phillippi flashed a grin. "On the money. No offense."

"None taken," Jake said, trading one lie for another. "But why'd you let me in if I'm still tainted?"

Phillippi put one hand on Jake's shoulder. "For the buzz, baby. A poker tournament is like a reality show, and every show needs someone wearing the black hat. There's a reception at eight o'clock in the High Seas Bar for all the VIPs and the fans that paid for the privilege. See you there."

All Jake wanted to do was order room service, sit on his balcony, and count the stars. "I don't know. I'm bushed."

Phillippi's face hardened, as did his grip on Jake's shoulder. "These people paid a shit-bucket-ful of money to rub shoulders with the players, and we're going to give them their money's worth. Aren't we, Jake?"

"Every dime," Jake said, pulling Phillippi's hand from his shoulder.

TWENTY

At eight thirty Jake stepped into the High Seas Bar. The first thing he noticed was that it was jammed with people. The second thing he noticed was that it was moving, descending like a gigantic, slow-moving, open-air elevator through three of the ship's decks.

He'd gotten on at the eighth deck, highest of the three the bar serviced. Long and oval shaped, the perimeter was defined by a waist-high glass wall topped with a polished wooden rail. The bar was at one end, the rest of the floor space dotted with seating areas. A jazz trio at the opposite end was playing "Blue Rondo a la Turk."

The music vibe said, *Be cool.* A banner suspended above the musicians proclaiming "Welcome to the Grand Slam Poker Challenge" and dotted with logos of the cruise line and the dozen corporate sponsors of the tournament said, *Screw the vibe and show me the money.*

Jake had barely felt the ship's movement, but the High Seas Bar was something different—going up and down while the ship was rising and falling on the waves. Sea legs were required. After a few moments he got his bearings and began snaking through the crowd.

It was easy for Jake to tell the players from the fans because the fans wore their ID card lanyards around their necks and the players wore their bracelets. It reminded Jake of high school, where cliques ruled, dividing jocks, nerds, geeks, Goths, and the chess club.

The newer players, the ones minted on the Internet and the satellite circuit, happily chatted up the fans. The seasoned pros clustered together, backs to the rest of the world.

Though he wanted to be somewhere else, Jake saw the reception for what it was—an opportunity to study the opposition. Ever since the World Series fiasco, he'd been absent from the regular US circuit. Looking around the room, he saw mostly strangers. He'd watched some of them play in televised events, but he hadn't sat across the table from them and observed their habits up close. That put him at a disadvantage. Tonight was a chance to make up lost ground.

He made the rounds, exchanging pleasantries with the people he knew, introducing himself to a few more. Then a meaty hand landed on his shoulder. "Jake Carter! Is that you?"

He turned to see Mitch Wheeling. Burly and bearded, he was from northern Saskatchewan and looked like he belonged out in the wild wrestling bears. He used his mountain man persona the same way Jake sometimes used his Kansas farm boy routine to distract opponents from his quick, calculating mind. Mitch only had one—minor league—tournament championship to his credit. But he was one of those increasingly rare players who simply enjoyed playing, regardless of the outcome. Jake liked him.

"How's it going, Mitch?"

"Can't complain." He clapped Jake's arm again. "It's good to see you're still playing. That World Series thing was bullshit."

"Thanks." He appreciated the sentiment, which not many of his fellow players had expressed.

A petite brunette approached, holding two glasses of champagne. Jake watched a goofy smile spread over Mitch's face as she handed him one. "Thanks, sweetie," he said, and leaned down—way down—to give her a kiss.

Hayley Wheeling was maybe half the size of her husband. The top of her head just reached his shoulder, and she was in four-inch heels. Jake had to smile, and not just because the two of them looked like an ad for a sitcom. The Wheelings were still as utterly besotted with each other as they were when Jake attended their spur-of-the-moment ceremony in a Las Vegas wedding chapel eight years ago.

For a moment he imagined Cassie looking at him the way Hayley was looking at Mitch—without craning her neck quite so far back, of course—and his heart actually skipped a beat. Jake was distracted from his thoughts as Henry Phillippi made his way through the crowd and onto the small stage where the jazz trio was playing. He signaled them to stop and pointed to the banner overhead.

"Ladies and gentlemen! Are you ready to play some cards?" The crowd burst into cheers and applause. "Then you've come to the right place. Welcome to the sixth annual Grand Slam Poker Challenge! All of the games will be broadcast throughout the ship and the final table will be televised on ESPN2. This year's challenge is especially exciting because it's taking place on the most incredible cruise ship I've ever seen—Sovereign Cruises' fabulous *Shangri-La*!"

More enthusiastic applause. Phillippi continued. "The game is Texas Hold 'Em. No limit. If you want to bet your entire stack on the opening hand, go right ahead. Your opponents will thank you." Scattered laughs. "Every one of you has posted your one and only buy-in of twenty-five thousand dollars. Once you're busted, you stay busted." Several players booed, prompting more laughs. "We'll keep playing until we're down to the final nine tables, and those winners will shoot it out at the final table for a grand prize of . . ." He held out the microphone, like the front man at a rock concert, encouraging the audience to sing along.

They obliged by shouting, "Five million dollars!"

The moving bar docked at the fifth deck. Players and fans began to drift away in search of other temptations the ship had to offer. Jake hung back at the rail, sipping a beer, enjoying a private moment lost in a crowd.

"I know you," a woman said.

She was short, thin to a fault, with a narrow, pinched face and a birdlike nose. Her gray hair was cut short and was as drab as the dull-blue pantsuit she was wearing. She was holding an empty glass, and Jake could smell the wine on her breath.

"And now I know you," Jake answered, extending his hand. "Jake Carter."

"You don't remember me, do you?"

Jake was better at remembering which cards had been played than he was at remembering people's names. "I'm afraid I don't. You'll have to help me out."

She narrowed her eyes at him. "It was at the World Series of Poker at the Bellagio. You remember that much, don't you? My husband was one of the ones you cheated. Cleaned him out. He was never the same after that. Just crawled into a hole and drank himself to death. You try any of that here and we'll throw you overboard."

Jake was stunned. A lot of gamblers drank. More than a few drank too much, some killing themselves with a bottle. He knew better than to take the blame for the death of the woman's husband, but her bitter words stung nonetheless. The last thing he wanted was to get in an argument he couldn't win.

"I'm sorry for your loss."

The woman's shoulders drooped, her anger turning to sadness, the wine soothing her. She sniffled. "Sorry won't change what happened."

Before he could answer, Henry Phillippi appeared.

"Margaret Cunningham," he said, putting his arm around her. "How are you, darlin'? Margaret's a regular on our cruises, aren't you, sweetheart?" Chin drooping, she nodded into her empty glass, her eyes watery. "C'mon, let's get that glass filled up."

Phillippi took her by the elbow and guided her toward a handsome young bartender, catching up to Jake as he was leaving the bar.

"Sorry about that," Phillippi said.

"Is putting up with drunken old women who accuse me being responsible for their husbands' deaths part of wearing the black hat?"

"Yes, and so is being on time. When I tell you to be at an event, you be there."

Jake turned and faced him. "Let's get something straight. I'm here to play poker. I don't work for you."

Phillippi drew a deep breath, his eyes blazing as he restrained himself, and patted Jake on the chest. "No, but if you want a seat at the final table, you'll do what I tell you."

TWENTY-ONE

Before leaving Helsinki, Cassie had another encrypted exchange with Prometheus, beginning with what Ana Cortez had told her.

Kendrick has jumped bail.

I'm aware.

Do you have a line on him?

The job is over. Not our concern. Unless there's something I should know.

Cassie was worried about Gina. Under the added pressure of life on the run, Gina was more likely to tell Kendrick how she had deceived her. And that would put both of their lives in danger.

His wife, Gina, is the weak link. We need to know whether she went with him. If she did, we need to find her.

Understood. Have you located the current target?

He's on a cruise ship in the Mediterranean called the Shangri-La. *I'm joining the cruise tomorrow when it docks at Monte Carlo. He can't possibly know that I'm looking for him, but he went to a lot of trouble to cover his tracks. Any chance we've got competition on this one?*

Prometheus's reply was unsettling.

Unknown. Will inquire. Watch your back. And remember, no attachments.

As Cassie traveled to Monte Carlo, Prometheus's reminder continued to reverberate. One side of her brain kept saying she wasn't becoming attached to Jake. The other side called her a liar. She'd had the same internal struggle over Gabriel Degrand. They'd met while standing in line at a deli and began complaining about their bosses. The next thing she knew, she'd given him her boss's password, her boss suddenly lost eight million dollars, and Gabriel wanted to introduce her to Prometheus. She'd known as little about him then as she did about Jake now.

She tried not to think about Gabriel or Jake, focusing instead on getting back to one of her favorite places, the French Riviera. Cassie's father was posted in Barcelona for several years and often took her there. She fell in love with the people, the beaches, and the glamour. As a young girl, she was starry-eyed at the rich and superrich, though she saw them differently now when they flaunted their jewels, art, and yachts. Since going to work for Prometheus, she'd listened to them tell their stories about the fabulous deals they'd made to acquire their baubles and toys, leaving out the illicit details that had put them on her radar. She would laugh to herself whenever she was about to give one of their stories a very unhappy ending.

She wasn't laughing as her connecting flight from Paris landed in Nice and her thoughts returned to Jake. It wasn't like Prometheus to be outflanked. He carefully vetted his clients, requiring that they not hire one of his few competitors and turn the job into a race. Either the client had ignored Prometheus's rule or it was the client who had competition, not him. Either possibility underscored his warning to watch her back and made her wonder once again, who was Jake Carter?

The airport in Nice also served Monte Carlo, since the principality's air service was limited to a heliport. A helicopter shuttle service ran regularly between them. Cassie stared at the deep-blue Mediterranean during the seven-minute flight, thinking about her next moves.

This job was a lot more challenging than recovering the Scarlet Star and the porn video from Alan Kendrick or the stolen Kandinsky from Andrus Vesik. There were no doubts about ownership in those cases, and she could hold each item in her hands. Jake was the only one who knew for certain whether he had cheated. The client's allegations were just that—allegations. She doubted that Jake had packed two million dollars in crisp hundreds in his luggage.

A driver was waiting for her at the heliport, and moments later she was at Port d'Hercule, grinning and staring at the *Shangri-La*. She'd been on a number of cruises, all of them on ships. The *Shangri-La* was a floating city.

"Jake Carter, you really know how to pick them."

"Excusez-moi?" the driver said.

She waved her hand, paying her fare with a generous tip. "Sorry. Just talking to myself."

Her cell phone rang as the driver tipped his hat. It was Zoey.

"Oh, I'm so glad you answered," Zoey said. "I'm about to lose my mind!"

"What's the matter?"

"The kids are home with sore throats, the dog shat on the carpet, and I missed my period. But that's not the worst of it!"

"Oh, no. What else could go wrong?"

"I'm out of wine!" Zoey laughed, a high-pitched cackle. "Just kidding. I miss you. Just wanted to hear your voice for a sec."

It was Cassie's turn to laugh, Zoey joining in until they were both breathless. "You're sure about not missing your period?"

"Not much chance of that with Harry working so hard at his new job and totally knackered when he's home. Thank God for my vibrator. Girl's best friend, and it doesn't roll over and go to sleep the minute I'm done."

"You're a mess."

"Don't I know it? How are you? Where are you? Tell me you're about to go off on one of your grand adventures."

Cassie stared at the *Shangri-La* again. "Well, I don't know how grand or adventurous it will be, but I'm in Monte Carlo about to board a cruise ship."

"Oh, my. A Mediterranean cruise. Top of my bucket list, that is. Care to trade places?"

Cassie sighed. It was a question she'd asked herself more than once. The stability and predictability of Zoey's life with a husband, kids, and a dog sometimes sounded more like a tonic than a toxin. "You wouldn't give up your life any more than I'd give up mine."

"Don't be so sure. Trade a life of dirty dishes for the Riviera? Sounds like a fair swap to me."

"You have a husband who loves you and children who adore you."

"And . . . ?"

"And a dog that craps on the carpet."

"Don't forget my vibrator—or yours," Zoey said, laughing again.

Cassie's phone beeped with an incoming call. "Sorry, Zoey. I've got another call I have to take. Talk soon."

"Don't have too much fun. Wouldn't want you going overboard and lost at sea."

"I'll wear a life jacket at all times."

"That should wow the captain and crew. Love you."

"Love you too."

The call was from Gunnar.

"Good news. I got you upgraded."

"From what to what?"

"An inside stateroom on the third deck with a pull-down bunk bed and two roommates to a grand suite on the fourteenth deck with a king-size bed and a balcony."

"How'd you manage that?"

"The previous occupants, Mr. and Mrs. Jensen, decided to quit the cruise when they got an offer to take an all-expenses-paid cruise around the world, leaving from Miami tomorrow. First-class airfare included."

"Gunnar, you are a genius."

"No, I'm just a generous soul with other people's money. I'll text you the confirmation. The target is on the sixteenth deck, corner suite, number 1602. Happy cruising."

He ended the call, and a moment later Cassie's phone pinged with a text that included a link to her reservation confirmation. She was the only passenger joining the cruise in Monte Carlo, so it took little time to check in. She received her digital bracelet, set her password, and made her way to her suite. It was one o'clock in the afternoon. The ship was scheduled to sail at seven.

She didn't have much of a plan A. Let Jake find her. Tell him she took his advice about going on vacation and let him squirm trying to explain why he wasn't in Vegas. Take advantage of their second "meet cute" moment and his obvious attraction to her to manipulate him into a confession. Plan B was everything in plan A except the confession and included watching him play poker, hoping to catch him cheating, confronting him, and using the threat of exposure to make him give up the two million. Plan C was everything in plan B except the cheating and included stripping him naked, tying him to her bed, and having her way with him until he begged her to take the money. A part of her was rooting for plan C.

She turned on the TV and found the onboard channels, with information about ship activities and ports of call. One channel was dedicated to the Grand Slam tournament, which would begin tomorrow once the ship had left port. Every day of the cruise was filled with seminars and poker lessons and opportunities to mingle with the poker pros over cocktails and wine tastings and even a night of karaoke. She had to smile at the image of Jake belting out "Born in the U.S.A." He seemed like a Springsteen kind of guy.

He was on the schedule for a meet and greet at eight tonight. That gave him the rest of the afternoon free. And where would a gambling man go if he had a few hours to kill? There were a number of casinos in Monte Carlo but there was only one Casino de Monaco in the world.

Cassie felt a strange sense of déjà vu as she walked up the steps into the famed casino, half expecting to see a tuxedo-clad James Bond with a beautiful woman on one arm and a bad guy in a headlock under the other. It was so familiar from the movies she'd watched growing up, waiting for the day that her boring diplomat dad would confess he was secretly a superspy. The closest she'd been was the plaza in front of the casino, her father telling her she wasn't old enough for a closer look.

The glittering Salon Europe was the room she'd most often seen on the screen. It was bigger than she'd imagined. Gilded arches stretched up to an engraved-glass dome. Huge crystal chandeliers cast a glow over row after row of gaming tables, each surrounded by eager gamblers intently watching the next spin of the roulette wheel or turn of the card.

The room was crowded with tourists dressed in jeans and T-shirts, as if they were at the mall instead of a palace, but they gave her cover as she moved around the room looking for Jake. Before she let him find her, she wanted to see whether he was paying attention to the game or watching over his shoulder for whatever trouble was coming his way.

She saw him as he entered the salon, moving through the throng with a casual confidence, patting people on the back as he passed, greeting them with a smile and an apology for bumping into them. Dressed in a dark sport jacket, gray linen slacks, and an open-collared white shirt, he was a man at ease and at home. He slid into a chair at a baccarat table on the far side of the room, clapping the dealer on the arm as if they were old friends. If he was worried about anything, it didn't show. The man didn't just have a poker face. He had a poker body.

She watched him play for an hour. He joked with the dealer and the five other players, feigning surprise when he won, congratulating the winner when he lost. A server placed a tall glass next to him filled with ice and a clear liquid, a slice of lime on the rim. He sipped at it as he played. Cassie guessed it was either gin or vodka, hoping he'd drink enough to get a little buzzed and let his defenses down. She'd use any advantage she could. This was the job and he was the target.

TWENTY-TWO

Alan Kendrick had left nothing to chance in planning his escape from New York. He'd chosen the golf course not only for its privacy, helipad, and marina but also because there were no surveillance cameras.

A shell company so far removed from him that it couldn't be traced back had hired the actors that posed as Gina and him. The same company had chartered the helicopter that picked them up. A different shell company even more removed owned the yacht. The two men that piloted the speedboat were part of the yacht's crew. And the boat was hidden away in the ship's belly.

His disappearance was the lead story on the network news and *The Daily Show* that night, and the next day it was on the front pages of the *New York Times*, the *Wall Street Journal*, and *USA Today* and fresh meat for the cable news crowd. He read each report on his iPad from a comfortable perch on the fourth deck of the yacht, enjoying the cool ocean breeze under a cloudless, radiant blue sky.

Christening it the Golf Cart Getaway, Jon Stewart said that Kendrick "had disappeared quicker than Fox News at a fact-checking conference." Though a lifelong Republican and devotee of all things O'Reilly, Kendrick chuckled. He was in the mood to take a joke. The

Times called it a daring escape worthy of Jason Bourne. *USA Today* called it a salute to illusionist David Copperfield. The talking heads on CNBC, CNN, and MSNBC agreed that Alan Kendrick had pulled off the perfect vanishing act.

The FBI trumpeted the immediate arrests of the imposters and helicopter pilot but was forced to release them, admitting that the trio had been duped. Even the address where they were supposed to go to pick up their checks after the job was done proved fictitious. The head of the US Marshals fugitive task force announced that they were following up on numerous leads and promised to hunt Kendrick down.

A shadow passed across Kendrick's table. He looked up to find Gina standing with the sun to her back. She was wearing a floppy hat and dark glasses.

"Sit down, darling." She didn't move. "I said sit down."

Gina took a seat. Kendrick raised his hand, summoning a waiter.

"Yes, sir. What can I get you?"

"I'd like a Denver omelet with hash browns. Make them crispy. Some fresh fruit—no berries. And black coffee. Oh, and orange juice—fresh squeezed, no pulp. Make sure it's chilled. Darling, what would you like?"

"Nothing," she murmured.

"You've got to eat something. I don't want you wasting away. Bring Mrs. Kendrick the same thing I ordered."

Gina waited until they were alone. "Why did you bring me?"

"Why do you think?"

"I don't know."

"Do you think I brought you because I'm so deeply in love with you that I can't imagine us being apart even for a day?"

Gina removed her sunglasses. Her right eye was swollen half-shut, the surrounding flesh discolored in a sickening hue of black, blue, and yellow.

"No. That's not what I thought."

"Smart girl. And I didn't bring you so I'd have someone to fuck or suck my dick. There were plenty of other women to choose from if that's all I wanted."

Gina blanched, wiping away a milky fluid oozing from the corner of her black eye.

"Then why?"

Kendrick leaned toward her, his arms folded on the table. "I brought you along because I need your help finding Cassie Ireland. And if you had been a little more forthcoming last night, your eye would look a helluva lot better this morning. Can't you put some makeup on that?"

"Why? I thought you'd like seeing what you did to me."

He sat back. "Gina, darling, you misunderstand me. I take no pleasure in hurting you. I asked you to tell me everything you knew about Cassie Ireland. If you had done that the first time I asked, your face would be as beautiful as ever."

"You're a horrible man."

"True or not, it changes nothing. I had hoped you would feel more like sharing this morning. Are you going to disappoint me?"

"What are you going to do—throw me overboard?"

Kendrick smiled. "In front of all these witnesses? No, darling. And besides, that would be such a waste. Tell me what I want to know and we'll both enjoy the rest of our voyage."

"I already told you everything. I met Cassie a few months ago at a charity lunch. We became friends. She was looking for an apartment and I suggested the Hendersons'. That's all."

Kendrick sighed, then lunged at her, hand raised, stopping inches from her face. Gina yelped and jerked backward in her chair, nearly toppling over.

"I had a dog once that kept begging for food. Wouldn't stop no matter how many times I told her not to beg. Finally, I hit her right in the chops. Knocked her halfway across the room. After that, whenever I raised a hand she'd jump to get out of the way. Just like you. But she never begged again. Why can't you be like the dog and do what you're told?"

Gina clenched her hands in her lap. She was crying. Tears drained from her eyes. Mucus ran from her nose. The waiter arrived, setting their breakfast on the table, avoiding eye contact with either of them. When he left, Kendrick tossed Gina a napkin.

"Wipe your face and quit sniveling. I'll make this easy for you. I'll tell you what I know and what I don't know about Cassie Ireland. Then you can fill in the blanks."

Gina sniffled and nodded.

"Cassie Ireland robbed me. She stole my money. She stole a very valuable gem from my collection. She stole some . . . home movies with a great deal of sentimental value. And she copied highly confidential information from a laptop computer I kept in the safe that the federal government wants to use to send me to prison for the rest of my life."

Gina's mouth hung open. She shook her head. "No. She couldn't have. She swore she . . ." Gina caught herself and looked away.

"Had nothing to do with it?"

Gina hung her head, then nodded. "Yes."

"Well, she lied. Made a fool out of you for trusting her. It took my people a while, but they were finally able to put it together. They found a thumbprint someone had added to the alarm system so that he—or she, as it happens—could turn off the alarm. Of course, we didn't know it was Cassie's. Not at first. But I remembered that she was in the apartment with you the night before when Jake brought me home. I was drunk but not that drunk. I got suspicious when we couldn't match the print to any database in the world. So we checked the Hendersons' apartment and found dozens of matches."

"I don't know what to say."

"Sure you do, sweetheart. Cassie knew where everything was—the alarm control panel, the panic room. She even knew what kind of equipment she'd need to drill the safe. I don't how she learned all of that. Do you?"

Gina shrank in her chair, wrapping her arms around her chest. After a moment she answered.

"I didn't tell you because I was afraid."

"Tell me what?"

She took a deep breath and then her confession came out in a torrent, every detail from the night before the robbery to the day Kendrick was arrested. He listened without comment, his face blank, taking it all in.

"Thank you for that. Thank you for telling me the truth."

Gina looked up at him, a flicker of hope in her eyes. "You're not angry?"

"Of course not, darling. I'd have been angry if you were in on it with her, but I knew that wasn't possible."

"Because I love you?"

"Because you're a stupid cunt who wouldn't have the brains or nerve to rip me off."

Kendrick stared out to sea, silent again until Gina interrupted his thoughts.

"What happens now?"

He looked at her. "In a few days we'll stop at a place in Portugal called Ilha de Tavira to refuel. Then it's on to Croatia."

"Croatia? Why?"

"Because, my love, they don't have an extradition treaty with the United States. It's a wonderful place to grow old—if you get the chance."

Gina began to cry. "You aren't really going to kill me, are you?"

He picked up his knife and fork. "I am if you don't eat your breakfast."

TWENTY-THREE

Jake spotted Cassie before he reached the baccarat table, catching a glimpse of her profile when the sea of tourists briefly parted, confirming his suspicion when he saw her reflection in the mirrored wall behind the bar as she cast a furtive glance at him. He didn't believe in coincidences, but his faith in the inevitability of a long shot eventually paying off was unshakable.

Before spotting her, he'd have put the odds that Cassie had actually called him out of the blue to ask for a second chance at better than 50 percent, the edge based on his irresistible charm. But seeing her across the Salon Europe pretending not to notice him was a reminder that he often found his charm more irresistible than women did. And the possibility that she just happened to wander into the casino at the same time he did was the long shot of all long shots.

All of which assumed she was here because of him, and he could be wrong about that. Whoever she really was and whatever she really did, she had a knack for showing up where the wealthy could be found—and robbed. He was working from a small data set, but it was all the data he had.

It made more sense that she was sizing up another victim rather than chasing after him, because she knew he wasn't in Alan Kendrick's league. Besides, he reasoned, why go to all the trouble to find him when she could simply knock on his door when he made it back to the Rex?

If she didn't want him to know she was there, she could easily slip away instead of lingering at the edge of the crap table half a room away, acting like she cared whether the shooter rolled a seven or an eleven. All of which made him think they were playing a game, only he didn't know the rules.

And if she did call his name across the crowded room, they'd both have some explaining to do about why she wasn't in Tokyo and he wasn't in Las Vegas. If the moment came, he'd let her do the talking, because if there was one thing he'd learned, it was that the first liar didn't stand a chance.

All these thoughts kept running through his mind as he concentrated on the cards coming out of the shoe. Multitasking was a job requirement for a professional gambler and it was one of his strengths, but one thing kept niggling at him. If Cassie had found him, how hard would it be for Theo to do the same thing? Especially now that he knew the final table would be televised on ESPN.

"La banque gagne le main," announced the dealer, prompting cheers and high fives from the winning bettors. Jake didn't care that he wasn't one of them. It was time to play Cassie's game.

He drained his glass and scanned the room until he found her at the roulette wheel, her back to him, her smooth, dark skin bare but for the thin white straps of her dress, muscles tense as the ball zipped around the wheel and finally landed on a number. She shot her fist into the air.

"Yes!"

In that moment everything slowed. He didn't see the wheel or the croupier or the crowd gathered around the table. He didn't hear the groans, whoops, and hollers of the other winners and losers. All he saw was Cassie and all he heard was a voice he hadn't been able to get out of his head.

She turned around, laughing, her gold-flecked eyes shimmering, clapping her hands in celebration, stopping when she saw him standing only ten feet away. She cocked her head, raised her eyebrows, and dipped her chin, letting her arms fall to her sides as if to say, *You got me.*

He walked toward her, smiling, until he was close enough to pick up her perfume, a distinctive blend of sandalwood and floral scents.

"Tokyo, huh?"

She shrugged and looked around the room. "This is a casino but we're not in Vegas."

"No, we aren't."

He waited, studying her face, trying to find her tell, but there wasn't one.

She took a breath, letting it out. "You were the one who said I should take some time off."

"Monaco is a long way from Japan."

"A little more than twelve hours—to Paris anyway. Then it's just a couple more to Monte Carlo. How long does it take to get here from Vegas?"

"I have no idea."

She crossed her arms over her chest, raising one eyebrow. "So, you weren't in Vegas."

"I was in Vegas but I flew to Rome, and let me tell you, that trip is a killer. Eighteen hours and change."

"And now you're in Monte Carlo."

"And tomorrow I'll be in Barcelona. I'm on a cruise where the main attraction is a poker tournament. Sort of the luxury version of the oldest permanent floating crap game in New York."

"You and Nathan Detroit, huh?"

Jake grinned. "Yeah. *Guys and Dolls* is one of my favorites. What does that make you? Sister Sarah Brown?" He looked her up and down. "That dress doesn't look like standard issue for the Salvation Army."

"No, but it's perfect for the *Shangri-La*."

Jake leaned his head back, mouth open. "Don't tell me you're on the same cruise. What a coincidence."

She nodded and smiled. "I do consulting work for Sovereign Cruises, and they call me sometimes when there's a cancellation. Something opened up last-minute and I took the spot, but I couldn't get to Rome in time, so I came to Monte Carlo to join the cruise."

"So . . . you being here has nothing to do with that phone call," he ventured. She looked at him blankly. "You know . . . the one about second chances."

Cassie furrowed her brow, concentrating for a moment, then brightening. "Oh, right. The agony of waiting days or even weeks for you to come back to New York was more than I could bear. I guessed that I'd run into you right here, right now, so I hopped on a plane and here I am. I'm so glad my plan worked."

He laughed. "Okay, okay. Sorry. My ego and I deserved that."

She reached out and touched his arm for an instant. "Yes, you did, but it's still good to see you."

"You too. You look . . ." He took in her tall, slim figure draped in a flowing white sundress. "Amazing."

"You don't look too shabby yourself."

Jake wondered whether she was flirting with him or just being polite, but she gave nothing away that would help answer his question. He broke off his stare and nodded to the roulette table.

"How's the wheel treating you?"

"I think our relationship has run its course." She moved past him to get a closer look at the table he'd left. "But I can't leave Monte Carlo without trying baccarat. Will you teach me?"

"Absolutely. All it takes is money."

Jake won and Cassie lost. They walked away after playing their last hand. Cassie slipped her arm inside his. Jake liked how natural it felt to be joined together but couldn't stop his gambler mind from spinning the odds against their meeting like this. He knew the difference between a long shot and a long con.

When they were outside on Casino Square, Cassie tugged at his sleeve, smiling softly as she turned to him.

"Tell me something."

"Shoot."

"How do you keep winning all the time? You must be cheating."

Jake flinched, immediately regretting his involuntary reaction. The question felt like an accusation even though he assumed she said it in jest. He hoped she hadn't noticed his tell but wasn't surprised when she did.

"Oooh, sore subject, huh? I was only kidding."

"That's okay. Nobody wins all the time, including me. But pros—the really good ones—win more than the average Joe. A lot more, or we'd be selling shoes or insurance for a living. Some people assume you're cheating when you're just better at the game than they are."

"You must get tired of hearing that."

"Goes with the territory."

"You don't seem the type."

"When it comes to cheating at cards, there's no such thing as a type. Given the chance, a lot of people will take it. Doesn't matter if they're rich or poor or if they're a doctor, lawyer, or rabbi."

She chuckled. "That's pretty cynical, don't you think?"

"Let's just say anyone could get fitted for feet of clay under the right circumstances."

Jake still couldn't read Cassie. Was her question about cheating innocent or was she trying to tell him that she knew about the rumors that had dogged him? Was she vetting him before letting him get close, or was something else going on that he had yet to figure out? He decided to shift the conversation.

"You know what else the cheating question is like?"

"No."

"It's like me asking you why you needed an alibi for the Kendrick robbery."

Her eyes flickered, barely noticeable but enough to tell him that he'd touched a nerve. She unlocked their arms, her voice turning cool.

"I told you that I didn't need an alibi."

"Which means that either you had nothing to do with the robbery or that you're such a good thief that you really didn't need an alibi."

Cassie took his arm again. "I see what you mean. Questions can be so unfair."

"You know they arrested Kendrick and he jumped bail."

She nodded. "I read something about that on the *Times* website. Living on the run can't be fun no matter how much money you have."

Jake had put up with her questions about cheating. He decided to remind her that she had a weak spot of her own.

"Maybe," he said with a mischievous grin, "he's not just running from the Feds. Maybe he's looking for the woman that robbed him."

Cassie turned to him and smacked him playfully on the shoulder. "Okay, mister. I get the point. No more questions about cheating or robbing."

"Good. What's next?"

"Something to eat, and you're buying."

They got an outdoor table at Salle Empire overlooking the gardens of Casino Square. Their conversation was easy and light. Jake told her funny stories about playing cards all over the world. She'd been to many of the same places. They agreed that Bora Bora was highly overrated as a dream getaway. She talked about the language and cultural pitfalls of being an international risk consultant and how she'd once tried complimenting a client in Mandarin, only to learn later that she'd actually told him that he had the face of a dead cow.

At 7:40 he noticed the time. "Crap. I've got to get back to the ship." He signaled their waiter for the check. He didn't want Henry Phillippi to chew him out again for being late.

"Hot date?"

"Already have one." He gazed at her and she ducked her chin, smiling. "I've got a meet and greet with the fans at eight."

"Wait . . . you have fans?"

"You don't have to sound so surprised."

She gave him her now-familiar half-amused, half-exasperated smile. "You really are impossible."

"That's what you love about me, right?"

"It's a good place to start, because the only way to go is up."

TWENTY-FOUR

They walked back to the *Shangri-La*, this time holding hands as if it were the most natural thing to do. The security guard scanned their digital bracelets and waved them through. As Jake made his way to the 360 Lounge, he kept expecting Cassie to say good night, but she kept hold of his hand.

"This is going to be pretty boring," he said. "Shaking hands, signing autographs—"

"And fending off groupies, I'll bet. Don't worry. I'll protect you."

"They're not . . ." he began, then stopped himself. "Okay, some of them are." Jake had always found celebrity hoopla embarrassing and he didn't want to subject Cassie to it. But he had to admit he was pleased that she wanted to stick around. "Don't say I didn't warn you."

The 360 Lounge normally featured virtual panoramas, such as Sydney Harbour Regatta and the northern lights, with video screens covering every inch of wall. Tonight was all about poker. The screens displayed highlights from past poker tournaments, including the World Series, featuring many of the pros working the room.

The waitresses were dressed in white shirts, black vests, and bow ties to look like casino dealers—if those dealers also wore short-shorts and lace garters. Mylar balloons in the shapes of hearts, diamonds, clubs, and spades adorned each table. Specialty drinks on offer included the Royal Flush and Ante Up.

Henry Phillippi was holding court, surrounded by players and fans, gesturing with a cigar in one hand and a brandy snifter in the other. He caught Jake's eye, tilting his head at Cassie, and gave him an approving nod.

Jake waded into the throng of fans, accepting hugs, posing for selfies, and signing anything that was put in front of him. He lost track of Cassie, occasionally catching sight of her in the crowd. She looked over as he was signing official Grand Slam Poker Challenge baseball caps for a group of college-aged guys. She smiled and raised her drink to him. Jake offered a resigned shrug in return.

"I saw you play in Hong Kong," a woman told him as she held out a small notebook for him to sign. "Maybe six years ago?"

He scrawled his name. "The Pan-Asian Tournament?"

"Yeah. You were great." She was tall with long red hair, green eyes, fine features, and porcelain skin, maybe early thirties. Her blouse was unbuttoned far enough to expose her breasts when she leaned a certain way, which she was doing.

After one reflexive—and appreciative—glance, he met her gaze. "Thanks."

"I was there with Danny Buckley. You remember him?"

Jake gave a short laugh. "How could I forget? He nearly wiped me out a dozen times."

"But you beat him at the final table." She moved a little closer, pressing one breast against his arm, and confided, "The asshole had just dumped me the night before. You completely humiliated him. I've always wanted to thank you for that."

"Happy to help." He glanced at the place where Cassie had been standing. She was gone. He held out a hand to the woman. "It's nice to meet you . . ."

"Kristen Templar," she said, and took his hand in hers. "It's nice to meet you too." She squeezed his hand, looking at him with bedroom eyes. "I mean it. I'd really like to thank you. I'm in Suite 932."

Jake swallowed and eased his hand from hers, resisting the temptation to look down. "That's very thoughtful, but I need my rest. Have to stay sharp for the tournament."

She licked her lips. "If you say so. But remember. Suite 932, in case you can't sleep."

She walked away, giving him a final come-hither look over her shoulder.

Jake went to the bar and ordered a beer. He suddenly found himself looking at his own much-younger face as footage from the last World Series of Poker he'd played in appeared on the wall behind the bar. The beer soured in his mouth with the memory of how that had ended.

He turned his back to the bar and found Cassie. She was holding a cocktail glass filled with a bright-red concoction and talking with Henry Phillippi. She laughed at something he said, briefly touching his arm. Jake recognized the gesture, suddenly wondering whether Phillippi—or perhaps the tournament—was the reason she was here. Phillippi controlled access to the nine million dollars in entry fees posted by each player. That was enough to put him in Alan Kendrick's league.

He smiled at the thought. What brass to pull something like that off. Maybe she'd need another alibi after all.

TWENTY-FIVE

Cassie left Jake to his fans and focused on Henry Phillippi. Gunnar had included a dossier on him in the materials he sent to her about the Grand Slam. She studied it on the plane from Helsinki to Paris. She knew the type. A man in full—as in full of himself, convinced of his importance, master of all he surveyed. At the moment he was master of a crowd of poker pros and groupies. Not what she would call a kingdom, but from the way Phillippi kept his chest puffed out, it was kingdom enough for him.

The easiest way for her to recover her client's money would be to steal Jake's winnings from the tournament, assuming he won at least two million dollars. She'd have to intercept the funds before Phillippi transferred them to Jake's bank account. And she'd need Phillippi's help doing that—without Phillippi realizing he was lending a helping hand.

She had another reason for wanting to get close to him. She wasn't going to steal Jake's money unless she was certain Jake had cheated her client. It was unlikely that Phillippi would know anything about that card game, but he might know enough about Jake to convince her one way or the other.

She watched as a steady parade of people approached him. Some got a clap on the back, others a two-handed handshake. He leaned in close to a few, keeping their conversation confidential. More often he looked over the shoulder of whoever was talking to him for someone more interesting—a habit Zoey called "better dealing." At the moment a pair of blue-haired women wearing glittery matching T-shirts proclaiming that whatever happened in Vegas stayed in Vegas demanded his attention. He nodded at them but looked at Cassie, twenty feet away, standing against the rail.

Cassie raised an eyebrow and shook her head, laughing just enough to tell him she was sorry for his predicament. It was all the encouragement Phillippi needed to abandon the women and make a beeline to her.

"I don't believe we've met. I'm Henry Phillippi."

"Nice to meet you, Henry," she said, extending her hand. "I'm Cassie Ireland. I was beginning to think those women weren't going to let you go."

He chuckled. "I'm happy to talk with all of our guests." He ran his eyes up and down Cassie's body. "Though, I admit, some more than others."

"Guests? That must mean you're one of the crew. Does the captain know you're out of uniform?"

He smiled, spreading his arms. "This is my uniform, but I'm not part of the crew. I own the company that's putting on the Grand Slam. You might say the captain works for me, because without the poker tournament this ship would be in dry dock."

It never failed, Cassie thought. It was easier to get a rise out of some men's egos than it was to get a rise out of their pants.

Cassie pitched her voice a little higher and her IQ a little lower. "Are you really in charge of the whole tournament?"

"That depends," said Phillippi, ducking his head toward hers. "Any complaints?"

She laughed and gave his arm a squeeze, letting her hand slowly slide down his sleeve, watching his eyes dilate. "Not at all! I've never been to a poker tournament before and didn't know what to expect. Nothing as impressive as all this." She gestured to their surroundings.

"Kind of you to say." He finished his drink and signaled for another. "I saw you come in with Jake Carter. Did he send you over here to ask me to stack the deck in his favor?"

"I came into the bar with him, but that doesn't mean I'm with him."

She held his gaze until he smiled. "That's good to know."

"Would he do that? Ask you to stack the deck in his favor. That would be cheating."

Phillippi turned serious, his jaw tight. "I run an honest tournament. Occasionally, a player might try to cheat, but I always catch them. I know all their tricks. As for Jake"—he shrugged—"there was some talk a few years ago, but it was just that—talk."

"You know what they say. Where there's smoke . . ."

He furrowed his brow. "That's a funny thing to say about the man you came with."

"I told you, I'm not with him, not in the way you imply. We met a month or so ago when I moved into his building in New York."

"And now you're on a cruise together?"

She laughed. "Small world. I decided to take a last-minute vacation and joined the cruise today. We ran into each other at the Casino de Monaco."

"So why ask me if your . . . neighbor . . . is a cheat?"

She pursed her lips. "Just trying to get to know him a little better even though we're . . . just neighbors."

Phillippi tilted his head back, looking down his nose at her, then nodded. "Well, let me tell you something about your neighbor. He doesn't have to cheat."

"He's that good?"

"I'm telling you he's that good."

Cassie felt the knots in her neck begin to loosen. "Thank you. That's very reassuring."

Phillippi glanced over her shoulder, then took her hand. "I'm afraid I have to tend to more of my guests. I hope we have the chance to visit some more. Perhaps dinner one night at the captain's table."

She gave him a sly half smile. "That sounds so crowded."

He grinned. "A private table then."

"Yes. That would be much nicer."

Phillippi leaned close and whispered in her ear. "I'll make all the arrangements."

He left her to talk to someone else, though Cassie was certain he didn't think his next guest was a better deal. Jake joined her a moment later.

"I see that you met Henry."

"Yes. He said nice things about you."

"Really? Like what?"

Cassie took his hand and smiled at him. "Just that you'd make a good neighbor."

TWENTY-SIX

Ana Cortez stood behind the chest-high concierge desk, elbows on the marble countertop, her chin in her hands. Her eyelids felt like they weighed twenty pounds. Her joints and lower back ached from walking the floor all night with her fifteen-month-old baby, whose colicky stomach had kept both of them up.

She'd come on duty at seven that morning and was counting down the last ten minutes before her shift ended at four o'clock. The thought of grabbing a quick nap on the sofa in the staff room before heading home was the only thing keeping her upright. She needed the sleep before tackling the laundry, cooking, and cleaning that were waiting for her. It had been a long, busy day of juggling demands and complaints from the residents, pampered rich folks used to getting what they wanted when they wanted it. They gave little thought to the burdens they placed on her shoulders. All she asked was that these final minutes would pass quickly and quietly.

The revolving front door whooshed open, the gust of air enough to rouse her. A man in his early thirties, a stranger to her, passed through the door and came toward her. He had slicked-back dark hair and an olive complexion, and wore a jet-black suit she recognized as Armani with an open-collared shirt. She noted his Bulgari watch, guessing that it cost more than she made in a year, and his thick platinum ring with a deep-blue sapphire that she was certain cost more than she made in ten years. They were the familiar trappings of wealth she saw every day.

But in her many years at the Rex, she'd learned to see past the trappings and listen to what her gut told her about people. Her first impressions were rarely wrong. And there was something about this man that sent a chill through her. It wasn't his confident stride. That was evidence of strength and conviction. It wasn't the smile he was showing her, though it was as phony as the artificially white sheen on his teeth. It was his eyes. She'd learned to fear the same off-kilter mix of amused viciousness in her father, who had looked forward to beating her mother, brothers, and her as much as he had enjoyed making them suffer.

Without realizing it, she took a step back. The man stopped in front of her, studying her. Then, as she finally did with her father, she stiffened her spine.

"Welcome to the Rex. May I help you?"

The man nodded as if to say, *Well done.* "I'm looking for Jake Carter. He lives here. Yes?"

She recognized his Greek accent. He rolled his *r*'s the same way Stavros, the building electrician, spoke.

What did a man who so easily triggered her childhood fears want with Jake? If the man had inquired about another resident, she might have told him the truth. But Jake wasn't like the others. He asked without demanding, thanked her and meant it, and, most of all, treated her like an equal instead of an indentured servant. Not that he was a saint. No gambling man was. She'd heard the rumors about him cheating but dismissed them, believing she was a better judge of his character. Every instinct she had told her to tell this man nothing, even though Jake had said to tell anyone who asked for him that they could find him in Las Vegas.

"We don't give out information about our residents."

"But he does live here."

Ana forced herself to keep her voice flat and calm. "I'm sorry, sir. We don't give out information about our residents."

A dark look flashed across the man's face, but he kept his tone polite. "That may be so, but we both know that he has an apartment on the fourth floor, don't we?"

Ana folded her arms over her chest. "If you knew that, why did you ask?"

"You know," the man said, raising his hand, pointing a finger at her, "I get the feeling that you don't like me. Why is that?"

Ana wanted to tell him why but knew better. "I don't know, sir."

The man shrugged. "I could take the elevator to the fourth floor and start knocking on doors."

"I'm afraid not. The elevators are keycard protected and only the residents and staff have keycards."

"Why are you making this so difficult?"

"I'm just following the rules, sir."

He fixed his eyes on her, boring in. "And I would like you to break the rules and tell me where I can find Jake Carter. I've been unable to reach him and we have urgent business."

She stared at him, not responding until he leaned over the counter, motioning her toward him. Ana held her ground, though she felt a tremor reverberating in her legs. He pointed to the name tag pinned to her blouse.

"Ana, I am a reasonable man. You know where Mr. Carter is but you won't tell me. I admire your loyalty, which is why I'm not going to offer you money for that information. I could take your keycard from you but," he said, glancing around, "I have no wish to put on a show for your security cameras. No. I think I will wait outside until you leave and then ask you again. Or I might follow you home and we can talk there. Maybe while you're fixing dinner for your children or waiting for your husband to come home."

Ana's stomach clenched and her legs wobbled as they used to do in the instant before her father struck her. She was ashamed of her weakness. She couldn't let this man anywhere near her family. Jake would understand. But her throat was closed and the words wouldn't form in her mouth.

"Hi, Ana! It's 3:59! I told you I'd start getting here on time." Milo strode up to the desk, backpack slung over one shoulder, then saw that Ana was with a guest and corrected himself. "Sorry, I mean Mrs. Cortez."

She could have kissed him. "It's okay."

The man turned to Milo, smiled, and extended his hand. "My name is Theo Kalogrides. I'm an old friend of Jake Carter. You must know him."

Milo grinned and shook his hand. "Yeah, Mr. Carter and I are tight."

Ana shook her head and wagged her finger back and forth, trying to get Milo's attention, but Kalogrides was standing between them, blocking Milo's view of her.

"When do you expect him?"

"Depends on how long it takes him to clean out every casino on the Vegas Strip. He left a few days ago, and I'll bet he has to rent a Brink's truck to bring back all the money he wins."

Kalogrides turned back toward Ana and cast her a venomous look, twisting the big sapphire ring. "Too bad I missed him. Maybe next time."

"Hey, you want me to give him a message?"

"No. I'd rather surprise him."

The man left. Ana glared at Milo.

"What'd I do?"

"That man was trouble. Mr. Carter should know he's coming."

She looked up Jake's cell number in the Rex's online directory and called him. She reached his voice mail and left a message. It was all she could do.

TWENTY-SEVEN

After the meet and greet ended, Jake walked Cassie to her cabin.

"It was such a nice surprise to run into you today," he said.

"A lot nicer than the first time you ran into me at the Rex."

"Hey, you still owe me an orange juice."

"As my sainted mother used to say, I'd rather owe you than cheat you out of it."

They laughed, held hands, and chattered as they walked about a whole lot of nothing. When they reached her cabin, she leaned her back against the door. He rested one hand next to her shoulder. She held his other hand. He took a breath, gathering in the fragrance of her perfume. She brushed an imaginary piece of lint off his chest. They tilted their heads together until they touched. And then they kissed—their lips brushed and then pressed together, mouths barely opened. She turned her head, whispered good night, and slipped into her cabin.

He went to sleep wondering what their kiss meant. Was it a polite gesture, no more meaningful than a firm handshake? Was it an offer, an invitation, a promise? He had no idea what she intended or, for that matter, what he wanted. His little head had cast its vote without a moment's hesitation, but his big head wasn't so certain. It had all been so unexpected, enticing, and easy—just like a sucker bet.

The next morning he sat at his balcony table, staring out at the Mediterranean, no closer to an answer. The rising sun painted the waves with a burst of yellow and orange as if it had been shot from a celestial cannon. The summer breeze was light and steady. The ship cut through the water so smoothly he wasn't sure they were moving. A trawler plowed along not far from their course. He liked his accommodations better.

Amado appeared on the balcony and placed a Belgian waffle with lingonberry syrup, fresh-squeezed orange juice, and fresh-ground coffee on the table.

"How was your evening, sir?"

"Nice. Very nice."

"Though I take it from making your bed that no one tucked you in."

Jake laughed. "Not yet. But I had one offer that I turned down and another offer I'd like to make."

"In my experience, sir, it's important to know the difference."

"There's a woman named Cassie Ireland who lives in my building at home. She moved in a month ago and we didn't get off on the right foot. But she's a terrific kisser."

"I would think that if she was a terrific kisser that you did get off on the right foot."

"Me too, but we didn't. We left town the same day. She was supposedly going to Tokyo and I told her I was going to Vegas. I was lying and I think she was too. Then I ran into her in Monte Carlo, and turns out she's joining the cruise. What do you make of that?"

"I think lying is a strange thing to share in common. I am unable to lie to my wife. She knows before my mouth opens. Is Ms. Ireland the one to whom you would like to make the offer?"

Jake nodded. "She's the one."

"Well, sir. It's early in the cruise. Much may happen before it's over. If there's nothing else, sir."

"I'm good."

Jake ate his breakfast and sipped his coffee before noticing that he had a voice message. It was from Ana. She had called a little after ten the night before—just past four in the afternoon New York time. With all the noise in the 360 Bar, he hadn't heard his phone ring.

The unfamiliar tremor in her voice and her rapid-fire delivery alarmed him. She was shaken and he'd never known her to be fazed by anything.

"Hi, Mr. Carter. It's Ana from the Rex. A man named Theo Kalgo something or other—I don't know what his name is, but I think he's a Greek. Dressed real flashy and he had this sapphire ring he kept twisting like he was afraid it was gonna fall off. Anyway, he showed up here this afternoon asking where he could find you. He said the two of you had some urgent business. I know you said I should tell anyone who asked that you'd gone to Vegas, but there was something about this guy that was just plain wrong and I didn't care what you said, I wasn't going to tell him anything. But then Milo let slip that you were in Vegas. Don't be mad at Milo. He didn't talk to this guy like I did, and the guy told Milo what good buddies you were, so Milo just naturally did what you told him. I know I'm rambling on and on, Mr. Carter, and I'm sorry, but I think he's on his way to Las Vegas to find you. Please watch out for him. Come back safe and tell me I was worried about nothing."

Jake only wished he could. But Theo Kalogrides gave him plenty to worry about. A smart gambler looked beyond the next card and knew what he was going to do no matter which card came up. Jake had followed that rule when he asked his friends to lay a false trail for him. Though he'd warned them about Theo and told them to stay clear of the hotels where he'd made reservations, he had to make certain they were safe. He sent a group text to his friends.

Theo is headed to Vegas. Don't take any chances. Take a trip on me—now. Thanks for helping out. Get back to me ASAP so I know that you're safe.

He watched his phone until it pinged, signaling that the message had been sent, then slumped in his chair. It was 8:00 a.m. in the Mediterranean, which meant that it was 11:00 p.m. the night before in Nevada—prime time for gamblers. And the last thing a gambler wanted was to be interrupted by his cell phone. Jake either kept his phone turned off or left it in his room when he was playing. He was certain his friends had done the same. Add in the effects of all-night poker games, booze, and the possibility of dead phone batteries, and there was no way to know when they would pick up his message. The Grand Slam rules banned cell phones from the tables, so he wouldn't be able to check for responses while he was playing.

"Shit."

Amado cleared Jake's breakfast dishes. "May I offer any assistance?"

"I don't think so. This is my mess. I pissed off the wrong guy and now he's coming after me."

"Should I assume this isn't a matter for the police?"

He was utterly unfazed. Jake wondered how often he'd encountered such "matters."

Jake nodded. "This guy has money. A lot of it. He also happens to be a vindictive psychopath."

"That is a problem. Does he know you're on this cruise?"

"Not yet. If things work out, he'll never know."

"Will things work out?"

Jake held up his phone. "I'll know soon enough."

"Very well. Should they not, what would you wish me to do?"

Jake gave him a quizzical look, his mouth half-open. "Amado, unless you're a Navy Seal under that butler outfit, the only thing I want you to do is to stay out of the way. I'm worried enough about my friends who are helping me. I don't want to add another friend to that list. Understood?"

"We are not friends, sir."

"What? Did I offend you?"

"Not at all, sir. It's the nature of the relationship—master to servant."

Jake stood. "Bullshit! I'm not your master. I'm . . . I'm . . ." He walked into the cabin and waved at the walls. Amado followed him. "I'm a guest in your home and you're a terrific host. So forget the master-servant crap. Lincoln freed the slaves in our country a long time ago. And now I'm going to free the butlers. Or at least one of them."

Amado smiled. "You are most amusing, sir."

Jake dropped his arms to his side and let out a sigh. "You're sticking to your butler story, huh?"

"Most definitely, sir, even if you are a guest in my home."

TWENTY-EIGHT

Cassie began her day with a solemn promise not to kiss Jake again—at least for a while. Her plan A was to exploit his crush on her and get him to confess. Last night's kiss almost derailed that plan. She was one hot breath away from dragging him inside her cabin and jumping straight to plan C. She wasn't prepared for the kiss or its aftermath. All she wanted to do was talk it over with Zoey, but Zoey didn't answer when she called.

Next on her list was checking in with Prometheus. She called him using an encrypted satellite phone.

"Where are you?" he asked.

"At sea. We'll be in Barcelona in the morning. Did you find out if we had competition?"

"The client denies hiring someone else."

"Do you believe him?"

"I've no reason to doubt him. It's possible someone is going after the target for reasons unrelated to our matter."

"It's also possible that the target didn't cheat the client," Cassie said, summarizing her conversation the day before with Jake, and Henry Phillippi's endorsement of him. "What proof did the client provide?"

"None really. We're hired to do a job, not to be judge and jury."

"But we're not mercenaries. We're supposed to do the right thing. I thought you vetted our clients."

"I did. Ours is a referral business, but that gate swings both ways. Past clients refer new clients, but new clients must come with additional references. This client's references were unimpeachable. Facts can be hard to come by, but reputations can be confirmed. Thus my suspicion that the target has other problems besides ours."

"That would explain why he disguised his travel plans. Anything new on Alan Kendrick?"

"Nothing. Either he's got an invisibility cloak or he's gone to ground—literally and perhaps unwillingly."

"You think someone might have killed him?"

"I don't, but the talking heads love conspiracies and Kendrick has enough enemies to stoke the flames."

"Is there anything else I should know?"

"Yes. Hackers have been nibbling around the edges of our network. Gunnar is handling it but we may have to go dark until we can strengthen our defenses. You'll be on your own if that happens."

"How will I know?"

"You'll know if you call for help and no one answers."

She ended the call with her questions about Jake still unanswered. A workout in the ship's fitness center opened her mind to another possibility. If someone else was chasing Jake, it didn't have to be a competitor. It could be someone who wanted the same thing as the client but was acting on his own.

Back in her cabin, she considered two scenarios while she showered and changed. In each there was the client and the rogue. The client lost the money to Jake, which the rogue had loaned to him. The rogue wanted to get his money back but didn't want to pay Prometheus's fee. The second scenario was the reverse. The client loaned the money to the rogue. The rogue lost the money to Jake and was trying to get it back on his own.

Both possibilities added to her sense that she was running in circles until she realized that she was focusing on the wrong thing. The client wanted as much of his money back as he could get even if that meant paying Prometheus half of the two million dollars. The other person, the rogue, might not care about the money. He might want something more valuable. If he was angry enough about losing the money, he might rather have Jake's life.

For a moment she wanted to race to the sixteenth deck, pound on Jake's door, and demand that he tell her what in the hell was going on before he got himself killed. The impulse told her as much about her feelings for Jake as the kiss they'd shared the night before. She thought back to Prometheus's question whether she could handle the assignment knowing that Jake was the target. She'd told him yes and she'd meant it. Her answer remained the same even if her reasons had changed.

She still had a job to do—recover the two million dollars from Jake. Prometheus hadn't made the assignment contingent on whether Cassie believed Jake had cheated the client, but that's how she was going to play it. If she decided Jake was innocent, she'd deal with Prometheus when the time came.

Her assignment also didn't include protecting Jake, but she didn't need permission to do that job. And for all his good looks and charm, she doubted Jake could throw a punch or take one, and she was certain that the only time he'd held a gun was when he played cops and robbers as a kid.

Given Jake's evasive efforts and the lengths Gunnar had gone to in order to get her on the cruise, it was unlikely that whoever might threaten him was already aboard. The only time Jake would be at risk was when they were off the ship. While at sea she'd continue her investigation, including figuring out how to steal Jake's money if that became necessary. But she wasn't going to let him out of her sight when they were ashore.

Henry Phillippi knocked at her door just as she finished dressing. Last night he was master of his domain. Today he was jittery and stammering like a nervous suitor.

"Good morning. I . . . ah . . . hope you had a pleasant night."

"I did." Cassie suspected why he was there but decided not to ask.

"You should check out the spa. I . . . ah . . . hear they've got a great workout facility. Probably should put some time in myself." He patted his stomach, tightening his soft belly.

"As a matter of fact I was there this morning."

"So . . . ah . . . I thought you might like to take a tour of the ship."

Jake wasn't scheduled to play poker until that evening. She intended to watch to see whether he was as good as Phillippi claimed. That left her day open.

"I'd love to."

He straightened like a flower turned to the sun, his eyes bright and hopeful. "Is now a good time?"

It was all Phillippi could do to stop from jumping up and down and clapping. Men are so easy, she thought. Tease them with what they want—or think they want—and you can make them bark like trained seals.

"It's a perfect time."

TWENTY-NINE

Phillippi's tour began in the engine room, located in the bowels of the ship. They worked their way up, circling each level. When they reached the fifth deck, he led her out past the helipad onto the prow at the far end of the bow. She let him stand behind her and put his hands on her waist, spreading her arms at his insistence in a ridiculous reenactment of the flying scene with Leo and Kate in *Titanic*. Holding the pose, she felt foolish, though the wind in her face and the ship's gentle rise and fall did make her feel airborne.

"How far down to the water?" she asked.

Phillippi gazed toward the top deck, then down to the surface. "Hmm . . . I'm no expert at these nautical terms, but the height of the ship is around seventy meters above the waterline, which is about two hundred and thirty feet. We're on the fifth deck, which is roughly a third of the way up, and I once heard someone say each deck was between ten and fifteen feet, so . . ."

Cassie looked at him over her shoulder and laughed. "You have no idea, do you?"

He laughed in return. "None. I'm guessing fifty-plus feet, but I wouldn't want to bet on it. I'll tell you one thing for sure. You don't want to jump, because the fall would probably kill you, and if it didn't you'd drown for sure before anyone noticed you were gone and the captain managed to turn the ship around and go looking for you."

Cassie shuddered. There was no land in sight, just the endless, unforgiving sea. The thought of being lost and buried beneath the waves was unnerving.

"Well, don't let go. And get me out of here."

She gasped for an instant as Phillippi surprised her with his strength, lifting her off her feet, swinging her around and setting her lightly on the deck.

"How's that?"

He puffed out his chest and put his hands on his hips, striking what he must have thought was the perfect pose for the hero who'd just rescued fair lady.

"Well done, Galahad. But after that I'm ready to go inside. Tell me, do you spend all day and night wandering the ship, or is there a nerve center for the Grand Slam?"

"There is indeed. One deck above the casino on the sixth deck, though I hardly use it."

"I thought you'd rate a higher floor."

"Simple cruise-ship economics. The engines are down below. The dining and entertainment venues that require the most space are on the decks immediately beneath the first level of cabins, along with the spa, the fitness center, and anything else that doesn't make money. The higher you go, the higher the rent, until you hit the top decks, where the sun is always shining and the women are always thin, beautiful, and rich."

"I'd love to see where you work."

He waved his hand. "Trust me, you wouldn't. I've got a laptop computer and a room the size of a closet."

"That's all it takes to run a multimillion-dollar poker tournament?"

Phillippi took out his smartphone. "Everything I need is right here. It's networked with my laptop. Every player's name, how much they've won or lost, and the wire transfer instructions for their banks. It's a digital world and this is a digital tournament. We uploaded the information for each player to their bracelets so they can keep track of where they stand, though the players can tell you down to the penny at any point in time. It's mostly bells and whistles, but we include the bracelets as a perk and the players love them."

"No more count rooms like the old days at a casino, huh? Guys wearing green eyeshades stacking chips and cash while some bent-nose character takes the mob's skim."

"Vegas still has them but I can't afford it—the count rooms, I mean. Maybe even the mobsters. Who knows? But the more space I take up, the more I have to pay the cruise line."

"What if you lose your phone or drop it in the toilet?"

Phillippi pointed to the sky. "It's all backed up in the cloud, plus I've got this." He held up his wrist, displaying his security bracelet.

"It looks just like mine."

"Only on the outside. Yours unlocks your cabin and lets you get back on the ship after you've gone ashore. Mine's like an external hard drive backup for my phone. It's a Bluetooth connection, like for a smartwatch."

The wheels were spinning in Cassie's head. Phillippi had left out an important detail. If his phone had all the players' wire transfer instructions, she was sure it also had the instructions for the tournament's bank. If she could hack his laptop or his bracelet, she could steal Jake's winnings from either Phillippi or Jake.

"Fascinating."

"It is, isn't it? Let's finish the tour. There's a gourmet lunch waiting for us when we get to the top deck."

Cassie looked at him. "You're quite the optimist."

"Hey, worst case I eat alone and have leftovers for tomorrow."

The lunch was delicious and the view was spectacular. Phillippi pressed Cassie to spend the rest of the day with him and to have dinner after the evening round of the tournament ended, but she begged off. He stopped pouting when she promised to have dinner another night.

Back in her cabin, she tried Zoey again, glad that she answered.

"Can't talk," Zoey said in a whisper. "I'm at the doctor's with the kids. Bloody sore throats and all. What I wouldn't give to be sunning myself on the top deck of your cruise ship."

"Careful, that's topless territory."

"No worries. I can take it if the rest of them can. C'mon now. I'm getting dirty looks for being on the phone."

"Okay. Just listen." Cassie told her about last night with Jake. "What should I do?"

"Just shag him, will you, and be done with it? Either you'll get it out of your system, or you'll marry the bloke and spend the rest of your life wiping runny noses and stinky bums. Gotta go. The nurse says it's our turn."

Cassie doubted whether she would get Jake out of her system so easily. She was even less certain that she would spend any part of her life wiping runny noses and stinky bums. The moments when she envied Zoey's domesticity faded when she thought about how exciting her life had been and the memories yet to be made.

She called Gunnar and told him about Phillippi's laptop and smartphone.

"You should break into his office and download everything on his laptop just like you did with Kendrick."

"No chance. I've been in the casino. There are cameras everywhere and there are probably more in his office."

"In that case you'll have to clone his smartphone."

"How do I do that?"

"Steal the SIM card, copy it, and put it back before he knows what's happened."

"Stealing it is hard enough, but how am I going to copy it?"

"Where will you be in two days?"

"Cartagena, Spain."

"I've built a device that does a nice job. Takes about half an hour. I'll get it to Cartagena and arrange for a drop."

"Thanks. By the way, Prometheus said that you might have to take the network down."

"Last resort. Don't worry. I'll be here if you need me."

That evening she watched Jake play, standing with other spectators in a ring around their table. He smiled when he saw her, but that was the only happy expression she saw during the game. Instead of carrying on his usual banter like he did with her, he was intense and quiet, studying the table before making his bets. She thought that was just his poker face, until he kept reaching into his pocket as if he was looking for something, shaking his head when it wasn't there. What was he looking for? Cassie swept the room and saw a sign prohibiting cell phones. Was he expecting a call? From whom, and why was he so anxious about it?

Whatever it was, it didn't affect his play. He cleaned out the other players and advanced to the next round without difficulty. Phillippi was right. He was too good to have to cheat. Afterward, she congratulated him.

"My, that was impressive."

"Thanks."

"I hardly recognized you. What happened to happy-go-lucky Jake? You didn't look like you were having much fun."

"Yeah, well, poker is my business. If I tell myself I'm just playing a game, I'll lose my edge."

"Really? I would have thought your frat boy shtick was your secret weapon."

"Frat boy shtick?"

"The Jake I know is a one-liner machine, always keeping things light. I didn't know you had such a serious side. Actually, you looked a little distracted, like maybe something was bothering you."

He studied her for a moment. "Like I said, it's my business, but now that I'm off work, how about I walk you to your cabin?"

Cassie sighed. "Not tonight."

He grinned. "Headache?" She shook her head. He frowned. "Second thoughts?"

"No. I've got work to do. I have to call a client on the other side of the world, and with the time difference this is my only chance to reach her. But let me make it up to you."

"How?"

"We're in Barcelona for the day tomorrow. You know the city?"

"Just the airport."

"Let me be your tour guide."

"That sounds like a pretty good second prize."

She kissed him on the cheek. "I'll meet you at the gangway at eight. Don't leave without me."

THIRTY

The next morning Jake waited for Cassie at the top of the gangway, pacing back and forth, checking his phone every few minutes. None of the fake Jakes had checked in yesterday. He'd tossed and turned all night while clutching his phone, kicking himself for his cockamamy scheme and worrying about what might happen to his friends. He should have stayed at the Rex and let Theo come to him. Instead, he'd run. That made him no better than Alan Kendrick.

When he woke up, there was a message from Greg Thomkins saying he'd checked out of the Bellagio and hadn't seen Theo. Brian Holt's response, a thumbs-up emoticon, arrived as he was getting dressed. Jake couldn't tell whether Brian was just acknowledging receipt of his message or confirming that he'd checked out of the hotel in Reno. He replied to Brian, asking for more information, and sent follow-up texts to Ryan Williams in Tahoe and Lucy Marshall in Biloxi, asking them to reply ASAP.

He looked up long enough to see Cassie slowly heading his way, carried along by the moving sea of passengers slowly marching toward the gangway. He hadn't believed her excuse about having to work last night and had wondered whether she would show up. She had been sending him mixed messages since the day they met, pushing him away, then drawing close, only to back off again. He was curious to see which Cassie he'd get today.

The morning air was cool, but the shafts of sunlight dodging scattered clouds promised a warm, beautiful day. He'd only touched down in Barcelona a couple of times on his way to somewhere else and was looking forward to Cassie's tour, though he'd enjoy it a lot more once he heard from the other fake Jakes.

Cassie finally made it to the gangway, looking like an ad for a travel magazine in white capris, blue-and-white-striped T-shirt, and straw sunhat. She joined him, linking her arm through his.

"Shall we?"

"Let's."

They walked down the quay and into the city. Despite Cassie's offer, he'd consulted the excursions coordinator about can't-miss sights and studied a street map so he'd know where he was going without looking like a tourist.

They were on Passeig de Colom.

"If we head this way, we can walk up Las Ramblas, right?" he said.

"Las Ramblas is nice but really touristy. I can take you somewhere better. I wasn't kidding when I said I'd be your tour guide. Or are you going to be a typical man who always has to lead the way?"

Jake winced. "I deserved that. Lead the way. How'd you come to be so familiar with the town?"

"My family lived here for a few years when I was a kid."

"How many is a few?"

They continued walking, Cassie now leading the way. "Five and a half. Dad worked in the foreign affairs division of the State Department, so we moved around a lot. After Barcelona we went to Frankfurt, then back to the States for a while, then Tokyo."

He shook his head. "I can't imagine growing up like that. Always starting over in a new place, learning a new language, making new friends. It must have been hard."

She shrugged. "Sometimes. But it was never boring."

Jake chuckled. "You want boring, try Kansas."

"That bad, huh?"

He felt the familiar mix of frustration, nostalgia, and guilt as he considered his hometown. "I shouldn't complain. Lakin's a nice place. Everybody knows everybody, and they all watch out for each other. As a kid I always felt safe."

"But you couldn't wait to leave."

"I left for college the day after I graduated from high school."

"I thought classes started in the fall."

"I signed up for summer school."

"And graduated at the top of your class?"

"And dropped out after my sophomore year because I was making too much money playing poker."

"What was the problem? You couldn't go to class and play poker at the same time?"

"Both were too easy—and too safe. I needed more action. So I took off for Vegas as soon as I turned twenty-one and I never looked back."

"Even at your hometown?"

Jake hesitated, looking down at the pavement. "I stay in touch with my folks. Been back a few times."

"But you feel guilty for not being a better son and wish you could make up for that."

He stared at her. "Do your tours always come with psychotherapy?"

"Okay, okay. Sorry. It's just that I saw something in your eyes when you mentioned your parents, like you owed them something."

They reached a metro station. "Maybe I do." He followed her inside. "Are you planning to tell me where we're going?"

She smiled. “It’s a surprise. Don’t you trust me?”

“I do. As much as you trust me.”

They took the metro to the base of Mount Tibidabo, just north of the city, then boarded a bright-blue tram, Barcelona’s version of a San Francisco cable car. Jake checked his phone while they were on the bus and again as soon as they got on the tram.

“Expecting a call?”

He shook his head. “A text.”

“From who?”

“A friend. Actually a couple of friends.”

“Must be important, because that’s about the tenth time you’ve looked at your phone since we left the ship.”

He slipped the phone back in his pocket. “Really? Hadn’t noticed. I promise to put it on silent once the tour starts.”

She poked him in the arm. “We both know you won’t. You’re a very difficult man.”

“Noted.”

As the tram took them up the mountain, Cassie lit up, her face radiant as she leaned out of the tram for a better look up ahead, tapping her hand on its side as if to urge it on. It was the first moment he’d seen her with her guard down. Though he was curious about what awaited them at the top of the mountain, he knew better than to ask.

He could have guessed all day and still not imagined what he saw when they stepped off the tram—an old-fashioned amusement park complete with roller coasters, bumper cars, and carousel. Tibidabo Park also boasted a panoramic view of Barcelona and the Mediterranean from an elevation of 1,700 feet.

THIRTY-ONE

Jake took it all in, doing a slow turn. "Wow."

Cassie couldn't stop grinning. "We'd come here on special occasions. Birthdays, straight-A report cards, that kind of thing."

"Sure beats Fun Time Mini Golf."

"Come on," she urged, pulling him along.

They passed a man in turn-of-the-century garb handing out balloons to happy children. "This place is over a hundred years old," she said. "It still has some of the original rides."

He watched a roller coaster car hurtle down a near-vertical drop. "That's reassuring."

"My sister used to torment me with these made-up statistics, like, 'Did you know that more than a hundred people die in roller coaster accidents every year? Amusement parks cover it up.' Scared the crap out of me."

"It's hard to imagine you being scared of anything."

"I was eight."

"Still . . ." She returned his crooked smile, accepting the compliment.

They worked their way up from mild rides like the log flume to the roller coaster that hung in thin air off the side of the mountain, coming at last to El Péndulo. It was a bungee jump with four seats suspended from a huge construction crane. They watched four passengers being secured into their seats with thick, padded restraints over each shoulder, their legs hanging free. The crane lifted them higher and higher until they were 165 feet in the air. It held them there for a long moment, then dropped the shrieking passengers in a virtual free fall, their legs nearly brushing the ground before their momentum sent them skyward again.

Jake and Cassie felt the rush of air as the passengers zoomed by, Cassie staring bug-eyed and openmouthed.

"I never made it onto this ride. I eventually worked up the courage to go on that crazy roller coaster, but not El Péndulo."

He looked up at the enormous steel frame, its joints creaking with every swing. "So, are you ready to conquer your childhood fear?"

"Why the hell not?"

All too soon they were sitting in the metal seats, hearing the click of the shoulder restraints locking into place. The metal arm jerked them forward, and they began to rise. Jake's heart raced, each breath coming faster. Cassie was jittery, humming an unrecognizable tune, her moist hand locked on to his.

The ride stopped at the top of the crane. They gazed at the Mediterranean coast, the shimmering blue sea melting against the sandy beach, cruise ships lined up at the port reduced to tiny white dots.

"You know the leading cause of injuries in amusement parks?" Jake said, tapping the padded bar across her shoulder. "Faulty restraints."

"Oh, you son of a—"

Her words were lost in screams as they plummeted, sweeping backward just in time to avoid smashing into the earth. They repeated their brush with death half a dozen times, making smaller and smaller arcs until they finally came to a halt.

Cassie smacked him on the arm as they exited the ride on shaky legs. They collapsed on the nearest bench, still breathless.

"I can't believe you said that!"

"I couldn't help myself. But you did it. Your sister will be so proud."

Her eyes moistened. "She would have." She rubbed her eyes. "She's been gone for ten years."

Jake put his arm around her, drawing her near. "I'm so sorry."

Cassie sniffled and sat up. "It's okay. I wanted to come here today for her."

"Then it's been a good day."

She patted him on the knee. "And you know what else? You haven't checked your phone in the last hour."

He took a deep breath, letting it out and nodding. "No, I haven't."

"Go ahead. I know it's making you crazy. You sure there's nothing wrong?"

Jake unlocked his phone, pressed his thumbprint on the screen, and let out another breath when he saw a text from Lucy. *All clear.*

"Good news?"

"Yeah."

"Crisis over?"

"Almost."

"So it is a crisis."

"You don't quit, do you?"

She shook her head. "Never. Not if it's important. Want to talk about it?"

Jake looked at her for a long, silent moment, trying to decipher the message she was sending, giving up when he couldn't get past her gold-flecked brown eyes.

"I'd rather get something to eat. Are you hungry?"

"Famished."

They went to a tapas restaurant in the park and feasted on ham, cheese, olives, and fried calamari.

As they finished, Cassie checked the time. "We should head back."

"I have a better idea. Let's stay here." He popped the last olive in his mouth. "Forget the cruise."

She eyed him, one eyebrow raised. "And the tournament? And the five-million-dollar prize?"

"There's always another tournament. At least I'd get out of this poker tutorial thing. It's the second day of round one, so I'm not playing tonight, but I'm supposed to give a private lesson."

"Is that so bad?"

"Not if they want to work on their game. But most people don't. They want a shortcut. They're convinced that guys like me know secrets no one else does, like how to turn a crappy hand into gold by saying magic words and sprinkling fairy dust on the cards. They don't want to hear about studying the players and the cards on the table and keeping track of what's left in the deck. And they sure as hell don't want to be bothered with a bunch of stuff about probabilities."

"Do they ever ask you how to cheat?"

"You keep coming back to that. How come?"

She shrugged. "Because cheating is the ultimate shortcut."

He paused, studying her, wondering again what she was after. "A few. I show them the door."

Her face softened. "I'm glad to hear that. Can you call in sick?"

"Henry Phillippi would feed me to the sharks."

"I don't know. He's been very nice to me. He gave me a tour of the ship. We did the Leo and Kate thing on the bow and he bought me lunch. I think he'd like to get in my pants."

"Is that the recommended route?"

She smiled. "There isn't one for him."

They left the park and returned to the *Shangri-La*. As they stopped at security to scan their ID bracelets, a helicopter touched down on the helipad. The Sovereign Cruise Line logo was emblazoned on one side. "Shangri-La" was painted on the other. And "Grand Slam Poker Tournament" was stenciled beneath both.

"Look," Jake said. "A flying billboard."

"I love helicopters. What a great way to see Tangier and the Strait of Gibraltar. But it's probably booked."

"I'll have my butler look into it."

Her jaw dropped. "Excuse me—your butler?"

He grinned. "Yeah. I know. I'm living large."

They walked into the atrium, which hadn't lost its power to impress. Jake turned to Cassie, no longer kidding around. "Thank you for today. This week's been pretty stressful and it was just what I needed."

He ducked under the brim of her hat, intending to kiss her cheek.

"I don't think so." She reached for his chin, turning him toward her lips instead.

He kissed her, taking his time without putting on a show for the people passing them by. "Like I said, just what I needed."

Cassie let out a sigh, one hand on his chest. "Me too. You know, in the work I do there's a crisis practically every day. I'm pretty good at finding a way out—if you want to talk about yours."

He was getting lost in her eyes again and as much as he wanted to stay lost, he held back.

"Let me see if my butler can scrounge up a helicopter for tomorrow and we'll go from there."

"Can your crisis wait that long?"

"It will have to. I'm late for my lesson."

He headed for the elevator, turning around when she called to him.

"Don't forget your fairy dust."

THIRTY-TWO

Cassie spent the evening sitting on her balcony. In the near distance she saw the profile of another cruise ship outlined in bright lights. A trawler lingered behind the *Shangri-La*, its lights muted in comparison. It was nice to know her ship wasn't alone.

She gazed at the night sky. Stars twinkle and planets shine, her father taught her. As a girl, she loved looking through his telescope to find Saturn's rings and Mars's dusky red surface and all the constellations. Tonight she was content to watch the heavens' celestial show with the naked eye as she replayed her day with Jake.

She had taken him right up to the edge of a confession or, she hoped, an innocent explanation. Instead of being pleased with herself, she was ashamed. Manipulation was one of her necessary fine arts. Never before had she felt so bad about being so good at her job.

There would come a moment, probably tomorrow or the next day, when he'd let her in and tell her everything. If the news was bad, she wasn't certain what she would do. If the news was good, she was even less certain. She'd chosen a life that left little room for what was happening between her and Jake. Whatever that was, she doubted it would survive when Jake learned that he was her target. He'd never believe that she had another reason for wanting to be with him. Even if he did, what man would want a woman who led such a life? Unable to see a way out, she felt foolish for having assured Jake of her expertise in crisis management.

She was relieved when her phone rang, until she saw that the caller was unidentified. Only a handful of people had her number, and their names always appeared on caller ID—but not this time. Her first thought was that Prometheus's network had gone down and either he or Gunnar was reaching out to her. But that would mean they were using an unsecure line, a risk they would only take under extreme circumstances. There was one other possibility, and she hoped she was right.

"Gina?"

"Cassie? Oh my god! I'm so glad you answered. I have to . . ." She was crying, making it difficult for Cassie to understand what she was saying.

"Deep breaths, Gina. Deep breaths."

Cassie heard her breathing, a steady in and out. The crying stopped. Gina cleared her throat. "I'm sorry for that. I've been holding it together, but I'm so scared and I didn't know anyone else to call and when I heard your voice . . . well . . . I guess I lost it."

"I don't blame you. Are you okay?"

"For now, but Alan . . . it's like he's . . . I don't know what he's like, except that he hit me and he never did that before and he's sort of joked about maybe killing me, but I'm not sure he's joking."

"Where are you?"

"In the bathroom."

Cassie fought hard not to laugh. "Can you be a little more precise? Whose bathroom?"

"Oh God. I'm such a mess. I'm on a yacht. Alan made me go with him and—"

Cassie knew what she was going to say and decided to make it easy for her. "And you told him about me."

She started to cry again but got ahold of herself. "I didn't want to. As soon as we got on the yacht, he yelled at me to tell him everything I knew about you. I told him we were friends—that's all. Then he hit me and gave me this hideous black eye. The next day he told me that his security people had found an unknown fingerprint in the alarm system and matched it to fingerprints in your apartment. That's how he knew you were the one who robbed us. The only thing he didn't know was how you knew so much about the alarm system and the panic room. I was afraid to tell him and I was afraid not to tell him."

"I'm glad you told him. The last thing I wanted was for you to get hurt."

"You're not mad at me?"

"I could never be mad at you. You should be mad at me. I got you into this."

"He's going to come after you. I don't know what he'll do if he finds you, but I think it will be worse than a black eye."

"Don't you worry; I can handle myself. I'm more concerned about you. We need to get you off that boat and away from your husband."

"That's why I called you. I'm afraid he'll throw me overboard if I go out on deck. This is crazy, but I don't know what to do."

"Where is the ship headed?"

"Croatia."

"Makes sense. They don't have an extradition treaty with the US."

"That's what Alan said. How do you know that kind of stuff?"

"I was a good student. If you sailed from New York, you've got to stop for fuel somewhere. Any idea where that might be?"

"Alan said we're stopping at a place called Ilha de Tavira, wherever that is. We're supposed to be there tomorrow."

"It's an island just off the coast of Portugal. Supposed to be a terrific resort, but I don't know if you can refuel a yacht there. Will he let you go ashore?"

"Maybe, but I don't think he'll let me go alone."

"Hang on a sec." Cassie went inside her cabin, opened her laptop, and pulled up the island on Google Maps, then searched for the closest marina. "Okay. Listen to me very carefully. There's a marina not far from the island. That's where he'll go. You've got to convince Alan to let you go ashore on the island while he refuels the boat."

"Then what?"

"I'll find you."

"How?"

"Are you calling me from a cell phone?"

"I'm not sure. I mean, I think it's a cell phone but I've never seen one that looks like this. It's an Iridium 955, whatever that is."

"It's a satellite phone. That's why you've got reception. Bring it with you. Since you called me, I've got the number in my phone. I'll call you when I'm close."

"What if Alan won't let me?"

"Gina, honey, just do whatever you did to become Mrs. Alan Kendrick and he won't say no. This isn't going to be easy. It might even be dangerous, but you can handle it. I know you can. You're stronger and tougher than you think."

The fear was back in Gina's voice. "I hope you're right. But if Alan is there—"

"I'll be ready."

THIRTY-THREE

Theo Kalogrides stood in the shadows of the port of Cartagena, Spain, waiting for the sun to rise and the *Shangri-La* to dock. Three days earlier he'd been in New York getting nothing but attitude from the Latin bitch at Jake Carter's building. He thought he caught a break when the dim-witted white kid who also worked there told him Jake had gone to Las Vegas.

Bad luck, he told himself, when he just missed Jake at the Bellagio. He got suspicious when the same thing happened in Reno, but he followed Jake's trail to the MontBleu in Lake Tahoe, because it was the only lead he and his crew had.

He thought his luck had changed when he learned that Jake hadn't checked out of the hotel. He asked a pit boss if he knew Jake Carter. The pit boss nodded. Theo asked him where he could find Carter. The pit boss shrugged. Theo handed him a hundred-dollar bill and asked again. The pit boss pointed to a poker table in the middle of the casino floor and told him that Jake was the skinny black guy who'd been riding a hot streak since the night before.

"The black guy? You sure?"

The pit boss folded the money and tucked it into his vest pocket. "I'm sure."

A cry went up from the poker table. The surrounding crowd began chanting "Jake, Jake, Jake, Jake," until a rail-thin African American with a shaved head glistening with sweat and a pair of wire-rim glasses resting halfway down his nose stood and exchanged high fives with his fans.

"I'm the baddest motherfucking poker player on the whole motherfucking planet, but it's time to cash out because I've won all the damn money there is to win!"

The crowd cheered again and applauded.

"Told you that was him," the pit boss said.

"So you did."

Jake Carter had given Theo reason enough to kill him when they played poker in Buenos Aires. It wasn't because he'd lost two million dollars to Jake. The money belonged more to his father than it did to him and, no matter how angry his father was, Theo knew there would always be more where that came from. Carter had to die because he'd done something far worse than take his money. He'd made a fool of him, and such an insult could not go unpunished.

Watching the black man gather his chips and walk across the casino floor to the cashier, Theo winced at his memories of Buenos Aires. How he'd stood in the corner of the restaurant's back room listening to his father yell at him over the phone, telling him he couldn't have another euro unless it was for a plane ticket home. How he could still hear the gasps and the laughter when Carter turned over his winning hand. How he could still see the smug grin on that cunt Mariposa's face as she slid his sapphire ring on her finger. And how he could still feel the hands of the goon who'd thrown him into the street like yesterday's garbage.

Soriano must have warned Jake after what he did to his sister. That memory made him smile. Maiming her was better than killing her, because not a day would go by that she didn't think of him.

And that's why Carter had led him by the nose across the United States from casino to casino, as if he were a child on a treasure hunt. Killing him would be better than cutting off a finger or a hand so long as he could see the expression on Carter's face in that final moment.

When he arrived home in Athens, he explained to his father that Carter had cheated him and vowed that he would get the money back. "You'll do no such thing," his father had said, reminding Theo that he'd caused the family enough shame to last a lifetime. "I'll take care of it," his father had said. There were people who did such things quietly and without trouble, the way he'd always done his business.

Let his father worry about getting the money back, Theo had decided. Theo would do what else had to be done.

Though he hadn't found Carter, he was a step closer. The black man would take him the rest of the way. He waited while the man sat in the bar, buying drinks and slapping people on the back. Theo had brought his boyhood friends Malek, Nicolai, and Christos with him. They were loyal and strong, and shared his taste for the rough edges of life.

An hour later he followed the man out of the hotel and onto the sidewalk that ran along Stateline Avenue. The man took a deep breath of the cool night air and began walking. It was well after midnight and traffic was sparse. Theo kept pace, gradually getting closer.

Malek was behind the wheel of a black SUV with tinted windows, creeping along behind them. As they approached an alley, he swung the SUV around them, stopping in front of the man. Nicolai jumped out of the driver's-side rear door and grabbed the black man as Theo shoved him into the car from behind. Nicolai slammed the door and climbed into the front seat, and Malek took off down the alley, stopping behind a Dumpster that shielded them from the street.

"I saw you in the casino," Theo said. "You were the big winner."

The black man looked at him, eyes wide. He backed away and pressed himself against the passenger-side door, trying the handle only to find it locked. He raised his hands chest high, palms out. "Look, man. All that money's in an offshore account by now. I don't have bus fare on me."

Theo smiled. "I don't want your money."

The man squinted at him and lowered his hands. "Then what do you want?"

"Information."

"About what?"

"Jake Carter."

The man paused, narrowed his eyes, and slowly shook his head. "Sorry, man. I don't know anyone by that name."

Theo pulled a gun from his waist and smashed the barrel against the man's face. Blood gushed from his nose. The man leaned his head back, pressing his hand against his shattered cartilage to stop the flow.

"Ahhh! Shit, man! Why'd you do that?"

"Let's just say I called your bluff. Inside the casino you told the whole world you were Jake Carter, but now you tell me that you don't know anyone by that name. We both know that Carter put you up to pretending to be him, so don't lie to me. He must have told you my name."

The man nodded. "Theo Kalogrides."

"That's correct."

"Oh, man! I shoulda listened to Jake. He told me you were coming and to get out of town, but I couldn't walk away from a hot streak."

"Why did you use Jake's name?"

"I don't know. He sent me one of his credit cards, so I was just having fun, playin' the role, you know what I mean? Man oh man, I shoulda listened to Jake."

"Yes, you should have. What's your real name?"

The man coughed as the bleeding slowed. He lowered his chin, feeling on the car seat for his glasses and avoiding eye contact with Theo. "Ryan Williams."

"Thank you, Ryan. Carter probably didn't tell you that he cheated me out of a great deal of money."

"Jake doesn't cheat."

"Then why did he run away and hide from me? Why did he leave you to face me all alone in the back of a car in the middle of the night in this shithole town?"

"Like I said, he told me to split, but I couldn't do it, not the way I was winning. Besides, Jake thought you'd give up looking for him if he ran you around for a while, but that's between you and him. It don't have nothing to do with me."

"Except here we are. So, let me ask you a simple question. Are you willing to die for Jake Carter?"

Ryan slowly shook his head. "No, sir, I am not."

"Then tell me where he is."

"I don't know." Theo raised his gun and Ryan covered his face with crossed arms. "I'm telling you, man, I don't know!"

"You said that Jake told you I was coming."

"That's right."

"When did he tell you that?"

"A couple of days ago. Sent all of us a text." Ryan reached into his pocket for his phone and tossed it to Theo. "Here. Check it for your own damn self."

Theo opened the phone and read both of Jake's text messages. He typed a reply—*Sorry. Been on a hot streak and didn't check my phone. I'm out now. No sign of Theo*—and pressed "Send."

"Thank you for your cooperation."

"Cooperation, hell! You fucking tortured me!"

"Oh, we've barely begun." Theo tapped Malek and Nicolai on the shoulders. "He's all yours."

Theo got out of the car and walked back to the street, where Christos had been keeping a lookout for the police or anyone else who might show an interest in what was happening in the alley.

"Anything?" Theo asked.

"It's dead out here."

An hour later Malek and Nicolai joined them in the Sports Book at Harvey's.

"Any problems?" Theo asked.

Nicolai shook his head.

"Good."

There were half a dozen sixty-inch flat-screen TVs hung throughout the Sports Book, each showing a different sporting event. On one screen ESPN was airing a report on the growth of poker tournaments being held on cruise ships. Theo's father had made part of his fortune building cruise ships, and Theo had grown up on and around them. He leaned forward, listening to the reporter.

The biggest of these floating poker tournaments is the Grand Slam being held right now on the Shangri-La *as it plies the waters of the Mediterranean Sea, stopping off at resorts from Monte Carlo to Tangiers. Many big-name players are entered, including last year's World Series champ, Joey Friedman, and former champs Miguel Garcia and J. T. Retzinger. Also, making his first tournament appearance since his last World Series of Poker ended in controversy several years ago is Jake Carter. ESPN will bring you the final table in just a few days.*

Recalling this astonishing gift of good fortune as he watched the rising sun illuminate the massive superstructure of the *Shangri-La*, Theo broke into a grin. His luck had finally changed, and, after a long flight, he was here to collect on it. He opened and closed his fists, imagining how it would feel to pummel Carter until his pretty-boy face was reduced to bloody pulp.

The key to winning a fight, he'd learned from his university studies and from observing his father, was to control the ground on which it was fought, whether it was on the battlefield or in the boardroom. There was no better place for his confrontation with Jake than out at sea on the *Shangri-La*. A cruise ship may be large, but in the end there was no place for Jake to hide where Theo couldn't find him, and there was only one way to get off. The immediate question was how Theo and his crew would get on.

The whoop-whoop of a helicopter lifting off from the ship claimed his attention. Theo followed its flight as it banked hard right before disappearing over the mountains that ringed the port.

THIRTY-FOUR

"See that?" Jake said, pointing at the helicopter as they stood on the edge of the helipad. "That's why it pays to get a cabin with a butler."

"Yes, but does he do floors and windows?" Cassie asked.

Jake looked at her, appalled. "There are some things a butler just doesn't do."

They climbed into the copter's plush cabin. Directly behind the pilot's seat there were two high-backed leather upholstered recliners. A floor-to-ceiling mahogany cabinet separated the chairs. Jake opened the cabinet doors. The bottom half was filled with snacks and refrigerated drinks. A monitor for movies and video games was built into the top half. Cassie plopped onto the cushioned bench at the back of the cabin, spreading her arms.

"Well, I'm glad he does helicopters. There's room for eight, but we don't have to share."

Jake chose one of the recliners, popping up the footrest. "I am ready for liftoff. Gibraltar, here we come."

Cassie decided to wait as long as possible before telling Jake that wasn't where they were going. For now she wanted him to enjoy the satisfaction of thinking he and his butler had made their trip possible.

Most cruise lines relied on charter helicopter services at each port. The *Shangri-La* used charters but also had its own chopper that met the ship at each destination. She chose that one because they could take off and land on the ship, avoiding the risks of being ashore.

She'd have preferred to go by herself but was sticking to her plan not to leave Jake alone when they were off the ship. She'd spent half the night mapping out how the day would unfold, as always planning as best she could for the unexpected.

It was dawn. The sky was clear and the Mediterranean was calm. Cassie had checked the forecast. Whatever problems they would run into, weather wasn't going to be one of them.

The pilot turned to her and gave a thumbs-up. The engine came to life. The rotors began whirling and the helicopter vibrated as it rose from the helipad, its nose slightly up. Once clear of the ship, the pilot banked and headed inland. Cassie peered out the windows at the handful of people on the dock. A man stared up at them, too far away for Cassie to make out his features.

An hour into the flight, Jake popped open a can of soda and a package of macadamia nuts.

"Ugh," Cassie said. "Too early in the day for me."

"You think this is bad, you should have gone on road trips with my dad. His idea of a survival kit was white-powdered doughnut and beef jerky."

Cassie pressed her hand against her stomach. "Yeech. That's not a survival kit. That's death by chemical preservatives."

"Actually, it all tasted pretty good."

"Maybe that was because you were on a road trip with your dad."

Jake closed his eyes for a moment, then opened them and nodded. "Yeah, that was a big part of it."

"What's your dad do?"

"Not much the last few years."

"Before the last few years."

Jake paused. "He and my mom had a farm equipment company. Sold to farmers in four counties. They did real well. Good enough to support our family and the families of the people who worked for them. They paid good salaries, provided health insurance and a 401(k). Not many businesses in Lakin could do that."

"Is he retired now?"

"The recession retired him. Farmers couldn't pay for the equipment, which meant my folks couldn't pay the bank or their employees."

"I'm so sorry. At least they all had their 401(k)s."

Jake shook his head.

"Oh, no. What happened to their savings?"

Jake tightened his jaw. "Alan Kendrick happened. Their investment adviser put the money in Kendrick's funds. Kendrick was supposed to invest it conservatively in blue chip stocks that paid dividends, but he put them in every highflier he could find and they lost it all—fifteen million dollars. They should have sued, but my folks aren't built that way and they'd have been stuck for Kendrick's attorney's fees if they'd lost."

Cassie scrunched her eyes. "But I thought you and Kendrick were buddies . . ." She paused, her jaw going slack. "No . . . you were trying to win back your parents' money from him."

"And their employees' money. It was pure luck that we lived in the same building. Otherwise, I probably never could have gotten close to him. But we weren't buddies. He was my whale, and I was slowly reeling him in until—"

"He was arrested and jumped bail."

Jake leaned back in his chair. "Bingo."

Cassie shook her head, looking around the cabin, out the window, anywhere but at Jake until she had to face him. "And you think I had something to do with that."

"This would be a lot easier if you stopped pretending that you didn't."

"You should hate me."

"That should be a lot easier too, but so far I can't make it work."

Cassie looked away again.

"You know what else would make this whole thing easier?" Jake said.

She met his gaze. "What?"

"If you told me the truth."

That was what Cassie had wanted to ask him to do since she saw him in Monte Carlo. Somehow he'd managed to put the onus on her first. She could stonewall him or tell him enough of the truth so that he'd be willing to come clean, but there was only so far she could go. Prometheus had one rule that she couldn't break—never telling anyone anything about him. Each word forming in her head felt like a land mine she was about to step on.

"And please don't tell me it's complicated. I hate that. It's a lame excuse for not telling the truth," Jake added, as if reading her mind.

The pilot's voice came over the intercom. "We're right on track, Ms. Ireland. I'll have you at Heliporto Miguel Barros by ten. I've confirmed that they'll have a car waiting for you, and you should make Ilha de Tavira before eleven."

Jake sat up and leaned toward Cassie, hands on his knees. "I thought we were going to Gibraltar. Where the hell is Ilha de Tavira, and why are we going there instead?"

"It's complicated," Cassie said.

THIRTY-FIVE

Peter Kalogrides, Theo's grandfather, started the family's shipbuilding business between the First and Second World Wars. His dream was to build elegant, luxurious oceangoing cruise ships, but he couldn't compete with the French, Italians, and British—especially the British after Parliament funded the completion of the *Queen Mary*. So, instead he built cargo ships—tankers, dry bulk and refrigerated ships—and became a multimillionaire.

Peter's son—and Theo's father—George, wasn't intimidated by the competition and started building cruise ships. They were so much better than anything else on the water that many of his competitors stopped building theirs and began buying his, turning Peter's millions into George's billions.

Though he grew up in his father's shipyard, Theo had no interest in the family business except as a means to support his lavish lifestyle. That didn't mean he was ignorant about cruise ships. He knew everything about them, from how they were built to how they were run, knowledge he'd never put to use until he found himself standing on the dock in Cartagena staring at the *Shangri-La*, one of the few ships his father hadn't built, thinking about how he and his crew would get on board.

They couldn't stroll up the gangway, say hello to the guard screening passengers, and tell him to have a nice day, not without each of them wearing one of the security bracelets issued to passengers. Nor could they buy tickets, since the cruise was sold out.

Getting on board wasn't enough. Theo needed to have the run of the ship without interference from the ship's uniformed security force. The officers kept a high profile, reassuring guests that there was very little crime on cruises but that if there was a problem, they would deal with it.

Theo knew all that, but he also knew that the right combination of temptation and fear would solve the problem. There were only two people on the ship that could give him what he wanted—the captain and the chief of security.

Hector Pavlis worked in Theo's father's security department. He had several bad habits that Theo financed in return for his help when the need arose. Pavlis had run deep background checks on both men while Theo and his crew made the long trip from Lake Tahoe to Cartagena. His report convinced Theo to focus on Alberto Navarra, the *Shangri-La*'s chief of security.

Navarra was born, raised, and married in Cartagena but now lived in Barcelona with his wife and children when he wasn't at sea. Blanca Vargas was his wife's sister—and Navarra's mistress. She lived in Cartagena and looked forward to his visits. He always stopped at her favorite florist to pick up a fresh bouquet before going to her apartment. Hector Pavlis discovered their relationship after hacking into Navarra's text and e-mail messages, which included the nude selfies they regularly exchanged.

Theo waited on the dock until Navarra came down the gangway, and followed him until he hailed a cab. Malek Goga was waiting for Theo with a car. They left for Blanca's apartment, knowing they would get there before Navarra, since he would stop at the florist. Nicolai and Christos were there already, keeping Blanca company.

When Navarra arrived, he let himself in with the key Blanca had given him the night before his wedding. He walked down the narrow entry hall, whistling and then calling to his lover.

"Blanca . . . Blanca . . . I'm here, my darling. Where are you hiding?"

He passed through the small, sparsely furnished living room and glanced in the kitchen and bathroom before opening the door to the bedroom. The flowers fell from his hand when he saw Blanca bound and gagged on the bed, with Malek and Nicolai sitting on either side of her, each twirling strands of her hair. Christos stood against the wall next to a dresser, picking at his fingernails with the blade of a knife. Theo sat in a cane chair next to the bed.

Navarra braced his hands against the doorframe, his eyes brimming with tears. He was in his early forties and fit but in no shape for what he saw. He looked first at Blanca, his face twisting with pain, then at Theo.

"Welcome home, Alberto," Theo said.

"Please . . . please don't hurt her."

"That is entirely up to you."

"I'll do whatever you want. I've got a little money in my wallet—not much—but I can go to the bank and get more, everything in my account. You can go with me. Just please don't hurt her."

Theo held up Blanca's cell phone, showing the last selfie Alberto had sent her. He was naked and had an erection. "What will your wife and children think when they see this picture?" Theo scrolled past the photo, showing him a photo of Blanca masturbating. "Or this one?"

Alberto fell to his knees. "Stop! What do you want? Just tell me and I'll do it."

Theo helped Alberto to his feet, throwing his arm over Alberto's shoulder. "I know you will, my friend. Let's go in the living room and talk."

THIRTY-SIX

Jake stood, arms crossed, looking down at Cassie. "Complicated won't cut it. You'll have to do better than that."

Cassie couldn't let him stand over her like she was the subordinate. She rose and moved away from him, her back to the side of the chopper.

"You're right. I should have been up front with you. I arranged for the helicopter."

"You? Amado, my butler, told me he took care of it."

"He tried but it was booked. I worked something out with the people who had reserved it and made sure you were the only one who could take it."

"Amado told me the helicopter wasn't available but that he would keep checking. The next thing I know, he said the other party's reservation had been canceled and he'd booked it for us. That was you?"

Cassie nodded. "Once you'd reserved it, I told the pilot that there was a change in the itinerary."

Jake pressed his fingers against his temples, then shook his head. "I'm trying to get my arms around this. Why did you go to all that trouble?"

"I didn't want you to know where we were going until we were in the air."

"Because?"

"Because I didn't want you to back out."

"Back out? Why would I back out?"

Cassie rubbed her hands together. She was uneasy edging so close to a line she couldn't cross, and the more she told him, the harder it would be not to tell him everything. Keeping control of the situation was essential, but that control was slipping through her fingers.

"Okay. Okay. You were expecting a fun, romantic getaway, and that's not going to happen. Heliporto Miguel Barros is a heliport in Portugal. We're landing there to refuel. We're driving from there to Ilha de Tavira, which is an island a few hundred meters off the coast. We're picking up a friend of mine there and then flying back to Cartagena."

"A friend? Who's this friend of yours that you had to keep it such a secret?"

Cassie paused, looking at him. Whatever was going on between them was about to change, and there would be no going back.

"Gina Kendrick."

Jake's shoulders slumped. He hung his head and dropped into his chair. She stepped in front of him. He took her hands and looked up at her.

"Lady, who the hell are you?"

The chopper hit a pocket of rough air and bounced Cassie off her feet and into Jake. The impact knocked his recliner backward, elevating the footrest and leaving her stretched out on top of him.

"Oh, crap!" Cassie started to push herself up, but he wrapped his arms around her, holding her tight.

"Uh-unh," he said. "Not until I get some answers."

Cassie sighed. His body felt good beneath hers. She was losing the battle raging inside her between duty and desire. They hit another air pocket, rocking Cassie's head into Jake's.

"Oww!" Jake yelped, sitting up and letting her go.

"Sorry about that, folks," the pilot said over the intercom. "We should have smooth air the rest of the way."

Cassie staggered backward onto the bench. They looked at one another, rubbing their foreheads, frowning at first, then smiling and finally dissolving in laughter.

"You're not going to tell me, are you?" Jake asked when they settled down.

"I'll tell you as much as I can when I can. For now let's just say I'm doing a favor for a friend. Is that okay?"

Jake grinned. "Yeah, because I don't think I can take another headbutt."

**

Ilha de Tavira was thirty-five kilometers from the heliport. The ten-year-old Dacia Sandero hatchback Cassie was driving made it feel like twice that distance. The two-lane highway called N270 cut through dry, open countryside. The car's air conditioning didn't work, and a hot wind stirred dust that swept through its open windows.

"You've been awfully quiet," Cassie said.

"I've been thinking."

"About what?"

"What you've told me and what you haven't told me."

Cassie was curious about what he'd figured out. "And?"

"Kendrick jumped bail and took Gina with him. If we're picking her up, that means she didn't want to go with him or, if she did, she changed her mind. Either way, she had to get away from Kendrick. And if we're picking her up on an island, she probably got there by boat."

"She could have flown into Lisbon. It's not that far away."

"I don't think so. Everybody is looking for them. It would be tough to get through airline security without being recognized."

"They could use fake passports," Cassie said, glancing at Jake to see his reaction, disappointed when he didn't flinch.

"Wouldn't do them any good with all the cameras. The authorities would be looking for their faces, not their passports. So she is—or was—on a boat. Kendrick must have made his getaway on a yacht big enough to cross the Atlantic. That means Kendrick is probably close by. He can't let her go because she could lead the cops right to him. And that means this could get dicey if he finds out what Gina has in mind."

"It could."

"And you do dicey?"

"If I have to."

"Is that why you brought me along?" He lowered his voice. "Am I the muscle?"

Cassie tilted her head toward him, looking down her nose. "Really? That's what you think?"

"Hey, be careful. I have a tender ego. Besides, I might surprise you."

"Trust me. You already have. What else are you thinking about?"

"Why you're doing this. Either Gina was in on the robbery with you . . ." Cassie shot him a sharp glance. He raised a hand in protest. "Yeah, yeah, I know. You had nothing to do with it. Or she wasn't in on it, but for some reason you feel responsible for her. Or you're the best friend ever. But if you are, you'd have called the FBI or Interpol or whoever and let them handle it instead of hoodwinking a poor, innocent gambler into helping you do your dicey."

Cassie smiled but didn't respond. Jake shrugged and let it go. They rode in silence the rest of the way to Tavira, the coastal town that provided access to the island. A winding inland waterway a few hundred meters wide divided the island from the mainland. From studying it on Google Maps, Cassie knew that the island was roughly eleven kilometers long and varied in width from 150 meters to a kilometer.

Cassie parked at the Quatro Aguas pier. They got out and stared across the water to the island. It had appeared tiny on the map, but knowing that Gina could be anywhere, it looked huge. They took a water taxi for the five-minute ride to the beach, which was crowded with vacationers.

"What now?" Jake asked. "There must be thousands of people out there. How are we going to find Gina in that crowd?"

Cassie pulled her satellite phone from the daypack she was carrying. "You know, I think this whole phone thing is going to catch on."

Gina answered on the second ring. "Cassie? You made it?"

"Yeah. We're on the island. Are you alone?"

"Alan sent a couple of guys from the crew to keep an eye on me, but I think I lost them."

"Great. We're at the landing for the ferries and water taxis across from Quatro Aguas. Can you meet us here?"

"I don't know. Those guys are probably creeping around somewhere near here looking for me. Alan will kill them if they come back without me. It would be better if you came to me."

"Okay. Where are you?"

"On a beach called Praia Dona Ana. It's north of Quatro Aguas. You can get here on a water taxi."

"We'll be there as soon as we can."

Cassie ended the call and they grabbed another water taxi. The driver gave her a huge grin when she told him where they wanted to go.

"I think he's in love with you," Jake said. "Not that he doesn't have excellent taste."

She smiled, elbowed him in the ribs, but didn't say anything.

It took fifteen minutes on the inland waterway separating the island from the mainland to get to the beach. Cassie paid the driver.

"We'll only be a few minutes. Can you wait for us?"

The driver nodded eagerly. They walked up a slight rise toward the beach and stopped when everyone they saw was nude.

"Oh, my!" Cassie said.

"My oh my. Now I know why the taxi driver was so happy to wait for us. Why did Gina pick a nude beach?"

"Kendrick sent two guys with her to make sure she didn't run away, but she said she lost them. I guess they were too shy."

They stared at each other for a moment. Jake pulled his shirt off and unbuckled his belt.

"Gina is waiting. How good of a friend are you?"

Cassie pointed her finger at him. "If you look, I'll kill you."

"If I don't look, I'll kill myself."

THIRTY-SEVEN

Cassie didn't mind being nude. She was comfortable with her body. She didn't mind being surrounded by hundreds of naked people. Having spent a lot of time on beaches in Europe and Asia, that was nothing new. And there was nothing less erotic than seeing hundreds of boobs, butts, and penises of all colors, shapes, and sizes.

Being nude and standing next to Jake, though, was altogether different. He had the kind of body she liked—lean with enough muscle definition to show that he took good care of himself. He walked to a nearby dispenser mounted on a wooden post and retrieved two large plastic bags for their clothes. Her heart skipped a beat as she watched him look at her and again when she couldn't help looking between his legs as he came toward her and handed her one of the bags.

"I guess neither one of has to kill ourselves now," he said.

"Happily not."

Cassie called Gina while Jake stuffed their clothes into the bags.

"We're here," she said when Gina answered.

"Now you know how I lost my bodyguards."

"Boy, do I ever. Where are you?"

"Do you see the blue tent in the middle of the beach?"

Cassie scanned the area, one hand shielding her eyes from the sun. "Got it."

"I'm in the water directly in front of it."

"Have you seen the guys from the boat?"

"Not in a while."

"Okay. Stay where you are. We'll be there in a minute."

"You keep saying *we*. Who's with you?"

"Jake Carter."

"You're kidding! Jake is going to see me naked?"

"Relax. He's naked too."

"Oh . . ."

"Oh is right."

The water taxi had dropped them at the northeast corner of the beach on the inland waterway. The sand spread out from there in an expansive, roughly half-moon shape, extending south to a rocky point jutting out into the water. It was low tide, and the beach stretched several hundred yards from where they were standing to the shoreline. The blue tent was angled to their left. A volleyball game was in progress on a patch of sand between them and the tent.

If Gina's escorts were nearby—and dressed—they would have to be somewhere along the inland side of the island, hiding in the scraggly line of trees and brush that defined the eastern perimeter. Cassie didn't want to have her back turned toward them as they approached Gina, so, carrying their bagged clothes, she and Jake quickly made their way west to the ocean's edge and walked south using the blue tent as a point of reference to find Gina.

"Where is she?" Jake asked.

"See the woman in the water up to her shoulders and holding a phone in one hand? She's about a hundred yards in front of us. That's her."

"Is she going to come out, or do we have to go in and get her?"

"Assuming that's a halfway serious question, she'll come out."

"It'll be just like Halle Berry in *Die Another Day* or Ursula Andress in *Dr. No*, only without clothes. Two of the best movie scenes ever."

"What are you? Ten years old?"

"Thirty-eight, but when I saw those movies they marked me for life—in a good way."

She looked at Jake, her jaw set. "If you look at Gina when she walks out of the water, I will definitely kill you and leave your body for the seagulls."

He cocked his head to one side. "You mean that, don't you? I'm touched."

Cassie wanted Gina to join them as they walked by, making their meeting as casual as any other to avoid drawing attention to them. As they got closer, she made eye contact with Gina and tilted her head toward the beach. Gina got the message and started moving. Their timing was perfect.

Gina came out of the water and fell in alongside them.

"Hi, Jake," she said.

Jake glanced over his shoulder back toward the plastic bag dispenser. "Hi, Gina."

"I told him not to look," Cassie said.

"Sorry, I already did." Cassie slapped him on the rear. "I'm not the only one looking. There are two guys standing next to the plastic bag dispenser, and I don't think they're lifeguards."

They stopped and turned toward the inland side of the beach. The men were wearing black jeans and black muscle T-shirts. One of them was watching through a pair of binoculars.

"That's them!" Gina said. "What are we going to do?"

Cassie asked her, "Where are your clothes?"

"In a bag by the blue tent."

"Let's go pick them up."

"Then what?"

"I don't know."

"I do," Jake said. "Just follow my lead."

Gina gathered her bag and they continued on in a straight line toward the two men.

"Do you mind telling me what we're going to do besides surrender?" Cassie asked him.

"Call it an exercise in crowd control."

Jake waited until they were fifty yards from the two men and then began shouting and pointing at them.

"Perverts! Perverts! Those guys are using binoculars on the kids!"

A woman playing in the volleyball game was getting ready to serve but slammed the ball into the sand and yelled.

"Let's get them!"

The players and a dozen others raced toward the two men, screaming and hollering. The men turned and ran, but not fast enough. The crowd descended on them, knocking them to the ground.

"We got them! Call the *polícia*," a man said.

Jake, Cassie, and Gina ran past the melee and jumped into the waiting water taxi. The driver was beaming and couldn't take his eyes off the women. Jake grabbed his arm.

"Hey, pal! Quatro Aguas pier. Get moving and keep your eyes on the water!"

The driver backed the taxi away from the landing, brought it around, and gunned it into the inland waterway heading north.

They dumped their clothes out of their bags and onto the taxi floor and scrambled to get dressed. Jake pulled on his boxer briefs and jeans and stood next to the driver, shirtless. Cassie picked up his shirt, intending to toss it to him, then saw his passport lying beneath it. She opened it, blinking twice to make certain she was reading it correctly. The name beneath Jake's photograph was Peter Donovan. She slipped the passport into her daypack just as Jake turned around.

"Hey, are you okay?" he asked her.

"Yeah, why?"

"'Cause you look like you're going to be sick. Too many naked people?"

She was sick, but that wasn't the reason, and this wasn't the time to confront him about his passport. She hoped he wouldn't notice it was missing until they were back on the *Shangri-La* and she'd had time to look at it more closely. She patted her stomach.

"Adrenaline overload. I'm fine now."

"But we're not. Look!" Gina said.

She was holding a pair of binoculars and pointing at a speedboat that had just entered the inland waterway from the north end of the island. It was slowly making its way toward them, observing the "No wake" signs. Cassie took the glasses from her. The boat was about a kilometer away. There were four men aboard. She focused the binoculars on one face at a time and put the glasses down when she recognized Alan Kendrick at the helm.

"Kendrick is on that boat."

"Alan?" Gina said. "He's supposed to be getting the yacht refueled."

"He must have overheard you when you called me. That's why he let you go. It was a setup. How fast can this tub go?" Cassie asked the driver.

"Twenty-eight knots, thirty if I push it."

"Push it."

Cassie turned and looked upstream. They were headed at an angle toward the mainland. In less than half a kilometer, the inland waterway turned right, running parallel between the island and the mainland.

"If we can make the bend before he sees us, we might have a chance."

She looked back at the speedboat. Kendrick was on his cell phone. He put the phone down and looked at them with a pair of binoculars, then started waving wildly. The speedboat's engine roared. The front end of the boat popped out of the water like a rocket launched right at them.

"Push it! Push it!"

The water taxi rounded the bend. There was a footbridge a couple of hundred meters away leading from the water's edge inland to a road.

"Let's get out there and make a run for it," Jake said.

Cassie nodded. "Do it!"

"No, no, no!" the driver said. "There's no landing. I'll get stuck."

Jake grabbed the wheel, but the driver wouldn't let go. They struggled for control as the taxi zigged and zagged across the channel until Gina tapped the driver on the shoulder. He turned toward her and she flashed her boobs at him. The driver gasped and let go of the wheel long enough for Jake to aim the taxi headlong into the sand at the end of the footbridge. The impact knocked the driver into Gina's chest. He smiled and fell to his knees.

Kendrick's speedboat came around the bend just as they jumped out of the taxi. One of the men opened fire and a fusillade of bullets slammed into the soft earth around them. Unharmed, they made it onto the footbridge and started running toward the road.

THIRTY-EIGHT

Cassie looked back into the channel. Kendrick would reach the footbridge in less than a minute. Half a dozen cars were parked on the opposite side of the road, which ran north and south. They ran to the cars and rattled the doors, but they were all locked. A narrower, dirt-packed road barred by a wrought-iron gate intersected the main road directly across from the end of the footbridge. The mix of scrub brush and a few lonely trees wasn't enough to provide cover.

Gina's phone rang. "I can't believe the son of a bitch is calling me!"

"You've had it on this whole time. That's how he tracked us," Cassie said.

She looked up and down the main road and saw a bus coming from the south. Jake ran out into the middle of the road, waving his arms. The driver honked his horn, screeched to a stop in front of the parked cars, and opened the door. Cassie stepped onto the crowded bus and saw Kendrick and his men at the far end of the footbridge. A young boy no more than ten was sitting in the front seat next to an elderly woman. He stared at Gina's phone.

"Here," Cassie said, handing the phone to the boy. "Call your mother." Then she said to the driver, "Sorry to bother you. We'll take the next one."

Gina was behind her. Cassie motioned her off the bus. Jake was waiting to get on. He glared at Cassie.

"Are you crazy?"

"You have a problem with crazy? Pick a car and get under it."

They rolled under the three closest cars and watched the bus's wheels disappear. A few seconds later, Kendrick and his men reached the road.

"They got on that bus. We missed them," one of the men said.

"Not really," Kendrick said. "All we have to do is follow Gina's phone. They're probably headed to Quatro Aguas to pick up their car. I've got men waiting there. Let's get back to the boat."

Cassie waited a few minutes before rolling out from under the car she'd chosen.

"C'mon out. They're gone."

"As much as I like what you did with Gina's phone," Jake said, "we're kind of screwed without the car. It's a long walk to the heliport."

"Fortunately, it's a short flight." Cassie called the pilot and gave him instructions. "Ten minutes and we're out of here."

Cassie alternated between counting off the minutes on her watch and scanning the sky for the chopper. Five minutes later she picked up the first sounds of its approach. Four minutes after that, Jake saw Kendrick's speedboat flying down the channel toward the footbridge.

"This is not good," Jake said. "Kendrick and his boys are back."

"The kid I gave the phone to must have gotten off the bus. They followed the phone and found him." Cassie looked to the east and then to the channel. The helicopter was descending toward them at the same moment Kendrick and his men reached the footbridge. "C'mon, c'mon, c'mon."

The intersection of the main road and the dirt road was just big enough for the pilot to land the chopper. They trotted back to the wrought-iron gate to give him room, arms over their faces to shield them from the dust and debris the rotors kicked up. The chopper hovered inches off the ground as Gina, Jake, and Cassie jumped in. Kendrick was a hundred feet from the road, flanked by two of his men, each aiming handguns at the helicopter.

"Those the bad guys?" the pilot asked Cassie.

"They're no friends of mine. Sorry about getting you into this."

The pilot grinned. "Hell, I haven't had this much fun since Afghanistan." He turned the chopper toward Kendrick and his men and lowered the nose, advancing on them. The powerful wash from the rotors blew them to their knees before they could fire a shot. The pilot flew directly over them before leveling out and taking off. "So long, chumps."

An hour later the pilot set down at a private airstrip. A car was waiting.

"Where are we?" Gina asked.

"Just outside Lisbon," Cassie said. "This is your stop. The man in that car will take you someplace safe where Alan will never find you. I'll come for you when this is all over."

Gina clutched Cassie's hand, her face crumpling. "No. Let me stay with you."

Cassie shook her head. "You've got to trust me. Now go."

"Let's go!" the pilot said.

Gina reluctantly climbed out. She'd made it only halfway to the car when she stopped and came running back toward the chopper.

"Damn it," Cassie said, then told the pilot to hold on.

When Gina opened the door, she handed Cassie a slip of paper with a series of numbers written on it.

"What's this?" Cassie shouted over the wash of the copter's rotors.

Gina leaned in tight. "The numbers for one of Alan's secret bank accounts," she shouted. "He left his computer screen open on the yacht. When I figured out what was on the screen, I thought the number might come in handy."

Cassie grinned. "Girl, you are too good for words."

Gina hugged her, then turned to Jake with a devious grin. "It was nice seeing you today, Jake," she said, and ran back to the waiting car.

"Well, I do believe you are blushing, Jake."

"I am, at heart, a modest man."

They took their same seats, Jake in a recliner and Cassie on the bench, as the helicopter lifted off.

Cassie said, "You did good back at the beach. Next time I need someone to start a riot, I'll call you."

"Thanks. Every good poker player knows how to misdirect an opponent, get him to do something that helps you, not him. You did the same thing leaving Gina's phone on the bus."

"Misdirection, huh?"

"Yep."

Gina unzipped her daypack and handed Jake his phony passport. "Kind of like this, Mr. Donovan. I found it on the floor of the water taxi. It must have fallen out of your jeans while you were getting dressed."

Jake sighed, tapping the passport on his thigh. "Yeah. Like this."

"Traveling under a false passport is a federal offense. You could go away if you get caught. That's not the kind of bet a good poker player like you would make."

"Well, sometimes I'm better at the table than away from it."

"Want to tell me about it?"

He shifted his weight and sighed again. "It's not a story I'm proud of. I was in Buenos Aires a few weeks ago. A friend of mine invited me to play in a high-stakes game he ran. One of the other players was a rich boy named Theo Kalogrides. I won two million dollars of his money."

"Two million? I guess you weren't playing for nickels, dimes, and quarters."

"No, but it turns out the stakes were a lot higher even than that. When he ran short of cash, his bank—or maybe his father—cut him off. He had this fancy sapphire ring worth a quarter of a million easy. He tossed it in the final pot and I won."

"And Theo didn't take it well."

Jake shook his head. "Not at all. He accused me of cheating. A lot of people do that when they lose too much. It's easier than admitting they're lousy cardplayers. And he threatened to kill me, which not as many people do but it happens. I never take it seriously, because rich guys generally calm down when they realize they're still rich."

"But this time was different?"

Jake opened his cell phone, scrolled to the photo of Mariposa's mutilated hand, and showed it to Cassie.

"Her name is Mariposa Soriano. She's a beautiful woman—smart, a terrific chef, and a pretty fair poker player. It was her brother Soriano's game. I didn't want Theo's ring, so I gave it to her, and Soriano gave me cash. The next day Theo took his ring back. Soriano sent me this photograph the same day I saw you in New York, just before you left for Tokyo. I decided that if Theo was coming for me, I wasn't going to wait around for him. Some of my buddies agreed to pretend to be me at different casinos to throw him off my trail, and I signed up for the Grand Slam."

"So why the fake passport?"

He shrugged. "Watch enough spy movies, and dumb shit like that seems like a good idea. I called in a favor from a guy I knew and—presto chango—I'm Peter Donovan. I didn't realize how much trouble I was in until I was on the plane to Rome. By then it was too late."

"Did Theo show up in New York?"

"Oh, yeah. Ana gave me a heads-up. I'd told her that if anyone asked for me, she should tell them I was in Vegas. Then I texted my friends and told them that it was time to start losing their own money again. It took a couple of days, but I heard from everyone. They're all okay and nobody saw Theo."

"So, maybe he cooled down after all."

"Maybe, but my gut tells me that any guy who'd cut a woman's finger off doesn't cool down."

"You can't stay on the *Shangri-La* forever. What are you going to do?"

"Running away made me feel like shit. I put my friends in danger and I broke the law all because I didn't have the balls to face up to Theo. When the cruise is over, I'll go back to the Rex. If he shows up, I'll deal with it."

Cassie felt the day's tension drain from every muscle in her body. Finding the truth was never easy. Prometheus had relied on his client's reputation to indict Jake. Cassie weighed that against the man she knew. Indictment dismissed. Case closed. She went to him and kissed him full and hard on the mouth.

"You're right. You will deal with it. If anyone should be worried, it's Theo."

THIRTY-NINE

Theo Kalogrides loved cruise ships because they had made his father rich beyond imagining. He also hated them because they had made him only as rich as his father allowed. He dreamed of the day his father could no longer keep him on a golden leash, smacking him across the nose like an unruly dog with each reminder of what a disappointment his only son had become. Respect, his father told him after each embarrassing escapade, was like money. Both had to be earned, two things Theo would never accomplish. Theo longed to tell his father that he was more disappointed in him for refusing to drop dead.

Losing the money to Jake Carter was the latest in a lifetime of fuckups. Even if he managed to get the money back, his father would only remember that he'd lost it in the first place. Better, then, to please himself than to try and fail to please his father, and nothing would please him more than killing Jake. The many therapists his father had forced him to see when he was growing up would tell him that killing Jake was a self-destructive way of working out his rage toward his father. Yes, but it would feel so good.

Cutting off Mariposa Soriano's finger had felt good. Beating Jake's imposter, Ryan Williams, had felt good. Letting Malek and Nicolai finish that job felt good the way he imagined an employer felt after handing out Christmas bonuses. And watching Alberto Navarra, the cruise ship's chief of security, dissolve into a pathetic puddle had also felt good. But killing Jake would feel better still.

Alberto Navarra didn't need to understand any of that. All he needed to understand—no, believe—was that his mistress's life and his future depended on doing exactly what Theo demanded. Navarra proved that he understood when he escorted Theo, Malek, and Christos onto the ship without requiring them to walk through the metal detectors, which would have revealed the weapons they were carrying. And he confirmed that he was a true believer when he gave them all-access security bracelets and notified his officers that the trio had been sent by the home office to carry out a confidential assignment requiring their full cooperation.

"Thank you for all your help," Theo told Navarra.

They were in a suite on the fifteenth deck that Navarra had arranged for Theo to use. It was one of a handful the ship held back for unexpected contingencies. Navarra squared his shoulders, having regained a bit of his self-confidence.

"You gave me no choice."

"You had choices and you made the right decision. But should you have second thoughts, remember that Nicolai will stay with Blanca until I tell him to let her go."

"When will that be?"

"When I decide. What are your next stops?"

"In two days we will be in Casablanca, and two days after that in the Canary Islands. In another two days we end in Lisbon."

"I'll say good-bye before we leave. There's only one other thing I need from you."

Navarra stiffened. "What?"

"I need access to the ship's computer system."

Navarra weakened, his shoulders slumping. "I . . . I . . . cannot do that."

"Oh, I think you will. You know what's at stake."

"I would do it if I could, but I can't. Our computers are part of Sovereign's network. There's a separate IT security team that monitors every keystroke. Anything out of the ordinary would be recognized immediately, and whatever you plan to do would be exposed."

"Alberto, you're overreacting. We're not terrorists. We're not going to hijack or blow up the ship. I need to talk to one of the passengers. Simple as that. All I need to know is what cabin he's in."

Navarra blinked and let out a breath. "Then you don't need to get onto the network. Just tell me his name and I'll get you his cabin number."

Theo smiled. "Your life is complicated enough, Alberto. I don't think you want it to be more complicated. Bring me a manifest with the names of all the passengers and I'll take it from there. Christos will go with you."

Navarra blanched. "Very well."

Twenty minutes later Theo knew that Jake Carter's cabin was one floor directly above him. That didn't mean he was any closer to killing Jake. Security cameras monitored the activity on every deck. He didn't want to be captured on video as the last person seen entering Jake's cabin before his body was found.

He went into the bedroom, closed the door, and lay on the bed, staring at the ceiling and thinking. Every scenario he ran through his head ended the same way, with his father's voice telling him he'd fucked up again. He paced around the room until a solution came to him. He would force Jake to return his father's two million dollars and he'd keep the money for himself, loosening his father's grip on him. Then Jake would die.

Between passengers and crew, there were almost six thousand people on board, and there were cameras everywhere. Getting Jake alone somewhere without surveillance would require more than Malek and Christos. Killing Jake on board the *Shangri-La* would depend on how much the chief of security loved his mistress. And no matter how much he loved her, neither Navarra nor Blanca would survive the voyage.

FORTY

Alan Kendrick lay flat on his back on the footbridge. The last thing he'd seen before the wash from the helicopter's rotors forced him to close his eyes was the Sovereign Cruise Line logo and the name of a ship called the *Shangri-La* painted on the sides of the chopper. He got to his feet and brushed himself off, remembering the mantra of one of his business school professors. *There are no problems, just opportunities.*

He did a quick assessment. Cassie and Gina were together on a cruise ship helicopter. The guy they were with looked like Jake Carter, but he couldn't tell for certain because of how far away they were. But it made sense that it was Jake. He and Cassie must have been in on the robbery together. Jake used poker to get close to him, and Cassie used girl power on Gina. It was a long con and he admired them for their effort—not that it would do them any good when he caught up to them.

There were still pieces that he didn't understand. Cassie took the cash and the jade, but why not the rest of the stones? Why bother with his videos if she didn't know what was on them, and if she did, how was that possible? And why download everything from his laptop's hard drive and turn it over to the FBI? The best explanation was that they'd been hired by one of his enemies to take him down, someone with the resources to pull this off and keep his involvement secret. The documents on his computer were for whoever hired them, and the money and jade were for them. Call it a windfall bonus.

Gina would either stay with Cassie and Jake or go to the authorities. Either way, he assumed the authorities would find out about the yacht and his plan to go to Croatia. The Mediterranean was the US Navy's playground, which meant there was no chance he could get to that safe haven by sea. The FBI and Interpol would be watching the Croatian border, so he'd have to find another sanctuary and figure out how he was going to get there.

Before he made it to another country that didn't have an extradition treaty with the United States, he needed a place to spend the night. He called the captain of the yacht and told him to set sail for Bermuda as soon as the rest of the crew returned to the ship. By the time the navy or the coast guard intercepted it, it would be thousands of miles away from him.

Although he was on the run, he wasn't without resources. His assets in the US had been frozen but he had plenty of other assets the government didn't know about. ATK Group was one of them. It owned and operated high-end resorts throughout the world, many of which included casinos. It was headquartered on the Isle of Man in the Irish Sea, where banking secrecy was a proud tradition. Edward Vaughn owned ATK Group. Trevor Howard was Vaughn's personal assistant and the only person who knew that Alan Kendrick was Edward Vaughn.

Using his satellite phone, Kendrick called Howard and told him what he needed and then took the speedboat to Quatro Aguas. Howard called him back an hour later.

"Howard here, sir. There's a heliport about thirty kilometers from Quatro Aguas. I've secured transportation for you from there to a secluded villa near Madrid. It has a helipad, and I've dispatched Brita and Conor Flynn to ensure your privacy. They should be there upon your arrival."

The Flynns were Irish siblings whose parents had fought with the IRA and trained their children to be ready when hostilities broke out again, as they were certain would happen. Until then Trevor Howard kept them on retainer, assigning them to accompany Kendrick on his European travels. Kendrick liked having them along because their fresh-faced, well-mannered demeanor belied what Trevor said about them—that they were ruthless and remorseless trained killers. Though Kendrick had never taken advantage of their skills, he'd often wondered what it would be like to wield such irrevocable power, the fantasy always giving him a fierce erection.

"It will be good to see them again."

"And I've taken the liberty of making sure you have an adequate wardrobe, food, and wine. I'm afraid it may not be up to your usual standards, but it's the best I could do on short notice. Should you require more long-term accommodations, I'm certain I can make arrangements for something more appropriate."

"And the research I asked you to do about Sovereign Cruises and the *Shangri-La*?"

"I will e-mail it to you. You'll have it by the time you arrive at the villa."

"Thank you, Trevor. Well done."

Kendrick hired a car to take him to Heliporto Miguel Barros. By late afternoon he was sitting by the villa's pool, reviewing the materials Trevor Howard had assembled on Sovereign Cruises and the *Shangri-La*. The important information concerned the Grand Slam poker tournament. Seeing Jake's name among the listed professionals confirmed that Jake had been with Cassie earlier in the day. Their use of the ship's helicopter convinced him that they were both on the cruise and removed any doubt he may have had that they had planned and executed the robbery together.

He was particularly impressed by Trevor's profile of Henry Phillippi. The man had turned an ignominious departure from Las Vegas into a highly profitable gaming niche. There are no problems, just opportunities. This was a man with whom he could do business.

Anyone else in his position would write Gina off as a bad investment and add Cassie and Jake to his list of scores to be settled after he'd found a new home. But Cassie's and Jake's presence on the *Shangri-La* presented him with a unique opportunity. While the ship was in international waters, no country had jurisdiction over it or him if he was on board. The captain was the law, but like any man or woman, captains could be bought.

More than anything else, Kendrick was a businessman. Angry as he was at Gina's stupidity and outraged as he was by Jake and Cassie's duplicity, he couldn't afford to let his emotions color his judgment. If he could resolve his immediate problem with them satisfactorily and settle in an extradition-friendly country, such as Dubai, he would have the rest of his life for vengeance. All he wanted from them for now was the name of whoever had hired them. He'd let them keep the money and the jade. The best time to have that conversation was now, and the best place to have it was on board the *Shangri-La*.

He called Trevor.

"I want you to reach out to Henry Phillippi and tell him that Edward Vaughn would like to discuss sponsorship opportunities for future tournaments. Give him this number and ask him to call me at his earliest convenience."

Kendrick's phone rang two hours later. After the introductions, Kendrick got to work.

"Bill Godwin speaks very highly of you," he said, casually dropping the name of the Grand Slam's biggest sponsor. "When I told him I wanted to boost our public profile, he suggested I give you a call. We're in the process of figuring out how to allocate a seven-figure budget."

He could hear Phillippi's smile. "I'm glad you did. ATK would be a perfect fit with the Grand Slam audience."

"My marketing people said the same thing, along with some gobbledygook about niche demographics that frankly went right over my head."

They shared a chuckle at the faux confession.

"I can definitely make sense of that for you," Phillippi was quick to assure him. "When can we get together? I've got another five days on this cruise, but I'm wide open after that. You name the time and place and I'll be there."

"Let me look at my calendar. I'm finishing some business in Madrid today and I've got a few days off before I have to be in Brussels . . ." Kendrick paused to let Phillippi come up with the idea.

"If you're that close, why don't you join me on the *Shangri-La*? The ship has a helipad, and you can be here in a few hours. You can be my guest for the final table of the Grand Slam. If you have room in your schedule, of course."

"That's very generous of you. I'll make room." Sometimes he didn't need money to get what he wanted. Just the promise of money. "I do have one favor to ask."

"You name it, Ed."

Kendrick flinched at Phillippi's informality. "For security reasons I prefer not to broadcast my movements. I'll have to ask you to keep my visit confidential."

"Of course! I'll arrange it with the captain and call you back with the details."

"Wonderful. And one last thing. I'll have a couple of my staff with me. I hope you've got a broom closet you can stuff them in."

Phillippi laughed. "I may even have two broom closets."

FORTY-ONE

Jake knew he should have been exhausted, barely able to crawl to his cabin by the time the helicopter touched down on the *Shangri-La* just after six. He'd had more adrenaline surges in one day than in a year's worth of poker, and that should have left him wrung out. But as soon as the rotors stopped spinning, he bounded out of the chopper and had to stop himself from sprinting the rest of the way to his cabin.

He felt more alive than he had in a long time. Cassie had a lot to do with that, but there was something more, something he'd never experienced. He'd thought about it throughout the flight back to the ship, finally realizing that it was the exhilaration from everything they'd done, from rescuing Gina to dodging bullets to diving into a hovering helicopter. Poker, for all its attractions, was at bottom about risking only money. Today had been about risking his life, and poker could match neither those stakes nor the payoff.

"Gotta go," he told Cassie. "I'm due at my table in forty-five minutes. Don't want to keep my money waiting."

"I'll catch up to you later."

One thing did trouble him. He'd opened up to Cassie, but she hadn't volunteered anything about the Kendrick robbery or the real reason she was on the cruise. The way she'd handled herself today convinced him that whatever she did for a living, it wasn't a nine-to-five job. He was okay with that. Punching a clock had never appealed to him. If she was a thief and was planning to hijack the Grand Slam prize money . . . Well, he couldn't wait to see if she could pull it off.

Amado had laid his clothes out for the evening—black slacks, black shirt, and black shoes.

"The man in black," he said to his butler. "Who am I supposed to be? Johnny Cash?"

"I'm not familiar with Mr. Cash. Is he also a poker player?"

"More like a guitar player. I like the outfit. Nothing says 'Don't call my bluff' like a man in black."

"My thoughts exactly, sir. If I may say so, Mr. Carter, judging from the smile on your face, you must have had quite a fine day with Ms. Ireland."

"That I did. There's nothing like starting a riot on a nude beach with two beautiful naked women and then being shot at while escaping on a helicopter."

Amado maintained his placid demeanor. "I'm sure that's the case. If I'm not prying, sir, may I ask whether Ms. Ireland approved of your activities with the naked women?"

"Approved? Hell, she was one of them."

"Of course. My mistake. Will there be anything else, sir?"

"Just wish me luck tonight."

"May you rake the big stacks, sir."

Jake cocked his head, his mouth half-open. "Amado, have you been hanging out at the poker tables on your day off?"

"It is a captivating game, sir."

"So it is. So it is."

It was also ridiculously easy, at least for one night. Jake stormed his way through his table, taking out the amateurs and pros that had the misfortune of catching him when he was hot. The cards fell his way, and when they didn't he bluffed with the ease and confidence of a man at the peak of his game. All the while he kept up a steady, cheerful patter, playing to the crowd, who oohed, aahed, and applauded as one by one his opponents busted out.

Henry Phillippi snagged him as soon as he left the table.

"That was quick, Jake—even for you."

Jake shrugged. "When you're hot, you're hot."

"And if you stay hot tomorrow you'll be at the final table the following night."

"That's the plan."

Phillippi put his arm over Jake's shoulder. "Tell me, your friend Cassie Ireland—are the two of you . . . you know?"

"A thing?"

"Yes, a thing."

Jake had asked himself the same question and didn't have an answer. Cassie had told him that Phillippi wanted her for her body, if not her mind. He was sure she hadn't discouraged Phillippi, not if she was setting him up, though he hoped she wouldn't make his dreams come true for a chance at a big score. It was an ugly image he wanted to crush.

"Yeah, I guess you could say that. We live in the same building in New York. I told her I was going to play in the Grand Slam, and she decided to surprise me by showing up in Monte Carlo."

Phillippi's shoulders sagged. "Good for you. She's quite a woman."

"Don't I know it."

He sighed. "Don't let her distract you too much. Nothing will kill a hot streak like a hot romance."

Jake watched him weave through the crowd, backslapping players and fans, then looked around the room for Cassie but didn't see her. He was too jazzed to go to bed, but he wasn't in the mood for the raucous crowd headed for the bars scattered throughout the ship. He felt a hand on his back and turned around.

"There you are," Kristen said, rubbing his arm. She was wearing a low-cut, slinky red dress with spaghetti straps and come-fuck-me stiletto high heels. "I've been looking all over for you."

He gently eased her hand away and took a step back. "And you found me."

She giggled, twirling her finger in the air. "Jackpot!"

Jake looked over her shoulder. Cassie was standing near the door, arms folded over her chest, brow furrowed, and her head tilted to one side.

"Sorry, not my game. Excuse me."

He met Cassie at the door.

"She's a pretty little thing, isn't she?" she observed.

"Yeah, as in pretty crazy."

"Not your type, huh?"

"Not even close. I need some air. Want to come along?"

She linked her arm with his. "I'd like that. Where to?"

"Hey, you're the one that had the Henry Phillippi personal tour of the ship. Lead the way."

She took him outside onto the fifth deck. They leaned against the rail, looking out at the sea. The waves were picking up, stirred by a strong wind.

"Looks like we're heading into some rough weather. Perfect end to the day we had," he said. "You really know how to do dicey."

She nodded. "It all worked out."

"Typical day for you?"

She looked at him, inscrutable as ever. "Not so much."

"I guess you're more the cat-burglar type than the nude-beach-riot, shoot-out-and-getaway type."

Cassie inhaled deeply, letting her breath out slowly. "Okay, let's get this over with. Ask your questions."

Jake straightened, scratching his jaw. "Did you rob Kendrick's apartment?"

"Yes, but you already knew that."

"Yeah." He took out his wallet and removed the surveillance photograph Ana had given him.

She studied the photograph. "There's no way you can tell this is me."

"Sure I can. It's your eyes. That's all I needed to see."

She chewed her lip. "Why didn't you tell the police?"

He smiled weakly. "Like I said, it's your eyes. Besides, I didn't feel sorry for Kendrick. Not after what he did to my parents and their employees. And I appreciated the irony of one thief stealing from another. No honor among thieves and all that."

"Romantic and noble with a taste for a little larceny. Quite a combination."

"Don't forget how good I look naked."

She shook her head. "Not likely."

"So, next question. Why Kendrick?"

"I can't tell you."

"Are the robbery and Kendrick's arrest connected?"

"I can't tell you."

"Why did you tell me to ask you questions you knew you weren't going to answer?"

"I was hoping you'd accept what I could tell you and respect that there was more I couldn't."

"And now I've disappointed you."

She stroked his cheek. "No. Not even a little."

He wrapped his hand around her wrist, lowering her arm. "Last question. Why are you here? Are you going after Phillippi and the Grand Slam?"

"That's two questions."

"For the price of one."

She eased her wrist from his hand and folded her arms over her middle. "No. I'm here because of you."

"If your body language wasn't so defensive, I'd say that was a good thing."

She studied him, her eyes narrowing. The breeze picked up, the ship gliding through the rising waves.

"My job is to recover assets that belong to people who have lost them. Usually that means the assets were stolen or were obtained through blackmail or extortion. Sometimes the client was cheated."

The picture she was painting was beginning to come into focus, and Jake didn't like it.

"Cheated? That's why you kept bringing that up. Someone hired you to come after me because they said I cheated them."

Cassie didn't hesitate. "Yes."

Jake shook his head and turned toward the sea. He felt like he'd been gut-punched. "Theo Kalogrides?"

"I don't think so. My employer never tells me our clients' names, so that I can't reveal their identity. This client probably gave Theo the money he lost to you. Theo told him that you cheated, so the client hired my employer. From what you've told me, Theo must have decided to get the money back on his own, plus a pound of flesh. And my employer said the client has an impeccable reputation, which also doesn't sound like Theo."

"Did it ever occur to you that I might not have cheated the little prick?"

"Yes, but there were the rumors about you and the World Series of Poker, and the way you snuck out of the country made you look guilty. I didn't know what to think. I tracked you to the *Shangri-La* to find out if you cheated Theo. If you did, I was going to find a way to . . . to steal his money back. And if you didn't, I was going to tell my boss to fire the client."

Jake scrunched his brow, his voice dropping and hardening. "You tracked me. Like I was a criminal. Like I was a goddamn thief."

Cassie raised her hands. "I'm sorry. I know how that sounds."

"I don't think you can. Not unless you're the one being accused and tracked. So how were you going to decide if I was guilty or innocent? I hear waterboarding is a favorite in certain circles."

Cassie glared at him. "I was hoping you'd just tell me the truth."

It was the final blow. Jake's eyes widened and he stepped away from her. "That's what all of this has been about? Pretend to care about me just so I'd confess my sins?"

Cassie squared her shoulders. "I was doing my job."

"Then get another one. Why are you telling me this? Why didn't you just steal my wallet or hack into my bank account or whatever the hell else it is you do?"

"Why aren't you listening to me? I wasn't going to do anything until I was sure you'd cheated Theo."

"You could have just asked me, but then you'd have had to take my word for it, and that wasn't going to work for you, was it?"

"Can you blame me? You're a professional gambler. You lie for a living."

Jake shook his head. "Well, at least we have that in common. Here's a poker tip for you, Cassie. Once you run a bluff, no one believes anything else you say. And for what it's worth, I did care about you, probably too much."

"I'm sorry." She reached for him, but he brushed her hand away.

"Our next stop is Casablanca. Do me a favor. Get off the ship and don't come back. In the meantime stay away from me."

FORTY-TWO

The High Seas Bar started its slow descent from the eighth deck. Jake stood below on the fifth deck, alone, waiting for its arrival. He wasn't certain which he wanted more—a stiff drink or a wall to punch.

He'd learned to live with the rumors that he'd cheated at the World Series of Poker by keeping a low profile and focusing on private, high-stakes games. It was a simple matter of adapt or die, because people would never stop whispering. But he never imagined that a lie like that would turn him into a wanted man. And he never dreamed that his ability to read people would fail him so miserably as it had with Cassie.

The closer the High Seas got, the more the thrumming din of voices and music, both turned up to the max, blended together in a deafening, pulsing beat. Throwing himself into that mind-numbing mix was the least bad idea he had at the moment.

"Noisy, huh?"

The comment came from a muscular, broad-shouldered man who'd materialized at Jake's right side. The man's accent was vaguely familiar, but Jake couldn't place it until he focused on the man's swarthy, olive skin. The man was Greek, which wasn't surprising given that they were on a Mediterranean cruise. A second man with a similar build and complexion appeared on Jake's left.

"Too noisy," the second man said with the same guttural accent.

The first man said, "The hell with all the drunks. Let's go to the Champagne Bar. It's a lot quieter."

Jake couldn't tell if they were talking to one another or to him, but having two bouncer-sized Greeks flanking him was enough to set off his alarm bells even if, after a quick glance around, he didn't see Theo.

"You know what, guys? I think I'll turn in. Enjoy your evening." He started to leave, but each man clamped one of his arms, holding him in place. He tried to pull free but they squeezed harder, making their message plain. "Look, I don't have much money on me but you can have it. Buy yourselves a couple of beers, and we'll all laugh about this in the morning."

The first one said, "Ha, he thinks we want his money."

"And he thinks we're thirsty," said the second.

"And," Jake said, "I think there's been some kind of misunderstanding, so before things get out of hand, why don't you let me go, and I'll forget all about it?" The first man pulled a handgun partway out of his pants pocket. "On the other hand, I hear the Champagne Bar is pretty nice. What do you say we check it out?"

Walking three across with Jake in the middle and their hands on his arms, they took the elevator to the tenth deck. The Champagne Bar was an enclosed, glass-walled semicircle with panoramic views of the ocean. Decorated in subdued earth tones, it featured a small bar, half a dozen three- and four-chair seating arrangements, dim lights, and soft music. No one was sitting at the bar and only one of the tables was occupied. A man sat with his back to them, facing the water. The two men nudged Jake forward toward him. He stopped when he came close enough to look over the man's shoulder and see that he was twisting a large sapphire ring around and around his finger. The man raised his head, and Jake saw Theo's reflection in the glass wall staring at him.

How Theo had found him didn't matter. What mattered was how Jake played the hand Theo had dealt him. Using his goons to bring him here was supposed to scare him. Theo's dramatic reveal of himself was supposed to stun him. It had worked, but only for a moment. If Theo intended to harm him, he wouldn't do it in the Champagne Bar.

The obvious play—the one he was sure Theo was counting on—was for Jake to stand there with his knees knocking until Theo summoned him. Suitably cowed, Theo would threaten to maim or kill him unless Jake gave him two million dollars. After what Theo had done to Mariposa, Jake was certain he'd want more than cash to go away. All of which meant that the obvious play was a bad one. He could walk away, but the wall of muscle standing behind him made that the dumb play.

He refused to fold. He couldn't raise. So he checked Theo's bet, turned, and crossed to a seat at the bar.

"What do you have on tap?" he asked the bartender.

"Nothing. They call it the Champagne Bar for a reason. I can pour you a glass of the house champagne."

Jake tapped his sternum. "The bubbly stuff gives me gas. You got any beer nuts or pretzels?" The bartender shook his head. "What about those little hot dogs on a toothpick that you dip in barbeque sauce? You got any of those?" The bartender shook his head again. "Can you call down to one of the other restaurants and have them bring me something?"

"I guess so."

"Terrific. I'll have a double cheeseburger with grilled onions and french fries. Make the fries crispy. I hate it when they get all soggy. Plus I'd like a chocolate milk shake."

The bartender grinned. "Anything else?"

"Yeah, call security." Jake pointed to the goons, making certain they and Theo could hear him. "Those guys forced me to come up here. I tried to tell them that champagne gives me gas but they wouldn't listen. Oh, and be sure to tell security that one of them has a gun in his pocket. If I had known that we could have guns on the ship, I'd have brought my bazooka."

The bartender's eyes darted back and forth between the men and Jake. "You're kidding, right?"

Jake looked over his shoulder. "Hey, Theo? Should I tell the bartender that I'm kidding?"

Theo kept his back to Jake, hesitating for a moment. "Malek, Christos . . . don't do anything to upset our friend."

"You know what?" Jake said to the bartender. "I think I'm going to pass on the burger. Kind of late for me."

"What about calling security? Does that guy really have a gun in his pocket?"

"Nah. I think he's just glad to see me." Jake slid off his stool. "Theo, you want some company?"

Theo moved to the table farthest from the bar. Jake took a seat across from him.

"You enjoying the cruise?" Jake asked him.

Theo studied his fingernails and played with his ring. "Yes, especially now. You know, this ring means a lot to me."

Jake had learned in Buenos Aires that irritating Theo was the quickest way to get him off his game. And getting him off his game was the easiest way to force him into making mistakes.

"I do, especially since you must have bought that one to replace the one you lost in Buenos Aires. Or did you find it in a box of Cracker Jack?"

Theo smiled grimly. "Actually, no. This is the same ring you stole from me. You might say I repossessed it . . . along with Mariposa's finger."

"Yeah . . . now that you mention it, I heard something about that. You must have been very brave to cut off her finger all by yourself. Or did Dumb and Dumber have to hold her down?"

Theo didn't take the bait. "You've been hiding from me. Putting those people up in hotels pretending to be you must have cost a lot of money."

Jake shrugged. "Two million dollars may not sound like much but it still goes a long way."

"Too bad one of your friends won't be able to spend it. I believe his name was Ryan Williams." Theo reached in his pocket for a cell phone. "Your friend loaned me his phone. He told me he got your text message but he couldn't leave because he was riding a hot streak, so I replied for him." He opened the text messages to Ryan's exchange with Jake and set the phone on the table between them. Jake stared at the phone, afraid to touch it. He squeezed his eyes shut and pressed his forearm against his belly to keep from getting sick. After a moment he opened his eyes and shook his head.

"You killed him for pretending to be me?"

"No. You killed him by letting him pretend to be you." Jake started to get up. "Don't go. Not yet. We have more to talk about."

"Fuck you. I'm going to—"

"Call the police? We're in international waters. The only police on this ship are the security officers, and they are, shall we say, my new friends."

"Then why didn't you let me have the bartender call them?"

"This wasn't the time or place for such a confrontation."

"I'll call the FBI and Interpol. They'll be waiting for you when we get to Casablanca."

"And what will you tell them? That I confessed to a crime for which there's no evidence to connect me?" He shrugged. "Except for this phone. It's only been on for a few minutes. Not enough time to track a signal, even if the Lake Tahoe police would go to the effort. And it will soon be at the bottom of the Mediterranean. Now, if you're done grandstanding, let's get down to business. You owe me two million dollars."

Jake was still reeling. He was the one who was off his game, not Theo, and he needed to get a grip. Maybe Ryan wasn't dead. Maybe Theo was bluffing. If he wasn't—if Ryan had died because of him—he didn't know how he would live with that. He was certain of one thing. He would find a way to make Theo pay for what he did to Ryan and Mariposa.

"I didn't cheat you. I don't owe you a dime. You're just a lousy poker player."

Theo sighed. "Let's agree for the sake of argument that you're the better player and take advantage of your skill. First place in the Grand Slam is five million dollars. Whatever you win is mine. We'll call anything over two million interest owed, and if you win less than two million, we'll call the difference the money you still owe me."

"What makes you think I'll go along with that?"

"A couple of reasons. There's room at the bottom of the Mediterranean for more than a cell phone. And if you don't care about your own life, perhaps you care about the lives of the two women I saw you with this evening. It's obvious that they are both fond of you. Personally, my tastes run more to the redhead than to the black woman, but that's just me."

Jake couldn't put Cassie's and Kristen's lives at risk, especially over money. Even if Cassie could handle herself, Kristen would be easy prey. He needed leverage but couldn't find any. Before he could respond, he heard a familiar voice call to him and knew that a bad hand had just gotten worse.

"There you are, Jake!" Kristen called from the entrance to the bar. "You are a hard man to track down, but lucky for you I don't give up so easily." She crossed the bar to their table, kissed Jake on the cheek, and turned to Theo. "Who's your friend?"

Jake stared at her, unable to believe her bad timing. She was the last person he wanted to see, and Theo was the last person he wanted to introduce to her. Theo solved that problem for him.

"I'm Theo. And you are . . . ?"

"Kristen Templar." She leaned over just enough to tempt Theo. "Nice to meet you."

"The pleasure is mine," Theo said, staring at her chest as she straightened. "Your friend Jake and I are discussing a business matter that I'm sure you would find terribly boring. Perhaps we can share a bottle of wine another time."

"Perhaps we can. Sorry to interrupt." She turned to Jake, pointing her finger at him. "I'll see you later."

When she was gone, Theo removed the SIM card from Ryan's phone and broke it into pieces. "Do we have a deal?"

Jake closed his eyes and shook his head. "Deal."

FORTY-THREE

Cassie tried to figure out how a day that had begun so well had ended so poorly. By the time they got back to the ship, it was too late to make it to the drop where Gunnar had arranged for her to pick up his package. She could live with that because she was convinced Jake was innocent, which meant she wouldn't have to steal his winnings. Gunnar didn't answer when she called to tell him. He always answered, and now she was uneasy, worrying that their network may have been compromised.

Her first instinct after she and Jake argued was to let him go and give him a chance to cool down, but she was afraid that time would only harden his anger. She followed him inside just as he got on the elevator with two men that towered over him. Each had a hand on one of his arms, pushing him along. When he tried to shake them off, they tightened their grip.

The elevator was one of a bank of three. The shafts and the cars were glass enclosed. Cassie was watching Jake's car rise, wondering where it would stop, when a woman's voice turned her away.

"You're Jake's friend, aren't you?"

It was the woman in the red dress who had been flirting with Jake.

"I'm sorry?"

"In the casino. I was finally getting somewhere with him when you showed up, and the next thing I know I'm history and he's taking you for a walk."

Cassie smiled, an idea coming to her that was a perfect cap for the day she'd had. "I'm Cassie Ireland and you are . . . ?"

"Kristen Templar, and if you and Jake are into threesomes, I'm game."

"I'll keep that in mind, but for now I could use your help just finding him. We can decide what to do with him later."

Cassie looked up again. Jake's elevator had stopped on the tenth deck. They took the next available elevator, exiting directly across from the Champagne Bar and in the center of a parklike setting, complete with trees and shrubs planted in a median. There were boutique shops on either side. It was late enough that the shops were closed, leaving the Champagne Bar the only place open.

"What now?" Kristen asked. "Where is he?"

"He has to be in the bar."

"Then let's go get him and get this party started."

"Not so fast. Maybe he's meeting someone and doesn't want to be bothered."

"Another woman? I don't know how I feel about a foursome. I've never done that."

Cassie raised an eyebrow. "I have a feeling you'll get around to it sooner or later. Okay, listen. I want you to go into the bar, say hello to Jake, get a good look at who he's with, and then get out of there. That's it. Don't stick around, don't mention me, and don't invite anyone to a party."

Cassie didn't like sending Kristen into the bar, but she didn't want to reveal herself to Theo, if that was who Jake was meeting.

Kristen was back a few minutes later.

"What did you find out?"

"The tree-trunk twins are sitting at the bar. Jake is at a table with some greasy-looking guy named Theo who said they were talking about business but he'd like to have a drink with me. Mostly, I think he wants to fuck me. Who is that guy?"

Cassie shrugged. "Beats me. At least he wasn't with another woman. Did you hear what they were talking about?"

"No, just that Theo said it would bore me to tears."

"How did Jake look? Was he in a good mood, a bad mood?"

"Actually, now that you ask, he looked like shit, like maybe he was going to be sick. And he didn't seem glad to see me, which I totally don't get."

Cassie saw no reason to explain. "Is that it? Did either one of them say or do anything else?"

Kristen thought for a minute. "No. The only other thing I saw was somebody's cell phone lying on the table."

"Whose phone was it?"

"It must have been Jake's because it looked like it was open to a text message somebody sent to him."

"The name of the person who sent the message is at the top of the screen. Did you see the name?"

"I only saw it for a second, but I think it was Brian or Ryan or something like that."

"Okay. That's good."

Kristen raised her hand. "Wait a minute. Now that I think about it, I'm not so sure it was Jake's phone."

"Why?"

"Because as I was walking out, I turned around to wave good-bye to him and I saw the other guy, Theo, pick up the phone and pull the little thingamajig card out of it—you know, the card that has all the stuff on it—and break it into little pieces. Why would he do that?"

"Maybe he wanted a new phone." Or more likely, Cassie thought to herself, Theo was getting rid of evidence. But evidence of what?

"If we're not going to hook up with Jake, I'm going to see what's happening on the High Seas Bar. I love the way it goes up and down between decks, don't you?"

"Better than a roller coaster, but I think I'll stick around for a bit. Thanks again for your help. I'd steer clear of Theo if I were you."

"Why? He seemed nice."

"Kristen, c'mon. You don't want to make Jake jealous, do you?"

She got a mischievous gleam in her eye. "I don't know. Maybe I do."

After Kristen left, Cassie hid behind a tree and waited. Ten minutes later Theo's goons came out of the bar and got on the elevator. She had to choose between following them and waiting for Jake. Without his muscle, Cassie thought Jake was safe enough with Theo.

She watched as the goons' elevator stopped on the fourth deck. According to the illustration of the ship's deck plan mounted on the elevator-bank wall, the fourth deck housed the ship's business and administrative offices, including the ship's purser, cruise director, casino manager, shore excursion manager, and a dozen others, along with the medical center and the security department. Cassie guessed that those last two would be the only ones still open. Neither man had looked ill, and she doubted that they were part of an undercover security team.

Cassie took the next elevator, getting out on the fourth deck. As she expected, the wide corridor was quiet and deserted. A directory across from the elevator showed that the medical center was at the far end to her left and that the security department was midway down the corridor to her right.

She headed toward the security department. Before she got very far, she heard the ping of an arriving elevator followed by fast-moving footsteps. She turned and saw a uniformed man hurrying toward her. His white shirt had bronze-on-black epaulettes, with four stripes on each shoulder. Having taken a number of cruises, she knew that each department on a ship had its own epaulette color. Bronze was reserved for security. Four stripes were reserved for the highest-ranking officer.

The officer raised one hand to his temple, tipping his head at her as he approached, his stern, pinched face and fast pace telling her he wasn't interested in her. But she was interested in him.

"Excuse me, can you help me?"

He stopped, sighed, and smiled, a quick stretch of his lips suggesting he was more irritated than pleased to answer. She read his name tag—Alberto Navarra, Chief of Security.

"Yes, madam. What is it?"

"I was looking for the infirmary. As soon as the weather kicked up, my husband got seasick and was going to see the doctor."

"I'm sorry your husband isn't well. I'm afraid the weather has taken a turn. There's a storm coming, but I assure you we'll all be fine. The medical center is at the other end of the deck."

"Thank you." They began walking in opposite directions when she stopped and called to him. "Chief Navarra?"

He stopped, his shoulders rising and falling as he turned around, his brow bunched, his eyes narrowed.

"Yes, madam?"

"Is everything all right? You look like the weight of the world is on your shoulders."

He flinched for an instant, opening his mouth as if to say something, then thought better of it, shook his head, and forced a smile.

"Everything is fine."

"I'm relieved to hear that. It's such a huge ship and with all these people and we're out in the middle of the ocean—or rather, the Mediterranean, which is a sea, not an ocean . . . Well, anyway, this is my first cruise and my husband says I worry too much and now he's in the infirmary and then I run into you and you look so troubled." She stopped and put her hand over her mouth. "I'm sorry. I'm babbling. You must think I'm an idiot, and here I am keeping you from what is obviously some very important business."

Navarra's features softened and he smiled again, this time in sympathy, and stepped toward her. "I apologize, madam. In my haste I have been rude and given you cause for concern where none exists."

Behind him a door opened, and Cassie caught a glimpse over his shoulder of a man looking down the corridor at them. It was one of the men that had been with Jake.

"Oh, that's not necessary. But it's such a relief to know that there's nothing else I have to worry about. I mean, I've practically worn out my worry beads. But looking at you, I can tell you're the kind of man who'd know just what to do if there was something wrong."

A pained expression passed over his face, giving way to his professional training. He gave her a quick bow. "My regards to your husband, madam."

Cassie lingered at the elevator long enough to see Navarra open the same door as the man she'd seen. She went to her cabin more worried than before. Theo was on board the ship and he brought help. And he'd made a connection—not in a good way—with the chief of security.

She called Prometheus to update him and ask for a background check on Navarra, but the call didn't go through. She tried Gunnar again and got the same result. Hoping it was just a problem with the satellite connection, she went back to her cabin to try reaching them on her laptop. When she logged on to Prometheus's secure network, instead of the home page she saw an image of a skull and crossbones interlocked with a viciously grinning clown face. The network had been hacked and taken down, just as Prometheus had feared. She'd called for help and no one answered. To make matters worse, when she logged on to the network, the virus had infected her laptop, freezing it and rendering it useless.

She thought about using a computer in the ship's business center but rejected the idea because she didn't know how long it would take and she couldn't trust the security on that system. That left her with one option—Zoey. Cassie punched in her number.

"Who died?" Zoey asked.

"Nobody, you dope."

"Then why in the bloody hell are you waking me up in the middle of the bloody night?"

"Because I need your help."

"You. Need. My. Help. The international consultant to the stars needs her poor little housewife friend to bail her out of whatever mess she's in?"

"Yes, Zoey, my darling. I come to you bereft of all hope. Now, will you cut the bullshit and pay attention? Because it's time for you to put your education to use."

"What education? My degree in art history or my on-the-job training as a professional nose- and bum-wiper for children of all ages?"

"None of the above. I'm referring to the self-taught skills that got you thrown out of at least two of our international high schools and at least one of your colleges. I hope birthing all those babies didn't kill too many of your brain cells. And I've got a couple of phone numbers I want you to keep trying, because I can't get through. The ship has lousy reception. They're private numbers for my company. Tell whoever answers to make sure my assistant is on call if I need anything."

"Shit, Cassie. Are you saying what I think you're saying?"

"Yes. I want to take you back to your golden years of hacking."

FORTY-FOUR

Alan Kendrick peered out of the helicopter at the helipad on the *Shangri-La*. They were close enough that he could see a man standing back from the helipad, shielding his eyes. He pointed him out to Brita and Conor Flynn.

"You see that man down there? That's probably Henry Phillippi. Yesterday he didn't know me from Adam. Today I'm his new best friend. As soon as I step off the chopper, he'll give me a two-handed handshake, clap me on the back, and tell me what a pleasure it is to have me on board. He's so anxious to get my money that if I had a bag of dog treats, I could get him to sit up, roll over, and lick his balls."

"And no doubt that would be a worthy use of dog treats, Mr. Kendrick," Conor said.

"It's Mr. *Vaughn*, my brother," Brita corrected him. "Edward Vaughn. Not Ed or Eddie—Edward."

"Thank you for the reminder, sister. And what will you say to him, Mr. Vaughn?"

"I will tell him that the pleasure is all mine and that I'm looking forward to exploring how we can help each other."

"And then?" Brita asked.

"We will persuade Mr. Phillippi to bring Cassie Ireland and Jake Carter to my cabin for what we call back home a come-to-Jesus meeting."

"And will they be meeting Jesus, Mr. Vaughn?" Conor asked.

"Only if need be."

The pilot banked right and brought the chopper in directly over the helipad, set it down gently, and killed the engine. Kendrick climbed down onto the deck, followed by the Flynns. Henry Phillippi ran to meet them, grasping Kendrick's hand with both of his.

"I'm Henry Phillippi, Mr. Vaughn. What a pleasure it is to have you on board the *Shangri-La* as my guests."

"The pleasure is all mine. I'm looking forward to exploring how we can help each other. Let me introduce my associates Brita and Conor Flynn. Conor is my executive assistant and keeps me running on time, and Brita lets me know when I've spent too much money, which, the way business is booming, is getting harder and harder to do."

"Excellent, excellent," Phillippi said, shaking hands all around. "I've got a suite for you on the eighteenth deck. That's our top passenger deck. It's more or less the penthouse. Actually, it's where I normally stay, but I found another cabin good enough for me but not you. Don't worry, because the maids have cleaned it up. It's got two bedrooms, so Mr. and Mrs. Flynn can share it with you if that's okay with you."

Kendrick saw no need to tell him that although the Flynns were siblings, not spouses, they always shared a bed, a detail he found as provocative as their professional skills.

"That will be fine. We have a lot of work to do, so close quarters is better than being spread out."

Phillippi showed them to their cabin. It was a two-bedroom, two-bath corner suite with a wraparound balcony, kitchen, and living room. Flat-screen televisions hung on the walls in every room, including the bathrooms. The refrigerator was fully stocked, as was the wine cooler. The Impressionist artwork was on loan from a private collection.

"What do you think, Ed?" Phillippi asked.

"Mr. Vaughn," Brita corrected him.

Kendrick waved his hand. "Oh, that's all right. Brita is a little more formal than I am. You can call me Ed. And these quarters are quite acceptable."

Phillippi smiled. "I've got one more surprise for you." He opened the door and escorted in a slight Filipino man. "This is Rizal. He'll be your butler. Anything you need, he'll take care of it for you."

Kendrick glanced at Brita, who gave her head a nearly imperceptible shake. "That's very generous of you, Henry, but I'll have to decline your offer. As lovely as this suite is, I'm afraid one more person will just make it crowded."

Phillippi shrugged. "Whatever floats your boat. Tonight is the Grand Slam semifinals. That will get us down to the final ten players, and they'll be going for all the marbles tomorrow night. ESPN is going to broadcast it, which translates to a few million viewers all over the world, plus another six thousand on this ship that can watch the broadcast on our closed-circuit TV. That's a lot of sticky eyeballs for ATK. I've reserved front-row seats for the three of you for tomorrow night."

"And we're looking forward to it. Before you and I sit down to talk about promotional opportunities, it would help us a great deal if we knew more about your passengers. I'm assuming the demographics of the people on this cruise are representative of your other cruises."

"Not a problem. We keep close track of everything. We can break it down by age, gender, nationality, and a hundred other metrics, right down to what they like for breakfast."

"If you could just e-mail that to Brita, she'll take it from there." Brita handed Phillippi a business card with her e-mail address. "Be sure to include the passengers' names and their cabin numbers in case we want to follow up and talk with some of them individually."

Phillippi blanched. "I don't know, Ed. We slice and dice all the data in the aggregate without identifying anyone. That's part of our privacy policy. I could get sued if any of my customers found out that I was passing that information to one of our advertisers."

Kendrick put his arm around Phillippi's shoulder. "Henry, we're on the same team here. We're all pulling in harness together. And if ATK is going to spend ten million dollars on your tournaments, plus a healthy bonus for you, that's got to buy us some wiggle room, don't you think?"

Phillippi's eyes lit up. "That will buy you a lot more than wiggle room."

Conor and Brita swept the suite for hidden cameras and eavesdropping devices as soon as Phillippi left.

"All clear, Mr. Vaughn," Conor said. "But there are cameras in the hallway. If we bring Ireland and Carter here, it will be on video. And the same will be true if we go to their cabins."

"What do you suggest?"

Brita said, "We might be able to hack into their video system and upload a loop of an empty hallway to run when we bring them in."

"Or," Conor said, "we could edit the loop in after the fact, but that means that if someone is monitoring the cameras, they might still see Ireland and Carter. That won't be a problem unless the same person checks the tape later and realizes that something has changed. I make the odds of that happening to be pretty slight, but it's still a risk."

"I'll leave it to the both of you to figure something out. I'd rather not leave the cabin. My face has been all over the news and someone is bound to recognize me, take a picture with a cell phone, and the next thing we know I've gone viral. Even though we're in international waters, I don't want to look out my window and see the US Navy alongside the ship."

"What about attending the final table tomorrow night?" Brita asked.

"That's the last thing I want to do. In fact, I'd like to get the hell off of this ship as soon as possible. So, get out there and find them."

FORTY-FIVE

Jake sat on his veranda, staring at the thunderheads on the horizon and the whitecaps on the water, unable to come to grips with Ryan Williams's death. He'd searched the Internet for some mention of it but found none, hanging on to the negative inference that Theo had been bluffing and that Ryan was alive. The other possibility, that Ryan's body hadn't been found, gave rise to grisly images of shallow desert graves and coyotes squabbling over Ryan's decaying flesh that had kept him from sleep.

The other fake Jakes had responded to his frantic text messages saying they'd heard nothing from or about him. Nor did they know how to reach his family or even whether he had any. Jake had never thought it important that their friendships existed within the narrow confines of a poker table, their ties dependent on the next turn of the cards. Now such disregard felt sinful.

Whose fault it was and how guilty he should feel were questions with shifting answers. He bounced back and forth between soul-crushing guilt and outrageous indignation. Yes, he'd set the events in motion by recruiting Ryan, knowing that Theo was dangerous. But it was Theo who'd really triggered everything, turning being a poor loser into a tragedy. Yes, none of this would have happened if only Jake had stayed in New York and faced Theo. But none of this would have happened if Theo had just gone home and licked his wounds. Each swing of the pendulum had one thing in common. Both left Jake in the grips of anguish and anger he'd never known.

It was almost enough to shut Cassie out of his mind, but she was still there. Just doing her job, she'd said—the truest of explanations and the worst of excuses. Betrayal and the loss of what might have been between them caused their own kind of pain. And yet now he had to protect her from Theo. He struggled with whether to tell her about the deal he'd made, deciding against it.

The time had come for him to settle things with Theo without dragging her or Kristen any deeper into their fight. Theo hadn't cut off Mariposa's finger just because that was the quickest way to reclaim his ring, and if he had killed Ryan, he wouldn't be satisfied with just taking Jake's winnings. Theo wanted his money and his life.

Jake ran through his options. He could tell the captain and ask for protection. The captain would ask for proof. Jake would show him the photo of Mariposa's maimed hand. The captain would tell him that the photo didn't prove Theo did it or that Theo had threatened Jake's life. At best he'd tell Jake to leave the ship when they docked at Casablanca. Theo would follow him, changing the playing field but not the odds.

He could kill Theo. The thought was preposterous. How would he do it? He'd need a gun. Where would he get one? Could he pull the trigger? What about the other two guys with Theo? Would he have to kill them too? Was he that angry? That afraid? How would he get away with it? Could he claim it was self-defense? Could he live with himself? There had to be another way.

All he could do for now was play poker. Theo would wait until Jake either busted out or won the tournament before making his next move. That gave Jake time to decide how to play his final hand.

"Mr. Carter, sir," Amado said, "your table begins in an hour."

Jake looked at his watch and tugged at the day's growth on his cheeks and chin. "Thanks. Guess I'd better clean up."

Amado followed Jake into the living room. "Sir, there's something I believe I should tell you, though I don't mean to alarm you."

Jake couldn't imagine being more alarmed than he already was. "What's that?"

"In many ways this ship is like the small village where I grew up. Everyone on the crew knows or wishes they knew everyone else's business. Gossip and rumors and occasionally the truth circulate like the air we breathe."

"And I take it that you've heard something that might alarm me."

Amado dipped his head in his usual quick, short nod. "Yes, sir. It seems that three men boarded the ship in Cartagena."

"Is that so unusual?"

"Not by itself. Passengers often join the cruise at different ports, just as Ms. Ireland did. These passengers, however, were not required to pass through security."

"How could they do that?"

"It seems that they were escorted by Alberto Navarra. He is the ship's chief of security, and I am told he instructed his officers that these men were on a confidential assignment and not to interfere with them. I am also told, sir, that the men are Greek and rather ill-mannered."

If Theo had the chief of security in his pocket, Jake would be a lot more than just alarmed. "What does this have to do with me?"

"I hope, sir, that it has nothing to do with you. However, given your concerns that a man or men may be in pursuit of you, I thought I should bring it to your attention. Especially, sir, since at least one of the men was seen to have a gun in his trousers."

Jake didn't want to involve Amado in his problems any more than he wanted to involve Cassie or Kristen. "Thank you, Amado. I'll let you know if I run into them."

Amado hesitated, clearing his throat. "If I may, sir."

"Yes."

"You were observed in the company of these men last evening."

Jake's jaw dropped. "Are you running some kind of shipboard spy ring?"

"Not at all, sir. News of the three men spread quickly throughout the crew. The bartender at the Champagne Bar is having a relationship with a young woman, a server who has been assigned to the poker tournament. She has brought you drinks on several occasions. Her cousin is a housekeeper and a . . . dear friend of mine. What one says, another hears and passes on."

"I still don't understand how you made the connection to me."

"I hope you don't mind, sir, but I had told my dear friend that I would be interested in knowing whether any such men joined the cruise at any of our ports, and if so, whether they took an interest in you."

"And that's all it took?"

"Yes, sir. We are all quite practiced in the exchange of information."

"Some of which is even true."

"Yes, sir. I hope I haven't offended you, sir."

Though Jake didn't like being the subject of gossip, he was impressed. "Why did you do it?"

"I am your butler, sir. Taking care of your needs is my job."

"Well, Amado. You've done your job, but let's leave it at that. This is my problem, not yours."

"Very well, sir. Forgive me for bringing it up when you have so much already on your mind."

Amado bowed and began to leave. Jake stopped him.

"Just in case you hear anything else . . ."

"Yes, sir. I will let you know. It's my job."

FORTY-SIX

It took Cassie less than an hour on a computer in the ship's business center to put together a profile on Theo Kalogrides from publicly available records. Most of the information came from tabloid stories about wild parties, huge gambling losses, and affairs with models and starlets.

One article included him in a discussion of how so many third-generation wealthy kids failed to live up to the expectations of the first and second generations, running through the family fortune rather than adding to it. Theo was featured in a sidebar focused on allegations that he'd beaten several girlfriends and assaulted two men, whom he'd accused of cheating him at poker. Theo's lawyer was quoted as denying all the charges and refusing to comment on confidential settlements reached with the victims. A photograph showed Theo being escorted from an Athens police station, flanked by his lawyer and his father, after one of the women pressed charges she later dropped. It was enough to convince her that Theo's father was Prometheus's client.

Next she searched for updates on Alan Kendrick. CNN was the first to report that, acting on an anonymous tip, the navy had intercepted a yacht in the Atlantic several hundred miles off the coast of Portugal but found no sign of him or Gina. Ownership of the yacht was buried in a web of shell corporations, with nothing to indicate a link to Kendrick. The FBI issued a statement that they were continuing to pursue all leads but had no actionable information concerning Kendrick's whereabouts at this time.

Uneasy, she walked the promenade on the top deck. There was no land in sight, just an endless expanse of sea. Kendrick was out there somewhere, but Cassie knew he was coming for her. She'd taken too much from him to let her go. She called Gunnar and Prometheus, but the secure network was still down. The *Shangri-La* was a refuge, but she worried it would soon become a trap.

And then there was Jake. He couldn't be so naive as to think that money would satisfy Theo. Not after what Theo had done to that woman, Mariposa, and what he'd probably done to Jake's friend Ryan. As well as Jake had performed under fire the day before, he was no match for Theo and his friends, especially if Theo had bought the chief of security. She had to get past Jake's anger and convince him to let her help him. He wouldn't listen to another apology but he would understand long odds and a stacked deck.

Or so she hoped when she knocked on his cabin door. Jake had told her he had a butler, but she couldn't tell whether he was joking until a short man with chestnut skin wearing black slacks and a white shirt, black vest, and gold necktie answered.

"Good evening, madam," Amado said.

"You're . . . you're Jake's—"

"Butler. Yes, madam. I am Amado. And you must be Ms. Ireland."

Cassie cocked her head. "And how do you know who I am?"

"Mr. Carter's description of you, while accurate, does not do you justice."

Flattered, Cassie took a deep breath. "Well, I'm glad Mr. Carter was at least accurate. Is he here?"

"He is getting dressed. Please come in."

Cassie did a slow turn, admiring Jake's suite. The bedroom door opened.

"Amado, did I hear someone knocking . . . ?" Jake saw Cassie, stopping in midsentence. A towel was wrapped around his waist, and he was still dripping from his shower.

"Yes, sir. Ms. Ireland is here."

Jake's eyes flashed. "I can see that. The question is why."

Amado disappeared into the bedroom.

"We need to talk," Cassie said.

"No, we don't."

"Look, you can spend the rest of your life being angry with me, but if you don't get off this boat alive, think of all the anger you'll miss out on."

"What are you talking about?"

"I'm talking about the two goons that took you for a ride in the elevator last night and delivered you to Theo Kalogrides."

Jake glared at her, sputtering. "After I told you to stay away from me, you followed me . . . and . . . and sent that dim-witted, oversexed Kristen into the bar to spy on me and flash her tits at Theo?"

Cassie folded her arms across her chest. "I didn't tell her to flash her tits."

"What is the matter with you?"

"What is the matter with *you*? Did you make a deal with Theo? Did you agree to give him his money back if he promised not to cut off your finger or do whatever he did to your friend Ryan? Are you so stupid that you think he'll keep his word?"

Jake turned his head to one side and closed his eyes for a moment. Opening them, he kept his voice low and controlled.

"Get out."

"You're outnumbered three to one. Plus Theo has the chief of security in his back pocket. That's a losing hand, and you know it. Tell me what's happening. I can help if you'll let me."

"Here's what's happening. You're going to leave, and I'm going to get dressed and go play cards. And if I don't fuck it up, I'm going to win five million dollars at the final table tomorrow and this whole thing will be over. And the day after that you're going to get off this boat at Casablanca, and the next time you see me will be at the mailbox at the Rex, unless I see you first."

Jake stormed into the bedroom and slammed the door. Ten minutes later he was dressed and left the cabin. Amado closed the door after him and turned around. Cassie stepped into the cabin from the veranda.

"That went well," she said.

"If you say so, Ms. Ireland. Is there something I can do for you?"

"Yes, there is. For starters, where's Mr. Carter's laptop?"

"I'm afraid I cannot allow you access to—"

"You can, Amado. And I think you will if you want help me save Mr. Carter's life."

Two hours later Cassie was in the casino. The center of the floor had been cleared of slot machines and blackjack, craps, and roulette tables, and in their place were nine green felt–topped poker tables. There were eight players per table, together with a dealer. The winner at each table would meet at the final table the next day.

The tables were arranged in an inner ring of four tables and an outer ring of five. The area was roped off. Spectators were lined up three and four deep around the rope, craning for a view of the action. Security officers were spaced every ten feet in a protective cordon.

Cassie was glad that Jake was seated at one of the inner ring tables, where he was less likely to notice her in the crowd. She milled around, more interested in those watching than in those playing. She saw Kristen standing at the rope across from Jake, wearing a shimmering green sheath cut to her navel, one side slit to her hip. Her eyes were lit and focused on Jake.

Theo wasn't there but his boys were, standing back from the crowd, hands in their pockets, shoulders relaxed. Amateurs, Cassie thought. Pros would be doing what she was doing—scanning the crowd for threats, separating people into categories—harmless, maybe, and watch out. They would be walking the room, never taking the same route twice, acknowledging each other with the faintest of nods that no one else would notice. They would be ready. She would see that in the way they walked, the way they carried themselves, shoulders slightly back, gait casual, and body coiled, eyes constantly sweeping the room.

Just like the man and woman passing each other for the second time.

She had an angular face with sharp cheekbones and jet-black hair cut short over her ears and was dressed in sleek black slacks and a form-fitting black top under a matching jacket. He had dark hair and a similar long, narrow face with a prominent nose. He wore a loose-fitting sport coat over a tight-fitting T-shirt that showed his wiry, muscled build. Seeing them together, Cassie picked up the siblings' resemblance. Watching their lips barely move as they put distance between themselves, she guessed that they were wearing comms units in their ears and were sharing their observations.

Cassie drifted through the crowd, grabbing a flute of champagne from a passing waiter, tracking the couple until she was certain of their intent. They were orbiting her, staying on opposite sides and gradually closing the distance—twenty feet, ten feet. The man reached behind his back beneath his jacket, palming a gun. Cassie locked on to the man, then the woman, each acknowledging who was prey and who was predator—five feet, then an arm's length. Cassie backpedaled toward the nearest security officer, tripping herself, falling backward into the surprised officer's arms, showering both of them with champagne. She clamped the officer's hands onto her breasts, slurring her words.

"Oh, honey! Thanks for catching me, but don't hold on so tight!"

The crowd erupted, laughing. Red faced, the officer stood her up, keeping his hands on her chest until she gently removed them with her fingertips, causing the crowd to explode again as her stalkers melted away.

FORTY-SEVEN

Cassie decided to name her stalkers Donny and Marie. She had nothing against the Osmonds, but those were the first sibling names that came to her mind. Giving them names gave her focus, and that was what she needed to answer the questions bouncing around in her head.

Who were they? She had no idea. In her business she ran across a lot of unsavory people who hired out for strong-arm work, but she'd never heard of a brother-sister team. If they had such a low profile, it would take someone with a lot of power, money, and connections to lure them out from under the rock where they hid.

Who sent them? That was easy. Alan Kendrick. He'd somehow managed to air-drop them onto a ship in the middle of the Mediterranean. She thought back to her conversation with Gina setting up their rendezvous on Ilha de Tavira, satisfied that she hadn't mentioned anything about the cruise. If Kendrick had been listening in, he could have traced the call to the ship. Possible, but he would have needed sophisticated equipment to do that, and she doubted that was part of the yacht's option package. Then it hit her. The ship's helicopter was a flying billboard for the *Shangri-La* and the pilot practically tattooed Kendrick when they made their getaway. He'd have to have been blind to miss the name on the chopper, and she'd been an idiot not to realize that sooner. And they weren't air-dropped. They came in on a chopper of their own.

Did Kendrick come with them? He was on the run from every law enforcement agency in the world. His only chance was to get to a country that didn't have an extradition treaty with the United States before he was caught. Only a narcissistic megalomaniac who didn't think the rules applied to him and was willing to risk everything in order to take his revenge would be that foolish. So, yeah, Kendrick was aboard and was waiting for Donny and Marie to bring her to him.

What would Donny and Marie do now? They definitely wouldn't go back to Kendrick and tell him that they screwed up, not without trying again. After the commotion she'd caused, the casino was out. It was a dumb play in the first place, trying to muscle her out of there with a gun in her back in front of all those people. They'd do what she would do: wait for her to leave the casino and then grab her. But they wouldn't wait together. They'd cover separate exits, the winner summoning the loser once she'd been captured.

Cassie counted the ways out. The main entrance to the casino was from the central passageway. There were entrances on either side, one of which led to the exterior of the fifth deck, where she and Jake had argued the night before. The other, she assumed, led to a separate passageway. There was a service entrance on the back end of the casino opposite the entrance. Servers were going back and forth through the double doors in a steady procession. It was the one exit Donny and Marie wouldn't be able to monitor. She was halfway to the doors when Henry Phillippi called to her.

"Cassie! There you are."

She turned around and there he was, grinning like a schoolboy. "Hello, Henry."

"My God, you look fantastic! If I didn't need Jake in the tournament, I'd throw him overboard and claim you for my own."

Cassie frowned. "I guess we're just star-crossed lovers."

He beamed at her. "Better star-crossed than not being lovers at all."

"Oh, Henry, did you forget your Shakespeare? Romeo and Juliet both died at the end. You don't want me dead, do you?"

He pressed his hand against his chest. "Never! There's someone I want you to meet tomorrow night at the final table. He's my special guest. Flew in a few hours ago."

Cassie's heart skipped a beat. "Who's that?"

"Edward Vaughn!" Phillippi beamed again.

Her heart regained its normal rhythm. "I'm sorry. I don't know the name."

"He's the president of the ATK Group. Big multinational outfit with resorts all over the world. He's going to do ten million dollars' worth of promotion for my Grand Slam tournaments. It's going to be huge. You'll love him. He's staying in my suite, which, I don't mind saying, is the finest one on the ship."

"How about that. He took a helicopter all the way out by himself just to watch people play poker."

"Oh, no. He didn't come alone. He brought his assistants, a husband and wife named Flynn. I don't remember their first names, but what the hell? They're not signing the checks."

Cassie's pulse picked up again. "I'm looking forward to meeting him."

Phillippi looked over her shoulder, found someone else to schmooze, and gave her a peck on the cheek. "Tomorrow night then."

Mr. and Mrs. Flynn. Their first names were still Donny and Marie as far as she was concerned. She took a final look at Jake. His head was in the game. She hoped he'd still be there when she got back.

Someone once told her that if you don't like what's being said, then change the conversation. The same thing applied to being stalked. Don't hide. Go hunting.

The service area at the back of the casino was filled with harried staff shuttling drinks and food to players and spectators. No one was in charge and no one pointed to the "Crew Only" sign and told her to get out. At the very back there was a stairway Cassie took down to the fourth deck, coming out into a narrow passageway with doors on either side. More crew members scurried past without challenging her.

She waited until the corridor was empty and tried several doors. One of them opened into a supply room, where she found several jackets hanging on pegs with "Shangri-La Crew" screen-printed on the back, along with matching caps. She grabbed a cap and pulled on a jacket, discovering cigarettes and a lighter in one pocket. Someone had left a pair of earbuds on a table, and there was a monkey wrench lying next to a toolbox. She put both in her jacket pocket, stepped back into the passageway, and followed the signs outside.

As best she could tell, the exit from the casino was directly overhead. That's where either Donny or Marie was waiting for her, and she didn't want to disappoint them. She headed toward the bow, found an exterior stairway, which she took to the fifth deck, and came out near the helipad.

Thick clouds obscured the moon and stars. The ship rose and fell through moderate swells. A brisk sea breeze filled the air with a fine mist. She put in the earbuds, turned against the wind, and lit a cigarette. With the brim of her cap pulled down, she rolled her shoulders back and widened her gait, keeping the wrench at her side. Turning the corner, she hoped Donny or Marie would think she was a male crew member listening to some tunes while breaking the ship's no-smoking policy.

Chairs for passengers to lounge in lined the exterior wall. Soft lights illuminated the deck, except at one spot, where there was a dark pool. Cassie doubted the bulb had burned out. More likely Donny or Marie had unscrewed it, creating a blind spot. Holding the wrench at her side, she continued toward the hiding place, nodding her head as if in rhythm with the music, and took a drag on the cigarette. A woman came out on the deck from the casino, and Cassie caught a man's silhouette as he stepped toward her from the darkness before retreating. *Hello, Donny.*

Cassie kept her pace steady, eyes half-closed, cigarette dangling from her lips. She came even with Donny, not looking at him. By the time he saw Cassie swinging the wrench, it was too late. She landed a bone-crushing blow on his knee, following up with a vicious punch just below his ribs on the centerline of his body, driving her fist upward like she was trying to push his stomach up into his chest. Breath knocked out of him, Donny gasped and hunched over.

Cassie caught him and frisked him until she found his gun. Sticking it in her pocket, she eased him into a chair, and blew smoke in his face to make it harder for him to catch his breath while jabbing him in the solar plexus with the wrench, causing him to gag.

It was over in five seconds. She flicked the cigarette over the side and stepped inside, shedding her props and tucking the gun under her blouse. She didn't know how much damage she'd done to Donny's knee but was certain she'd done enough to slow him down. And she'd sent Kendrick a message—this wasn't going to be easy.

FORTY-EIGHT

It took Jake until 1:00 a.m. to close out his table. The crowd standing around the rope line had thinned down to the diehard fans. They applauded vigorously when he stood and accepted congratulations from the last player he'd wiped out. Jake acknowledged them with a wave.

He scanned the room. Malek and Christos were sipping drinks at one end of the bar. From the other end Henry Phillippi offered a salute. Jake did a double take when he saw Cassie sitting on a stool next to him. She whispered in Phillippi's ear and made her way toward him.

Jake sighed. Seeing her made it harder to stay angry. He had to admit that she wasn't wrong to have suspected him. Not after the fake Jakes and the fake passport. And though he didn't think of himself as a liar, he'd run so many bluffs that it was sometimes hard to tell the difference.

"Congratulations on making the final table," Cassie said.

"Thanks. Listen, I've been thinking—"

Cassie cut him off. "Alan Kendrick is on board. He brought a couple of psychos with him to fetch us."

Jake shook his head, laughing. "You don't know when to quit, do you? Next you'll be telling me that he's paying Phillippi to look the other way."

"Ten million dollars, according to Henry."

"You're unbelievable."

Cassie stared at him, her face stone-cold.

Jake's eyes widened. "You're not making this up."

She shook her head.

"Ten million. Really?"

"Ten million. Only Henry thinks Kendrick's name is Edward Vaughn and that the money is to advertise the Grand Slam tournaments and that Kendrick is actually going to pay him. Kendrick must have seen the ship's logo on our helicopter and bought his way on board."

"Have you seen him? Does he know you know?"

"I haven't seen him but I borrowed this from one of the psychos." She took his hand and pressed it against the gun at her waist. "So by now Kendrick knows that we know."

Jake brushed his hair back with his hand. "Christ. Now what?"

"We quit acting like a couple of teenage lovers who've had their first fight and figure out what we're going to do about them. You have to win the tournament so you can make good on whatever deal you made with Theo, and you can't very well do that if Kendrick's killer kids are on the loose."

Jake ducked his head, thought for a moment, and then looked at Cassie. "Theo gets whatever I win. Less than two million, I make up the difference."

"In return for what?"

"In return for leaving you and Kristen alone."

Cassie backed up a step, her mouth ajar. "What about you?"

"I know he's not going to be satisfied with just the money. Not after"—he paused, his throat tightening—"not after everything that's happened. But that's my problem, my fight. I'll handle it."

Cassie's eyes glistened. "That's the most stupid, noble thing I've heard in a long time."

Jake smiled. "Well, you know me. I'm nothing if not stupid and noble. What's your plan?"

"Alberto Navarra is the chief of security. We tell him he's harboring an international fugitive, and if he doesn't call for help we'll go public."

"You met Amado, my butler. According to him, scuttlebutt is that Navarra brought Theo and his boys on board and didn't make them go through security. We can't trust him."

"I know about Navarra. I followed Theo's goons after they left the Champagne Bar. They were waiting for Navarra in his office. We're not going to trust him. We're going to threaten him. Besides, we don't have a choice."

Jake tilted his head toward Malek and Christos. Phillippi was standing in front of them, arms gesturing wide, blocking their view. "What about them? How do we pay Navarra a visit without them tagging along?"

"Henry loves doing me favors. I asked him to keep them busy while we go out the back way."

Cassie led him through the service area, down the stairs to the fourth deck, and through the warren of side passageways, until they entered the main corridor near the medical center. They hurried to the security office, opened the door, and stopped cold. Theo Kalogrides was sitting behind a desk, his feet up. Alberto Navarra was standing against a wall, eyes downcast and his hat in his hands. From behind, Malek and Christos shoved them into the room and closed the door.

"Is this where we say that the enemy of my enemy is my friend?" Jake asked.

Cassie answered. "If you ask me, the enemy of my enemy is still my enemy."

Theo swung his feet to the floor. "And I just want us all to be friends."

"Hate to disappoint you," Jake said.

Theo shrugged and stood. "Be my friend, be my enemy—I don't care as long as I get my money." He turned to Cassie. "Theo Kalogrides. I don't believe I've had the pleasure."

"Cassie Ireland, and don't worry, because you won't."

"Ha! You see what I told you, Jake? Stick with the redhead. Now what's all this about the enemy of my enemy? Who is this mysterious person, and why is he my enemy?"

"His name is Alan Kendrick," Cassie said. "He came aboard earlier today. He's looking for us, and if he finds us you'll never see a dime of your money."

Theo looked at Jake. "You and I, we made a deal. Tell me what she's talking about."

Jake shrugged. "We've had some, you might say, business dealings with Kendrick that he's not happy about. In fact, he'd like to kill us."

"And he brought help," Cassie said.

"So," Jake said, "that makes Kendrick your enemy, and if you're smart that makes you our friend."

Theo stood. "When it comes to my money, I can be a very good friend."

FORTY-NINE

Theo assured Cassie and Jake that he would take care of Kendrick. He assigned Malek to stand guard outside Jake's cabin and sent Christos to do the same for Cassie should Kendrick try to grab her and use her for leverage against Jake.

Amado listened closely as Jake explained how Malek, a man as large as a tree and whose boss would probably try to kill him after the tournament ended, had become his bodyguard. He nodded silently when Jake confirmed the gossip about Alberto Navarra and told him about Kendrick and the Flynns.

"Thank you, sir, for taking me into your confidence."

"For now let's keep the emphasis on confidential. If this thing should somehow turn out okay, you'll have a great story to tell your grandkids. If it goes south, someone has to be around to tell what really happened."

Despite Jake's insistence that he go to his own quarters, Amado spent the night holding a butcher knife and sitting in a chair he'd pushed close to the cabin door.

**

Wearing his usual final-table garb—dress jeans, black shirt, and a black sport coat—Jake navigated his way through the crowd gathered outside the theater waiting for the final table to begin. Kristen elbowed her way to him and planted a kiss on his lips, to the delight of people who captured the moment on their cell phones. Tiffany Wells, an ESPN reporter, stuck a microphone in his face.

"Jake! How's it feel to be back at a final table? If you win, are you afraid that the other players will think you cheated?"

He wanted to cram the microphone down her throat but forced a smile. "I'm just glad to be here."

"Sure, but what about the cheating?"

"I'll answer that if you'll tell me when you stopped snorting cocaine."

She bristled. "I've never used cocaine."

"Exactly my point. Hope you enjoy spending the rest of your life denying it."

Moments later he stood in the wings of the Crystal Theater, waiting to be introduced, along with the other players who had qualified for the final table. The auditorium seated fourteen hundred people, and its stage could accommodate Broadway productions and high-flying aerial acts. It was so huge that it rose from the stage and orchestra level on the third deck to the first balcony on the fourth and the second balcony on the fifth.

Today the stage was bare except for a poker table surrounded by cameras. Another camera hung from a wire to provide an aerial view. The game would be broadcast on huge screens mounted on either side of the stage and on the ship's closed-circuit television and worldwide on ESPN2. The broadcasters' makeshift booth was in the orchestra-level box closest to the stage.

When Malek escorted Jake to the theater, Amado followed them. Looking out in the audience, Jake saw him sitting in the second row directly behind Cassie, who was flanked by Theo and his boys.

Henry Phillippi escorted a man and a woman to front-row seats at the opposite end of the row from Cassie. Jake caught Cassie's eye as she tilted her head toward them and mouthed, *That's the Flynns.* He chuckled as the brother hobbled to his seat, wearing a brace on his left knee. Before taking their seats, they played a game of death stare with Malek and Christos that ended in a draw.

The auditorium filled with people holding signs Phillippi's staff had handed out displaying the names of the finalists. As he introduced them one by one, those holding signs for each player burst into raucous applause, whistling and foot stamping as if at a presidential nominating convention. The excitement was enough to make people ignore the ship's increasingly wobbly ride as a summer storm kicked up outside.

The crowd rose in a standing ovation as the players stood around the table at their assigned seats. Joey Friedman, a showboating former World Series champion, gave the raise-the-roof signal, exhorting people to cheer for him. J. T. Retzinger tugged his black cowboy hat down and grimaced. Samuel Nkosi, known for his fierce demeanor, glared at the crowd and his competitors. Mitch Wheeling, wearing dark glasses, drummed his fingers on the back of his chair. Miguel Garcia strutted once around the table, flexing his pecs and flashing his blinding white smile. Victor Robbins turned his baseball cap around with the bill in the back and slid into his chair. Jim Bob Denton let his barrel-sized gut rest against his chair and mopped his brow. Vanessa Duke was the ninth player. The only amateur, she was a former applied mathematics professor at MIT. Gray haired and stocky, she wore her glasses on a chain around her neck and didn't crack a smile, even when Phillippi told the crowd that this was her first final table.

Phillippi took the dealer's seat and cracked the first deck of cards. "Settle down, folks. Settle down. Let's take our seats and play poker."

Jake knew how unpredictable a final table could be. He'd played in one that lasted eighteen hours and another that was over in two when a kind of madness had gripped the players, everyone tripping over one another to be the first to go all in. The other men had played with one another long enough to have a good sense of each other's games. He'd been off the circuit long enough that they couldn't be certain what to expect from him. Vanessa was a wild card. Amateurs often mistook a hot streak for talent, but she didn't strike Jake as someone who would make that mistake. Though she came across as a stern schoolmarm, he wouldn't be surprised if she sliced a few of them into tiny strips and hung their flesh out to dry.

Not much happened during the first two hours. Players felt one another out, watching for tendencies while pretending not to notice anything at all. Samuel Nkosi and Vanessa were the last two players in the next hand. The pot had grown to a hundred and fifty thousand dollars, the largest of the night. Nkosi took a run at Vanessa, going all in. The common cards were an ace, a king, a seven, and a pair of sixes. She called. Nkosi turned over a pair of kings, giving him a full house. Vanessa didn't move until he started to scrape the chips toward him and then showed her pair of aces in the hole, giving her a stronger full house. The crowd went crazy and Nkosi went home.

FIFTY

Phillippi called for a half-hour break every three hours. By the second break, five players had been eliminated. Jake, Joey Friedman, J. T. Retzinger, and Vanessa Duke were the survivors. They stood and stretched along with the crowd.

Theo, Malek, and Christos were huddled together, giving Cassie a chance to check her phone. She'd had it on silent and it had vibrated just before the break, signaling receipt of a text message. It was from Zoey.

Bad news—Brian/Ryan is Ryan Williams. He was beaten to death. The police say he'd won a lot of money at a casino in Lake Tahoe and was probably the victim of a robbery. So sorry. Tricky news—hacked Navarra's e-mail, phone, and credit card records. He has a wife in Barcelona and a mistress in Cartagena named Blanca, and they're sisters. Beastly. Still can't get through on those calls. Will keep trying. Should I be worried?

Cassie was sick about Jake's friend, but there was nothing she could do about that. There was still a chance to dig Theo's claws out of Navarra. He must have found out that Navarra was having an affair and blackmailed him. Cassie surveyed the theater until she found Navarra lingering near the stage. He looked away as she approached him. Dark circles hung beneath his eyes and his cheeks sagged.

"Chief Navarra. I don't have much time, so I'll make this fast. I know about your affair with Blanca and I'm guessing that Theo is using that to force you to cooperate with him."

What little color he had in his face faded. "But . . ."

Cassie held up a hand. "Never mind the but. The other night when I ran into you in the passageway, I meant what I said. You're a man who knows the right thing to do. Please don't prove me wrong, or you'll have more than adultery on your conscience. You'll have my life and Jake's."

She returned to her seat, not giving him a chance to reply. Theo was waiting for her.

"What were you and the chief talking about?"

"I told him that I'd pay him double whatever you're paying him if he'd put a bullet in your head. Triple if he'd give me his gun and let me do it."

Theo laughed. "And what did he say?"

Cassie glared at him. "That once he's been bought he stays bought."

"The chief is a shrewd man. Unlike your friend Jake, who is a coward. He ran from me and still he will pay me what he owes and more."

"What about Kendrick? Is he a shrewd man?"

"Indeed. We had a talk last night. It turns out that we both want the same thing in the end. He understands that it is sometimes better to wait a little longer to get what he wants." Cassie flinched. "You seem surprised."

"I am, but I should have known better. Why would Kendrick do you a favor?"

"Oh, he isn't doing me a favor. I'm doing him a favor. I'm going to let him stay at my vacation home in Dubai until he finds a place of his own. Consider you and Jake as my housewarming gifts to him."

"Dubai doesn't have an extradition treaty with the United States. That's quite a favor. Since you were going to turn us over to him after the tournament anyway, why did you have Malek and Christos stand watch outside our doors?"

Theo smiled. "I wasn't keeping Kendrick out. I was keeping you and Jake in."

There was nothing Cassie could do but watch the final table when play resumed. The big screens switched back and forth between the cards on the table and the players' faces. Joey Friedman couldn't resist mugging for the camera. J. T. Retzinger couldn't turn his perpetual frown upside down. Jake's and Vanessa's faces could just as well have been cast in concrete.

**

Phillippi dealt the next hand. The seven of hearts, three of clubs, and ten of hearts showed up in the flop. Jake had an eight and nine of hearts in the hole. It took him a moment to calculate his odds of winning at better than 50 percent. But that was without knowing what cards the other three were holding. Still, he liked his chances of drawing to a flush on one of the last two cards.

Joey Friedman sat to Jake's left and had the first bet.

"Fifty thousand."

Everyone called. Phillippi turned up the next card—four of clubs. Jake watched Joey out of the corner of his eye, catching a quick upturn at the corners of Joey's mouth. Club flush, Jake decided. No way to know how high. Joey bet again.

"Hundred thousand."

Vanessa and J. T. folded. Jake ran the odds again. With both of them going for a flush, his odds had dropped to less than 50 percent, even lower if Joey's hole cards were higher than his. Jake called. Phillippi turned over the last card—jack of hearts.

"All in," Joey said.

Jake took his time. There was no way Joey could beat him. He wanted to savor the moment.

"Call."

He shoved his chips into the pot. Joey turned his cards over, thumping his hand on the table. "C'mon, man. Let's see 'em, already."

The crowd gasped, then applauded furiously when Jake revealed his straight flush. Joey paled and put his head on the table.

**

Vanessa went head-to-head against J. T. in the next hand, taking him out when her trip queens beat his trip eights.

"This could be it," Theo said, and opened his cell phone.

"Who are you calling?" Cassie asked. "Your daddy?"

Theo rested the phone on his leg, grinding his teeth. "I think I'll stick around after I turn you over to Kendrick. He says that the Flynns have special skills, and the brother, Conor, owes you, although he was pleased to get his gun back."

"Stop before I pee my pants."

"Have it your way." He picked up his phone. "When Jake finishes off that dyke, five million dollars is going to be instantly transferred to my bank account, and I can't wait to watch that happen." He tapped on his phone, opening up his account.

"Pot's right," Phillippi declared as he dealt the cards.

Cassie couldn't take her eyes off the big screen as Phillippi revealed the flop—nine of spades, six of clubs, and three of diamonds. She knew enough about the game to realize that those were lousy cards. Jake's hole cards would have to be fantastic for him to pull out this hand. She expected him to fold if Vanessa bet serious money.

"Check," Jake said.

"Two fifty," Vanessa said, adding a quarter of a million to the pot.

Murmurs swept through the audience, punctuated by the odd "Damn!" and "Holy shit!"

Jake didn't hesitate. "Call."

The next card was the three of hearts.

Theo leaned across Cassie and tapped Malek on the leg. "Look at that, a lousy pair of threes. They're both bluffing."

"Three fifty," Vanessa said.

"She's trying to buy the pot," Theo said.

Jake studied the cards. The camera flicked back and forth between the two of them. Vanessa didn't blink or twitch. Jake didn't move.

"Call."

The crowd oohed, a few people standing, rubbing their palms against their thighs. Phillippi turned up the final card—three of clubs.

"Trip threes on the board," Theo said. "Fuck! She's probably got a pair in the hole. Jake doesn't have a chance."

Vanessa didn't hesitate. "All in."

Everyone in the audience got to their feet but no one made a sound. Jake leaned back in his chair, hands on the table. It was so quiet, Cassie could hear the buzz in the stage lights.

"What the hell. Call."

Vanessa turned over a pair of aces.

"Son of a bitch! A full fucking house!" someone yelled from the balcony.

The crowd grew quiet again. Jake looked at Cassie and grinned as he turned over the nine of hearts and the three of spades.

"Four threes," he said.

The eruption was thunderous as people shouted and high-fived one another. A confetti cannon showered the stage.

"He did it!" Theo said, pushing Cassie aside as he made his way to the stage.

Cassie followed him, getting to Jake first when Phillippi intercepted Theo.

Jake grabbed Cassie in a bear hug. "How about that, babe?"

She pulled away. "Since when am I 'babe'?"

"Since I just won five million bucks . . . even if it isn't mine. I still won."

"Don't be so sure about that."

"About what? Winning? What the hell do you think the confetti is for?"

"I'm talking about the 'even if it isn't mine' part. Let's get out of here. Now."

He put his hands on her shoulders. "Hey, hey, hey. The money goes to Theo, right into his bank account. That's the deal we made."

She shook her head. "I sort of changed the deal."

"How?"

"I hacked into your security bracelet and changed the settings back to your bank account."

Jake put his hands on the sides of his head. "You changed it! He's going to kill us if Kendrick doesn't kill us first."

"Yeah, well, they were going to kill us anyway."

People swarmed toward the stage. Theo's shrieking voice cut through the commotion.

"Where's my money! Goddamn you, Carter! Where's my fucking money! I'm going to fucking kill you!"

"I think you really pissed him off," Jake said.

Screams broke out at the front of the theater as a man barreled through the crowd, knocking people to the ground.

"That's Kendrick," Jake said.

"And he's no happier than Theo."

"What did you do to him?"

She shrugged. "Stole fifteen million from his secret bank account on the Isle of Man."

"Cassie Ireland! Where the hell are you!"

Kendrick and the Flynns charged the stage from the right side. Theo, Malek, and Christos came at them from the left. Amado shoved a chair in their path, causing Theo to stumble and Malek to trip over him.

"Time to go?" Jake asked.

"Yeah. We're late already."

FIFTY-ONE

They ran backstage. Jake made for a side exit.

"No good," Cassie said. "We'll be trapped with everyone trying to get out of the theater. This way."

She weaved around equipment and curtains to the very back and tried the handle on an unmarked door. It opened into a small vestibule with another door. She locked the first door and opened the second. They stepped outside, nothing between them and the stern. Black, roiling clouds obliterated the stars. A stiff wind swept rain across the deck. They pressed themselves against the wall as the stern rose ten feet and then dropped back in the water.

Jake shouted above the wind, "Did you know about the door?"

"No, but most cruise ships have them. They're called secret decks because the doors are unmarked and they aren't for passenger use. We just got lucky."

"We can't stay out here until we get to Casablanca."

"Afraid you'll melt? C'mon."

They half walked and half ran the length of the boat to the bow, drenched by the time they found the stairway Cassie had used to sneak up on Donny. They took it from the third deck to the fourth, went inside, and took cover in the same supply room she'd used the night before.

"I prefer a cabin with an ocean view," Jake said, "but this will do."

"Shut up."

Cassie grabbed him from behind his neck, pulled him to her, and kissed him fiercely, then shoved him away.

"What was that for?"

"It's the best and last apology I'm going to make."

Jake grinned. "Apology accepted, but I doubt that's the best you can do."

She raised an eyebrow. "At the moment it is."

"I hope you have some kind of plan, because I'm getting tired of running for my life."

"You'll get used to it. And I do have a plan, sort of. We can't hide forever, because they'll find us, especially if Navarra helps them. If we keep roaming the ship, they'll find us, and when that happens, passengers could be caught in the cross fire."

"Cross fire means guns, and we don't have any. So, what do we do? Order guns from Amazon? Overnight delivery won't be much help. And a few marksmanship lessons would be helpful. An online video maybe."

"We'll borrow the guns, and if the shooting starts, aim at them, not me."

"Wait a minute! You're serious about the guns, aren't you?"

"Can't bring a deck of cards to a gunfight."

"Whoa, slow down, Annie Oakley. I've never fired a gun, let alone shot someone or, worse, killed someone. Don't you think you're asking an awful lot?"

"I'm not asking you to do anything except to not shoot me."

"So you're going to kill them—Theo, his boys, Kendrick, and the Flynns. Just gun them down. You make it sound like you've done this before."

She held his gaze. "Jake, there are six people out there that want to kill us. They have guns. They will shoot us if they can and shoot us again to make sure we're dead. We're past talking with them. And, yes, I have done this before."

Jake took a step back, shaking, then nodded his head. "Okay, okay."

"In the meantime we'll have to settle for these." She took two screwdrivers from the toolbox and gave one to Jake. "And put these on." She handed him a crew member's jacket and cap and took a set for herself.

"Theo and Kendrick aren't going to believe we're crew members. The crew wears uniforms. We're wearing jeans."

"They'll pay attention to the jacket and cap first, and that ought to buy us enough time to make a move. If not—well, look around the room. This is as good as it gets. All we need now is a fire alarm to pull."

"Gee, I feel like I'm back in high school."

Cassie elbowed him in the stomach on her way out the door. "Dope."

"Double dope."

The few crew members that passed them in the corridor nodded and continued on. They came to a break room. There was a fire alarm on the wall next to the door.

"When I pull the alarm," Cassie said, "the captain will instruct all the passengers to report to their muster stations. That will keep them contained and out of the way at least until security and the crew can confirm that there isn't a fire. And it will leave the security office unguarded. If there are any weapons to be had, that's where we'll find them."

"Then what?"

"We find a place away from the passengers that we can defend and wait for Theo and Kendrick to come to us." Cassie pointed to the alarm. "Care to do the honors?"

Jake grinned. "Are you kidding?"

He pulled down on the handle, and the *wah-wah* of the alarm reverberated around them. Red lights flashed on and off in the corridor. They stepped into the break room and closed the door.

Ten seconds later the alarm stopped and the captain's voice came over the ship's PA system.

"Attention, this is the captain. May I have your attention, please. The sound you just heard is our fire alarm. This is not a drill. Until we can confirm whether there is a fire, we will follow our muster procedures. Please proceed to your muster stations immediately. Do not go back to your rooms for any of your belongings or attempt to find someone else. Our crew will check every cabin and facility on the ship to make certain that all passengers are accounted for. Any delay on your part in proceeding to your muster stations will only add to whatever danger may now exist. We appreciate your cooperation. I will report to you as soon as we have more information. That is all."

Cassie and Jake listened as crew members ran past. When it was quiet, they came out and followed the signs to the main passageway. They peeked around the corner. The security office was twenty feet away. The door was closed. Navarra and Malek were approaching from the opposite direction with Kristen between them, each with a firm grasp on her arm. Cassie and Jake ducked back into the side passageway.

"Goddamn, Theo," Jake hissed. "The son of a bitch! We can't let them take her."

"I know. Zip up your jacket, pull your cap down low, and don't look at them. If we get past them, we'll take them from behind. Which one do you want?"

Jake didn't hesitate. "Malek."

Cassie and Jake trotted into the main corridor, heads down. They passed the trio without notice, pivoted, and attacked. Cassie took Navarra out at the legs and pinned him to the floor. He didn't resist.

Jake jumped on Malek's back, wrapping his arm around Malek's neck and yanking his head back. Malek roared, clawed at Jake's arm, spun around, and smashed Jake into the wall, taking a step forward and then driving his body and Jake into the wall a second time.

"Motherfucker!" Kristen yelled, and kicked Malek in the balls. He slumped to his knees. "Goddamn motherfucking asshole!"

She grabbed the sides of his head and drove her knee into his chin, knocking him out. Malek collapsed facedown, with Jake still on his back. Jake looked up at Kristen.

"Where'd you learn how to do that?"

"Watching wrestling with my dad," she said, grinning, breathless, and wild eyed. "He always said it was fake. Guess he was wrong."

Jake crawled off Malek and pulled a gun from his waistband. He handed it to Cassie. "You keep it so I don't accidentally shoot one of us."

Cassie let Navarra get to his feet but kept the gun on him. "Guess I was wrong about you knowing the right thing to do. Open your office."

"What do we do with him?" Jake asked, pointing to Malek.

"Tie his hands behind him with his belt."

"That won't be necessary," Navarra said. "There are plastic handcuffs in my office. We'll use those."

Navarra secured Malek's wrists with the cuffs, dragged him inside the office, and closed the door. Malek began to stir, and Navarra kicked him in the head, silencing him.

"So, I wasn't wrong about you after all," Cassie said.

"You were both right and wrong. I let these men humiliate and intimidate me. But no more. I called the police in Cartagena and I called my wife. Blanca is safe and my wife is very angry. I told her how sorry . . ." Navarra stopped in midsentence as the door swung open.

"I've been looking for you," Christos said.

FIFTY-TWO

He leveled a gun at Navarra and shot him in the eye. The bullet exploded out of the back of his head in a red mist as his lifeless body crumpled to the floor. Christos swung the gun toward Kristen.

"Noooo!" Jake screamed, and dove at Christos, driving his shoulder into Christos's gut.

The gun fired harmlessly into the ceiling as they tumbled into the main passageway. Jake grabbed Christos's gun hand as they hit the floor with a thud. Grunting, Christos bucked, rolling Jake onto his back, forcing the barrel toward Jake's face. The floor shot upward, launched by the heaving waves, sending Christos listing to one side. Jake rolled with him, the pitch and yaw of the ship throwing him back on top. He bent Christos's wrist down and away in the same instant Christos pulled the trigger, then collapsed on Christos's chest, muffling the crack of the gun.

"Oh my God!" Cassie screamed.

She ran to Jake and pulled him onto the floor. His shirt was blood splattered, and he was slack jawed—but alive.

Christos's arm lay across his body, the gun still in his hand, the barrel smoking, the wound in his heart gurgling and oozing. His eyes were open, his gaze fixed and glassy. He coughed once. Blood ran from the corners of his mouth and he was dead.

"Did I . . . did I kill him?" Jake asked.

"Technically, no, since he pulled the trigger. But I'll give you an assist."

"Hey!" Kristen said. "What in the hell did you people get me into?"

Jake got to his feet. "I'm sorry. I never meant for any of this to happen." He took off his bracelet. "Go to my cabin. It's 1402. My butler, Amado, will be there. Tell him I sent you. He'll take care of you until I get back."

She softened. "Promise you'll come back?"

"Promise."

She pointed at Christos. "What if I run into his buddy, Theo?"

Cassie handed her Malek's gun. "You know how to use this?"

"No, but no one will know that."

They watched her walk toward the elevator bank, hips swaying, tapping the gun against her thigh. An elevator pinged. She waved at them before getting on.

"I like having her on our side," Jake said.

"As long as she keeps walking."

"Jealous?"

"No. She's not your type, but one amateur on the team is enough."

"Amateur? Who you calling an amateur?"

Cassie picked up Christos's gun and checked the magazine. It was empty. She'd started to search his pockets for more ammunition when another elevator pinged. Donny and Marie stepped out and turned toward the security office, followed by Theo and Kendrick. Seeing Cassie and Jake standing over Christos's body lying in the middle of the corridor, the siblings drew their guns and began firing. When the ship's rolling caused their shots to go wide and high, Marie sprinted toward them, with Donny half running, half skipping after her, dragging his bum leg. Theo and Kendrick overtook him, shoved him aside, and tore after them down the corridor.

"Run!" Cassie said.

They flew back the way they had come, darting into the jumble of interior passageways. When Cassie started grabbing door handles as they went, opening them and slamming them shut after each turn, Jake looked at her, eyes wide.

"They can hear the doors," Cassie explained. "They'll have to check each room."

Rounding a corner, they sprinted down a straight length of hall toward an exit. When they looked over their shoulders, Marie sprung into view and squeezed off a pair of rounds that shot sparks from the metal door they were scrambling for.

"Well, that worked," Jake said.

"One assist and now you're a critic?"

They shouldered through the door and into the raging storm, clinging to the rails of the landing of a steep, narrow stairway. Cassie pointed her hand up, and he began climbing after her to the fifth deck.

"We should split up," Jake called.

She wheeled and looked him in the eye. "Never!"

Cassie had just reached the next level when Marie burst through the door beneath them. The ship bounced wildly on the waves, forcing her to pocket her gun and grab both stairway rails.

"C'mon, Jake!" Cassie yelled.

Jake ignored her. Bracing his forearms on the rails and extending his legs like battering rams, he shot down the slippery rails and crashed into Marie's chest with the soles of both feet, knocking her into a dazed heap, and then raced up the stairs to where Cassie was waiting.

"I can't believe you just did that."

He grinned. "Me either. But it was awesome."

Cassie looked past him down the stairs. "Not awesome enough. She's back, and so are her friends. Come on!"

Jake glanced back just in time to see Theo leap past Marie onto the stairs, then charged up after Cassie. Just as he reached the top, the bow shot up high and then plummeted into the water, sending Cassie skittering onto the deck and sliding face-first toward the helipad.

Jake managed to grab the deck railing just past the top of the stairway. Shielding his eyes from the rain as he climbed, Theo didn't see him crouched there. As Theo topped the stairs, Jake lunged for his legs, smashing him to the deck and sending his gun spinning away across the floor. Jake dove past him, clutching Theo's gun, and jumped to his feet on the heaving deck. Theo rose, grinning, his face cut, blood drooling off his chin. He reached into his jacket and drew another gun. Jake shot him once in the chest, then kept pulling the trigger until the gun jammed.

As Theo staggered on wobbly legs, Donny appeared behind him, grabbed his collar, and threw his body across the deck, then stepped toward Jake and held his gun on him. Jake dropped Theo's gun. Marie joined her brother, training her gun on Cassie, who had managed to get to her feet on the open deck. No one moved and no one spoke. Kendrick cleared the stairs, bracing himself against the rail as the ship swayed in the sea and the rain tore at them.

"You two are bigger pains in my ass than the entire fucking FBI," he shouted over the gale. "Take them over there, next to the rail. But don't throw them overboard—not yet anyway."

Donny and Marie herded them across the deck to the portside rail, guns pressed against their ribs. The rain stung like icy BBs, and the ship rolled side to side like a teeter-totter.

"What do you want?" Cassie shouted at Kendrick.

"I want to know who hired you," he shouted back. "I want my money back. And I want you to die."

"You can't have all three," Jake said. "Kill us and you'll never get the first two."

"Well, then. I'll settle for number three."

Donny and Marie pushed them up on their tiptoes, leaning them over the rail.

"Hang on! Hang on a second!" Jake bellowed back at him. "How do we know you won't kill us if she tells you who hired her?"

"Don't you mean who hired both of you? And don't pretend you weren't part of this all along."

"Me?"

"Yeah, you. From what our dead Greek friend told me, you're a lot better poker player than you ever showed me."

"He was never part of this," Cassie shouted. "I'm the one you want. Let him go and I'll tell you who hired me. I'll tell you everything, including how I used my screwdriver to break into your crummy safe."

She slid her hand in her coat pocket, tightening her grip on her screwdriver. Jake did the same.

"Sure," Kendrick said. "Tell me who hired you, and Jake goes home."

"Cassie! Don't do it! You can't trust him. Either way, he's going to kill us."

"I've got to take that chance, Jake."

Kendrick stood on the deck, balancing himself as the ship rose and fell. "I'm waiting. Give me the name. I'll know if you're lying, and if you are, the Flynns will shoot you where you stand and throw you overboard."

"First you let Jake go."

"Cassie, I'm not stupid."

"Sign of good faith then. Tell Flynn to move him away from the rail. That's all—just a few steps."

Kendrick studied her for a moment, then motioned to Donny, who steered Jake midway between the rail and Kendrick. Searching for anything resembling help, Jake looked up at the sixth deck and found it. Amado and Kristen were watching from the rail, each of them holding life jackets handed out at the muster stations. He caught Cassie's eye, tilting his head at the pair. She glanced up and then looked back at Jake.

"Don't look at him. Look at me," Kendrick said. "Last chance, Cassie. Who hired you?"

Before she could answer, a howling, swirling gust of wind swept across the bucking, bouncing deck. Just behind Jake, Donny lost his footing, landing on his bad knee, his gun hand on the deck. Jake stomped on his hand, but Donny swept his other arm across the back of Jake's legs, knocking them out from under him. Jake yanked his screwdriver from his pocket as he went down and drove it through Donny's gun hand, pinning it to the deck. Donny screamed.

Marie screamed louder. "Conor!"

She was distracted enough for Cassie to slam her hand against the rail. Marie's gun fell to the deck as Cassie plunged her screwdriver into Marie's thigh and shoved her away.

Jake had scrambled to his feet and was running to Cassie as Kendrick pulled his gun and fired. The crack of a gunshot cut through the wind, and a bullet ricocheted off the rail between them. Conor yanked the screwdriver free of his hand, then took aim, with both hands gripping the gun. Marie stood next to him, adding her gun to their arsenal.

Jake and Cassie looked down at the water and up at Amado and Kristen, then at each other. Jake nodded.

"Really?" Cassie said. "You think that will work?"

"I'll bet my life on it."

"Finish them!" Kendrick said.

And they jumped.

FIFTY-THREE

Cassie hurtled toward the boiling sea, casting a last look skyward as Amado and Kristen launched their life jackets into the air. The blinking rescue lights on the jackets flickered like tiny falling stars chasing them into the Mediterranean.

Hitting the water felt like crashing through a brick wall. The sudden, shocking cold made her gasp reflexively, inhaling a mouthful of salt water. She shed her suddenly heavy jacket and kicked as hard as she could, a jolt of pain shooting from her right ankle through her lower leg, the impact having broken one or the other or both. Ignoring the pain, she kicked again. Making it to the surface, she coughed and sputtered. Her vision cleared in time for her to see the lights on the *Shangri-La* disappearing into the gloomy night.

Eight-foot waves carried her up and down like mini–roller coasters. She tried to brace her good leg against her injured leg in a vain effort to stabilize the fractures, crying out each time the broken bones moved.

At each crest she looked for Jake and shouted his name. At each trough she was driven underwater, gritting her teeth against the pain to kick to the surface, starved for air. Exhausted to the point of surrender, she spotted a small, blinking light. Pulling her arms through the water with all she had left, she swam to the life jacket, slipped it on, and closed the three clips in front, her fingers clumsy.

"Jake! Jake! Where are you?"

No response. He either couldn't hear her or he was dead, a possibility she refused to accept. Not after everything that had happened. Not before . . . what? She didn't know where their relationship could go, only that she wanted the chance to find out.

She heard her name, barely audible over the wind and rain. Then she saw him swimming awkwardly toward her using a sidestroke, barely able to raise his right arm out of the water. She swam as quickly as she could, grabbed his shirt, and pulled him close.

"Are you all right?"

He nodded to his right shoulder. "I think I dislocated it when I hit the water. Getting rid of that jacket was a bitch. Otherwise, I'm good. You?"

"Broken ankle or leg or both." She looked around at the open water. "But we're alive."

They clung to each other, his good arm around her neck, her hands clasped behind his back, their faces inches apart. Cassie's life jacket provided enough buoyancy to keep their heads above water, the two of them bobbing like a cork in the turbulent sea, pelted by rain.

"Amado would have raised the alarm right away," Jake assured her. "They know we're out here. The captain will turn the ship around and come back for us."

"At a speed of twenty-five knots, the ship will be miles away before that happens. By then the current will have taken us even farther away. We couldn't be more lost if we'd been abandoned on Mars."

He grinned. "Aren't you in a bad mood all of a sudden."

"I'm just being realistic."

"Realistic? Are you kidding me? We just survived getting shot at and jumping five stories from a moving ship in a raging storm, and you're worried about a little thing like being lost on Mars? How about a little optimism?"

"Optimism? All right. We picked the best possible time of year to be adrift in the Mediterranean. The surface temperature of the water probably doesn't get much below seventy degrees all summer. That gives us some time before we have to worry about hypothermia."

"How much time?"

She sighed. "Three to twelve hours before exhaustion or unconsciousness. But as long as our life jackets hold up, we can survive longer."

He stared at her as a blast of wind sent them twirling like a top. "That's interesting information to have at your fingertips."

"I spent a couple of weeks in survival school. For work."

"How did you decide to get a degree in asset recovery?"

A tall wave crashed down on them. Cassie lost her hold on Jake and the water began dragging her away, but he kept a tight grip on her vest. She grabbed his sleeve, pulled herself back in, and wrapped her arms around his neck, breathing in fast, hard gulps.

"It's okay," he said. "I'm as scared as you are."

They rested like that for a long time, not talking. The sea gradually calmed and the clouds disappeared, the moon and stars shining down on them. He tapped her on the shoulder. She lifted her head, looking at him.

"You were going to tell me about asset recovery school."

She took a deep breath, knowing it was time and even if it wasn't there might not be another time.

"Six years ago I was Gina. Not married to a creep like Kendrick but working for one." She shook her head. "I was so goddamn proud of myself. I came out of Harvard with my brand-new MBA and went to work for a hedge fund run by a guy named Howard Platt."

"I remember that case," said Jake. "He laundered money for a drug cartel, didn't he?"

"Among other federal crimes. I didn't see it, didn't want to see it, for way too long. Then I met a man named Gabriel Degrand. In line at a deli. We were both picking up lunch for our bosses. At least that's what he said. We started talking trash about them, comparing notes about which boss was worse. We flirted a little, but he didn't ask for my number and I didn't ask for his. For the rest of that day I wished I had. About a week later we ran into each other again, and he invited me out for coffee. Then dinner. He wasn't even that good looking, but really smart and funny . . ."

The tone of her voice told Jake everything. "You fell in love with him."

"Yes. I told him all about how disillusioned I was with my dream job on Wall Street and my growing suspicions about my boss. Gabriel encouraged me to find evidence and said he'd help me blow the whistle, that he knew people in the DA's office. He convinced me to steal Platt's password and give it to him. Turns out that was all he really wanted."

"He pretended to be in love with you?"

"At first, but not at the end."

"So he came clean."

"He had to," said Cassie. "When he recruited me."

"As an asset recovery—"

"Specialist. With my help, Gabriel recovered almost eight million dollars for his client. Later, he anonymously tipped the feds with what they needed to take Platt down."

Jake let out a low whistle. "Sounds familiar."

She nodded. "Felt pretty good. Still does."

"And it only works if you completely trust . . . What was your boss's name again?"

She hadn't mentioned it, and he knew she hadn't. But since they were both going to die out here anyway, Cassie didn't see the harm. "Prometheus. And I do trust him. Completely."

"Lucky man," said Jake. They floated quietly for a moment, then he asked, "So, what happened with you and Gabriel?"

She kept her voice calm and deliberate. "He died."

Jake pulled back to arm's length and looked at her. "Shit. I'm sorry. That's terrible."

"Yes. It was."

"How did it happen?"

"Does it matter?"

"It does to me. I killed a man tonight—two if you count the assist on Malek. I close my eyes and I see Theo's dead eyes staring at me. Makes me wonder if that will ever stop."

"It will. Don't forget that both of them would have killed you if you hadn't killed them first."

"Was it like that for you?"

She shook her head. "No. It was pure revenge. We were alone. I had a gun. He didn't. He killed Gabriel and I made him pay for it. That's not what happened today."

"It sort of was. They cut off Mariposa's finger and they probably killed my friend Ryan."

"I'm afraid they did kill him."

"How could you know?"

"Kristen saw his name on his phone when she was at your table in the bar. I had a friend of mine run down what happened to him. I'm sorry."

Jake looked away. "Me too."

"It's not your—"

He swung back to her. "Of course it is." He put his head down.

They stopped talking, drifting on the gentle swell of the waves, their bodies pressed together for warmth. After a while Jake raised his head.

"What happened to the money from the Grand Slam and Kendrick's account?"

Cassie smiled. "Thought you'd never ask. The Grand Slam money is in your bank account. Kendrick's is in a new account you opened in the Caymans."

"I opened? How'd I manage to do that?"

"You didn't, but it's in your name and it will be there until you give it to your parents. I used your laptop."

"You stole my laptop?"

"No, dummy. I borrowed it after you thought you threw me out of your cabin. Only I hid on the veranda until you left, and then I had a chat with Amado. Once I told him what I was doing and why, he was very helpful. I hope you tipped him before we went overboard."

He stared at her. "You are really something, you know that?"

She nodded. "Yes, I do."

"It's going to be tough sending them the money from out here."

"Not really. I made them beneficiaries on the account. If you don't send them the money within the next year, the bank will do it."

"You were that confident we'd get out of this mess, huh?"

Cassie shrugged. "You're the gambler. You should understand hedging your bets."

He took this in, quiet, then faced her again. "I wouldn't have bet on us finishing up like this."

"Is that supposed to be a farewell? Because if you think I'm finished with you . . ." She stopped as she saw his eyes suddenly go wide.

"Boat," he said.

"What?"

He grabbed her face and turned her toward a pair of distant lights cutting through the darkness. "It's a boat!"

They waved their arms and screamed until their throats were raw. As the boat approached, they saw that it was a trawler with outriggers on either side keeping it steady in the waves. A man stood on the prow, waving a flashlight in their direction to let them know they'd been spotted.

It finally drew up beside them, a rope ladder hanging down the side. Two men helped Cassie up the ladder. She was so happy—and so cold—she didn't feel the pain in her leg. Jake was next.

"How did you find us?" Cassie asked one of them.

The sailor spoke flawless English. "We've been following you since you left Monte Carlo. We were told to stay close to your ship in case you needed us."

"Told? Who told you?"

"Look at the side of the boat."

Cassie leaned over the edge, grinning. The name of the boat was *Prometheus*.

They collapsed onto the deck, surrounded by several large, very fragrant tubs of fish. Another man threw a rough blanket over them. Jake pulled her close and she wrapped her arms around him.

"What?" she asked.

"I guess you're not finished with me yet."

A NOTE FROM THE AUTHORS

Thanks for adding *All In* to your library. Readers depend on readers to recommend good books, and authors depend on readers to generate positive word of mouth for their books. If you liked *All In*, please leave a review on Amazon, Goodreads, or any other online platform of your choosing, even if it's only a few words. It will make a big difference, and Joel and Lisa will be very thankful.

ABOUT THE AUTHORS

Photo © 2014 Roy Inman

Joel Goldman is the bestselling author of the Lou Mason thrillers, the Jack Davis thrillers, and the Alex Stone thrillers. He was a trial lawyer for twenty-eight years. Goldman wrote his first novel after one of his colleagues complained about a partner, prompting him to write a thriller featuring that partner, kill the son of a b*tch off in the first chapter, and spend the rest of the book figuring out who did it. And he never looked back. Goldman is also the cofounder of the crime fiction imprint Brash Books. He lives with his wife and two dogs in Leawood, Kansas.

Photo © 2012 Kat Shadian

Lisa Klink started her career in the world of *Star Trek*, writing for *Deep Space Nine* and *Voyager* before coming back to Earth for shows such as *Martial Law* and *Missing*. In addition to writing for television, she's scripted a theme park attraction and authored graphic novels, short stories, and three novels in The Dead Man series. Klink is also a five-time champion on *Jeopardy!*